BREAK THE YOUNG LAND

Center Point
Large Print

**This Large Print Book carries the
Seal of Approval of N.A.V.H.**

BREAK THE YOUNG LAND

50094

T. V. OLSEN

CENTER POINT PUBLISHING
THORNDIKE, MAINE

This Center Point Large Print edition
is published in the year 2004 by arrangement with
Golden West Literary Agency.

The text of this Large Print edition is unabridged. In other
aspects, this book may vary from the original edition. Printed in
Thailand. Set in 16-point Times New Roman type.

ISBN 1-58547-462-2

Library of Congress Cataloging-in-Publication Data

Olsen, Theodore V.
    Break the young land / T.V. Olsen.--Center Point large print ed.
        p. cm.
    Originally published under the pseudonym of Joshua Stark. Garden City, N.Y. : Doubleday,
1964.
    ISBN 1-58547-462-2 (lib. bdg. : alk. paper)
        1. Norwegian Americans--Fiction. 2. Immigrants--Fiction. 3. Ranchers--Fiction.
    4. Farmers--Fiction. 5. Kansas--Fiction. 6. Large type books. I. Stark, Joshua, 1932-1993.
    Break the young land. II. Title.

PS3565.L8B74 2004
813'.54--dc22

                                                                                    2004001606

CHAPTER ONE

"MJÖLK, DADA." THE LITTLE GIRL HELD UP HER EMPTY cup. "More *mjölk*."

"No, no, Kjersti. Milk. Say Milk." Borg did not quite conceal his irritation that Sigrid was still teaching the child Swedish words. He took the cup and set it aside, frowning gently. "There is not much milk for our porridge. Don't be greedy, eh?"

Sitting by his feet, three-year-old Kjersti stuck her thumb in her mouth and nodded gravely. Borg's irritation died as he turned to the simmering kettle hung on an iron rod laid across two forked sticks with a low fire built between them. He ladled out the porridge into four bowls, adding milk to each, and called, "Magnus!" as he set one bowl down by Kjersti. He handed her a spoon, saying sternly, "Wait till it cools." He picked up a second bowl and tramped over to his brother Lars who sat on a wooden box by the front wheel of his wagon, which was drawn up behind Borg's.

An old army greatcoat was pulled tightly around Lars' thin, hunched shoulders and a bright quilted blanket covered his useless legs. Though the chill of the prairie night had not set in, he was shivering slightly; his tight-lipped sallow face barely lifted as Borg came up. His pale brown eyes touched with a brief and indifferent rejection the bowl Borg held out, then shifted away.

"Inga will make my meal; it's her duty."

Against impatience Borg made his voice mild: "Tonight our wives have other woman's work. We shift for ourselves, eh?"

"I'd like to shift for myself." Lars' cold stare held an ancient unrelenting bitterness, and Borg thought wearily, *Ah Lars, why bring the old hate into a new country; at last can't there be an end to that?* But his weathered face showed nothing, hardened against old hurts, and he only stood holding out the bowl till his brother, muttering under his breath, took it.

Borg returned to the fire, shuttling a glance outside the wagon circle to where Magnus, his son, had turned loose their oxen and horses. Finished with this task, he was talking with another youngster; their clear laughter rang out boyish and buoyant. "Magnus!" Borg called again, sharply, then sat cross-legged on the ground and picked up his bowl.

Magnus came sauntering up, a tall loose-jointed boy of eighteen with a hint of his father's compact beef through chest and shoulders. He sank down with indolent grace by Kjersti, observing idly, "What abundance graces our table." He spoke English without accent and with a sardonic ease.

Borg growled, "Eat, don't make the smart talk."

Magnus dug hungrily into his bowl, pausing to rub a hand over his sister's tow head. "Hey, *flicka,* don't burn your tongue."

Kjersti cautiously tasted her porridge and made a little face. "It's not so good like *Mor's,* Magnus."

"Lumpy too," Magnus said around a full mouth. He

chewed judiciously. "Ma's is better because she always says grace."

"Say your grace in your head," Borg told him, "and keep your smart tongue still, sonny. Maybe you think you got too big to whip, eh?"

Magnus' light gaze briefly met his, and lowered. They ate in silence, Borg feeling the usual baffled anger. The rift between Lars and himself was an old story, but understandable—this son of his who hid a moodily sensitive nature behind mockery, he had never understood.

Magnus was sharp and clever and reluctantly obedient, yet different—as different from both parents as day from night. In more than one exasperated moment his mother had thrown up her hands and predicted that he'd come to no good end. Borg had reasoned in his careful methodical way that it wasn't so simple; his own young manhood was not so far behind that he couldn't appreciate the restless angers and self-doubts of youth. Yet Magnus was a complex boy, beyond him in thought and feeling, and Borg, wanting deeply to understand, could only wonder what Magnus wished of his life. . . .

A muffled scream roused him from his scowling thoughts. Inside the compound formed by twenty-three wagons drawn in a close circle, the smoke of cooking fires furled away on a low evening breeze: the people sat about eating or quietly talking. The sun had now westered above the horizon, and it softly gilded the canvas wagon tops and the hand-woven blankets or sheepskin sleeping robes thrown over them. Out on the grass a cow lowed gently into the sudden wedge of tranquility cut by the scream. The people listened a moment, their glances pulled toward Lars Vikstrom's wagon, then resumed their talk at a lower, muttered pitch.

Borg scraped his bowl clean, set it aside and stood up, stretching his stiff muscles, then walked over behind his brother's wagon. There Sigrid was tending a pot of boiling water, also tearing one of her precious sheets in half and twisting each half into ropes. She brushed a stray lock of pale hair back from her forehead as she turned—a small, buxom, roundly formed woman of thirty-seven. Her large eyes were blue as a summer fjord, as kind as heaven. And her tired smile, he thought, was the loveliest on earth.

"Not your good sheets, *litagod*," he chided, and she smiled again at the endearment.

"Mr. Vikstrom, she has lost much of her water, *ja?* In a dry delivery she will be called on for extra labor and this will make it easier. The sheet can be sewed again."

"Don't talk, hurry with it." Inga's voice came with peremptory sharpness. Borg moved over to the wagon and peered into its dim interior. Helga Krans lay gasping quietly, her thin waif's face as pale as the pillow under her head. Her light brown hair lay in sweaty limp strands on her brow and cheeks, and her eyes stared wide with pain. A girl in childbirth . . . herself hardly more than a child.

Inga kneeling beside her held the girl's knotted fists tightly in her own strong hands, and to Borg's quiet, "How does she do?" his sister-in-law snapped waspishly, "How can I tell? How many brats have I carried?"

Borg gave a wry grin, knowing her acid way too well to take any one statement as a gauge of her temper. Her piercing dark eyes sent him a brief glare, and she bent back to Helga as a whimper escaped the girl's tight lips. "Let it out, *flicka*," Inga murmured with a gentleness that surprised him. "When it comes again, let it out strongly, the pain."

Still there was some understanding of Inga, who had shared her husband's bitter cross for a dozen years. She was a "black Swede," black-haired with dark brown eyes, a tall handsome woman rugged as a Valkyrie. Her skin was deeply tanned and her body, at thirty-two, was well-formed and firm-fleshed, never having been dragged down by children.

"Helga," Borg said gently, *"hur mar du? Fint som snus?"*

The girl's eyes rolled painfully to focus on him. A wan smile as she whispered, *"Ja, tack."* Her eyes closed, and he studied her with a deep pity. Fresh from Sweden by less than a year, wracked by birthpains in a strange land whose language she hardly spoke, a man could only guess at what lay in her mind.

Sigrid, jogging him with an elbow, said briskly, "Here, mister, tie these ends to this hoop, and make them tight."

Borg knotted an end of each twisted rope to the bent willow sapling that formed the last supporting hoop for the canvas roof, tying them at opposite sides. This while Inga made swift deft knots at the other ends,

9

thrust them into Helga's hands.

"Now pull, little one, and help us."

Almost at once, with her sharp scream, the ropes tightened. Inga muttered, "The pains are coming more quickly. Soon. It will be soon."

"It's shameful, all the attention that girl's getting," said a shrewishly shrill voice. Enid Nansen had come up behind Sigrid. She stood arms akimbo, her slatternly form stiff and her long face vindictive. "A girl who did what she did—"

Sigrid's lips tightened as she turned, but her voice held soft. "She did wrong, Enid, but we must do the Christian thing."

The woman let her hands fall, something vicious in the gesture. "*Gud bevara*—don't lecture me on Christian duty, Sigrid Vikstrom! My husband and me take this hussy into our house only from goodness and charity, we needed no hired girl, and see how she pays us. Oh, the slut! Oh, the disgrace and all the people laughing at us—"

Sigrid's round face had flushed, and she said sharply, "Charity! Yes, tell us of charity, Enid. Then maybe I tell you what Our Lord said to the Pharisees—"

"Oh, shut up!" Inga cut in now. "Disgrace—Christian duty! You both make me sick! What do you know of loneliness, of real need, eh? So a girl in love was too generous with a man who wasn't worth it—not that any man is! Who are you to spit on her—"

"Inga," Borg broke in very quietly. She glared at him a moment, then said in her bitterly normal tone. "All right, Vikstrom. But get that hag away from here

10

before I break an arm for her."

Enid Nansen reached for a sputtering reply, but her husband Gunnar, a thin nervous man with a face like a tired sheep's, now moved quickly over and took her arm. "Come on, come on," he cajoled, careful to avoid Borg's cold eyes as he tugged his wife toward their wagon.

Borg, frowning, moved off a few paces; Sigrid hesitated, wiped her hands on her apron and stepped up to him, having to tilt her head well back to meet his eyes, since Borg stood six and a half feet without his boots.

"Now I have made Herr Vikstrom mad."

"Maybe the wife of the wagon leader should not bicker with the other women. She has duties besides her Christian one, eh?"

She lowered her eyes, but laughter crinkles formed at the corners of her mouth. "I have made Herr Vikstrom very mad."

Borg grinned and dropped a big arm around her shoulders. "Old woman."

She smiled gravely. "Has Mr. Dart come back yet?"

Borg turned his head, facing across the rolling, seemingly limitless Kansas grassland. "Not yet. Don't worry for Nathan. This is his country. His home, eh?"

His glance down at her surprised an indrawn look softly pinching her face. "But not ours," she murmured now, "Borg."

"It will be." He tilted her chin up with his thumb. "Ah sure, a new wild country. Now it is all strange. But we'll make it a home, old woman, eh?" He knew the fear in her too well, let the force of his love meet it, his arm shaking her gently. "Believe it, Sigrid, believe in me."

"In you—always." Briskly she shrugged away his arm. "Now don't wait around where you're in our way. Put Kjersti to bed, and mind that she says her prayers."

He tucked Kjersti inside her eiderdown in their wagon, received her sleepy kiss and "'Night, Dada." As he was climbing down, Nathan Dart rode in, drumming his moccasined heels Indian fashion against his roan's bony flanks. He slipped to the ground like a noiseless shadow, quietly greeted Borg.

"How's the little gal? Baby come yet?"

"Not yet, Nathan."

"Pity no tellin' who the man was," Nathan Dart said quietly.

Borg shrugged. "Him we likely left behind in Wisconsin. You found the place?"

Nathan Dart nodded.

The party had struck early camp because Helga had gone suddenly into labor. Dart, not wholly sure of his bearings on a prairie without distinctive landmarks, had gone to scout well ahead. Now, lifting an arm, he pointed toward a low cluster of hills to the northwest.

"Tonight's your last camp on the trail, Mr. Vikstrom. Yonder over them hills is Liberty, Eb Haggard's town." His arm swung due west. "Look sharp down them last slopes where they dip, you'll maybe see sun hittin' water. Cherokee River."

Borg shaded his eyes with his hand, squinting to the horizon and downward. He nodded slowly . . . so this was the place, the river bottomlands, and knowing

12

they were this near he felt the excited fret of sharp impatience.

Then dropped his hand with a grin. "Liberty. A good sound, Nathan."

"That she is."

Dart grinned too as they regarded each other, two different men with a common understanding. Borg Vikstrom, a horny-handed giant in his prime, with the power of a young bull contained in his great chest and shoulders and long arms. Toughened, but not yet bent, from a lifetime of pushing a plow and swinging an ax. He had the long bony face of his Norwegian ancestors, the forehead high and square and the sky-blue eyes deepset under a straight ridge of sun-bleached eyebrows. His cheekbones were high and sharp as an Indian's with the skin taut as smooth leather across them, and the fine wrinkles around eyes and mouth had appeared early in life. Under a battered slouch hat his hair was a tawny mane which fantailed shaggily over his ears and neck. His blue faded workshirt, the sleeves rolled high on brown muscle-corded arms, was mottled with the salt of old sweat, and his dusty shapeless trousers were stuffed into rundown boots.

He dwarfed Nathan Dart, who had served as guide and scout for this wagon train of mixed Norwegian and Swedish immigrants clear overland from southern Wisconsin. Dart was worn and weathered and colorless. His face was ugly and wizened as a monkey's and his hair was like old hemp. His skin was dyed to the texture of dried saddle leather from fifty-odd years of plains, wind and sun. His manner was modest, his voice a hushed drawl, and his appearance was wholly deceptive.

Through the grueling long weeks of the trek, the party had found Nathan Dart a Godsend; he knew the country and the trails, the ideal campsites with good water. He knew the vegetation and wildlife like the palm of his hand, and he was equally at home in woods or prairie. When Sofie, the brindled cow who had plodded the whole way tied behind the Vikstrom wagon, had sickened with larkspur poisoning and swelled up like an inflated bladder, it was Dart who saved her. Deftly sticking his Bowie knife in her side, to Sigrid's shocked objection—but soon Sofie was well. When a roving band of Pawnees had caught them at the nooning two days ago and arrogantly demanded ten cows, it was Dart who went out to sign-talk them, calmly bluffing them off with a little sugar and tobacco.

Dart had proven himself worth his weight in gold— but long before that, at their first meeting in Koshkonong, Wisconsin's great Norwegian settlement to which Dart's wanderings had brought him, Borg had felt the inner resources of this gray little man.

There had been the mutual liking at first sight, but it wasn't till after a few drinks and words that each had sensed a deeper vein of kinship. With no more than a vaguely shared notion apparent at first, neither being a man of words, they'd come to realize a common purpose that might have been an unwatered seed in each man for years, finding its catalyst in this meeting. Borg's Viking forebears had profoundly believed in

Fate, guiding their lives by omen and portent, and he wondered a little. But maybe that was too high-sounding.

Maybe Dart had put it best, saying simply, "I like folks. I just come from a place called Kansas, Mr. Vikstrom. Prairie land, wide, free, and open. Man can lay his sights for miles an' see nothin' but buffler grass. Some call it barren an' useless, savin' to Injuns and buffler, maybe cattle. Reckon the ranches'll come now the railroad's opened up shippin' points for the Texas drovers. Buffler'll be gone in a few more years with the Injuns losin' ground an' the hide-hunters trimmin' down the big herds. Be Texas all over maybe, few big cattle spreads waxin' fat and sassy, lot of one-loop outfits barely hangin' on.

"Only maybe not. This child's been studyin' the lay of her. Like to see that country turned over to people. Solid family folk, I mean. Enough so's they can be comfortable, not so many they're barkin' shins on each other. Want to see 'em get the feel of her big and free, raise their kids with the feel. Rough mean country, but opens a body up, brings out the best and worst. I make her a challenge. She'll show her good once she's halter-broke.

"It's croppin' I got in mind, and I could be wrong. Some says the prairie weather's too harsh, the land's good for only graze. Maybe so. Only there's soil under that buffler grass, roots and blades growin' and dyin' for hundreds of years built her deep and rich. Like to see a land put to its best use.

"Hell, I ain't no farmer. Grew up on the Texas

15

Caprock and dabbed loops on mean longhorns most my life, ate dust on drives to Joplin an' N'Orleans. But I seen the Pacific Ocean in my time. Dug gold in California an' rid with Sherman an' Sheridan—hated that goddamn slavery—an' after the war, for the hell of it, packed off to Mexico with Jo Shelby and the New Confederacy. This dog's seen his days. I'd bet the poke I gambled away in Sacramento that Kansas country'll belong to the ones who sink their stakes deep an' hang on. Kansas an' farmin', there's a gamble. Hell, yes. Only say you get a man knows the country, another who knows his trade; have 'em throw what they know, along with some guts, together. There's half your fight won."

It had been, without a doubt, the longest speech of Nathan Dart's life. Warmed by whiskey and opening up to a man with like feelings. That man was Borg Vikstrom, a workaday farmer who, except during the war, had never traveled fifty miles beyond the immigrant village where he'd grown up.

CHAPTER TWO

WATCHING BORG'S FACE, NATHAN DART CHUCKLED. "Before you champ that bit to pieces, whyn't we ride over and take a pasear on them bottomlands? Couple hours good light left."

"You have not eaten, Nathan."

"Chawed some jerky, filled my belly with water by the river." At Borg's wry face, the scout showed his gray quiet smile. "Puts grit in a man's craw, hoss, and we ain't sunk our wells yet. Anyways I'm like you, too het up for grub to settle light. Want to throw on your hull?"

Borg nodded, glancing around to ask Magnus if he cared to ride along. Then saw his son across the compound standing by Olof Holmgaard's wagon with Olof's daughter Greta. He eyed them a thoughtful moment . . . Magnus was coming to manhood fast, and Borg wasn't wholly pleased with the way he flitted like a bee from flower to flower. His too-quick wit and words with too many girls could make him trouble.

Still, Borg mused, passing his glance to the Hultgren boys, who squatted by their wagon wolfing their meal, Magnus was sowing his oats with considerable restraint next to those lads. Syvert Hultgren had been the first Koshkonong man to rally to Borg's call for followers. Syvert, eight years older than his brother, Arne, was a bundle of loose-reined energy which made him a hard willing worker, also a troublemaker. Restless and taciturn and surly, hot-tempered and a hard drinker, he set a poor example for eighteen-year-old Arne who idolized him. Pitying these orphaned boys, Borg still regarded their presence on the party with watchful displeasure; in a strange new country they could hardly afford the luxury of troublemakers.

He shrugged these thoughts away, walking out from the camp to unhobble Hans, his bay gelding. Hans playfully swelled his barrel as Borg threw on the saddle and Borg carefully kicked him in the belly; Hans unwinded with a baffled snort and tried to nip him. Borg rode back to Lars' wagon to tell his busy wife where he was going. Getting her impatient nod, he rode around past Lars with a troubled glance at the bleak tightness of his brother's face.

They set off due west, he and Dart, with the dipping sun against their faces, a brassy red ball which turned the buffalo grass to a muted golden. Nathan had told him how the grass stood green and lush in the spring, the summer heat searing it soon to a golden brown, curling it down against the earth. In the fading light of this early fall day, the analogy of gold caught at a man's fancy . . . Borg remembered his father telling how he'd come to America half-believing in streets of gold. His father, broken in spirit by financial and family troubles in the old country, had desperately wanted to believe in America's rich promise. Yet both he and his wife had died young, wresting a home from the Wisconsin wilderness.

Borg had resolved to tear gold of its own sort from the American earth, and could wonder with the thought whether he wasn't breaking himself on his own empty dream. What made a man of forty, a settled farmer and family man, suddenly tear up his roots and bring his family into a raw undeveloped country to start over?

He had been slow to tell Sigrid his decision, knowing how it would be; she had fought tears and chagrin as he'd tried to explain his feelings. But there was no explaining it clearly, not even to himself.

True that for years he'd supplemented their slender income by working winters in the logging camps, and that the lumber barons, having denuded southern Wisconsin, were moving operations up north—still the family could make do. True that Borg's farm had been developed in an area of pines, not hardwoods, and the pin needle loam was too acid for good crops—still they had gotten better returns in recent years. True that the long Wisconsin winters made for a short growing season—but they were descended from Northmen, toughened by adversity.

Maybe it was only that a man had to find a deeper meaning in his life than the drudgery of everyday routine. Sigrid, being a woman, could find that meaning in her religion and home and family. But maybe for a man, the thing must have a physical challenge, watered by a little blood and sweat, to find fruition. . . .

After a steady hour's ride, they drew near the river, and now Nathan Dart pointed upstream to where its southward flow straggled through a deep cleft between two rounded hills. "Liberty's over that divide yonder. Eb Haggard built her in a crook of the river so's the drovers could hold their cattle on the bottomlands. Plenty fine grass there to fatten up beeves before dickerin' with buyers. Beeves shed a lot of tallow on a thousand mile or so drive, extra pounds mean good prices."

Borg nodded. "You have not said much about this Mr. Haggard."

"Thought I told you a sight."

Nathan had told of how Eben Haggard had come last year to Gopher Wells, a miserable cluster of sod shacks on the prairie. Of these, two were a store and a horse relay station for a once-a-month stage layover; the rest were inhabited by ne'er-do-wells who'd staked out a few sections of land along the Cherokee bottoms. Haggard had bought up for a song whatever squatter's rights they might possess, then built his town, and gave Gopher Wells the ringing new name of Liberty. Prior to this he'd dickered the Kansas & Colorado Railroad, which had lost money building onto the empty prairie past Lawrence, into extending their line to his proposed town. The railroad would make a fortune shipping cattle from this new railhead; all Haggard asked in return was a five-dollar fee for every stock car loaded at his depot, also that they build a half mile of siding for loading.

This was good business, but—"I meant of the man," Borg said.

"Well, he's a book fella, lawyer I'd say, but made him a tidy sum land speculatin' around Austin, Texas. Yankee from Boston hisself, sharp as razor soup. Reckon he sounds sort of dry and dusty, but you'll see otherwise." Dart paused thoughtfully. "Got a way about him. Fact when I talked to him six month ago he was fired up with the notion of bringin' settlers from back East—owns a lot of undeveloped land that's doin' nobody good just layin' there—and he sort of fired my idea about Kansas farmin'."

Dart gave his dry gray smile. "Our party's camped on Haggard land. Twenty thousand acres of it, with the Cherokee here formin' the west boundary."

Borg whistled. "I'll look forward to meeting this man."

"You will, tomorrow when we ride in to dicker for the land." Dart grinned again. "Ever meet a New England hoss trader?"

Borg shook his head.

"You will."

They were pressing down the last grassy slopes above the river, and now Borg halted, dismounted and threw reins. He breathed deeply, studying the lay of the land, the sluggish yellow flow of the river, then sank on his haunches and dug his hands into the earth. With mounting excitement he saw the crumbling black rich grit, rubbed it between his hands, smelled it and felt almost an impulse to taste it. Nothing thrilled him like the touch of rich soil, and he had never seen better. Like Eben Haggard, Borg Vikstrom had a plan, and in this earth he'd found its first step solidly realized.

Grinning like a boy he rose and dusted his horny hands on his pants. "Good land, Nathan. This is the place."

But Dart was studying a sparse grove of cottonwood low along the upriver bank, and following his glance Borg saw smoke wisp up from a hidden fire. At the same time a lone horseman paced over a rise, halted with his sighting of the smoke, then rode down toward it and the trees swallowed him.

Borg glanced at the scout. "Someone living here, maybe?"

"Just a break-up camp is my guess, and that other fella'll join him for the night. Plains hospitality, son."

On the heel of his words came a wild yell, and they saw the horseman spur out of the grove at a hard run.

21

Another man was stumbling after him. In the dimming light Borg watched a puzzled moment before realizing with a shock that the rider was pulling the second man on a rope. Now he fell in his lurching run, and the rider dragged him face-down along the bank with another rebel whoop.

Nathan Dart slammed a heel into his roan's flank to turn the animal at a sharp angle toward the river, and Borg saw that he meant to head them off. Mounting swiftly, he followed Dart downslope.

They reached the bank and pulled up as Dart dragged his Springfield from its scabbard. As he levered it to loud cock in the still dusk, the rider broke to a skidding halt a few yards away. Close up, he was a tall rangy scarecrow of a fellow with a bristling yellow beard. His eyes were a vapid washed-out blue, and his jaw sagged loosely, stupidly. *This one's wits are addled,* Borg thought narrowly.

Dart dismounted and curtly motioned the man to the ground. Borg got down, too, tramping over to the second man who lay face down, breathing in shallow painful gasps. He was a withered small stick of a man, and Borg felt the light-boned frailty of him as he lifted him enough to slip off the noose. And turning him on his back then, saw that the man was an Indian. An old Indian with skin like seamed and sun-blackened parchment, his straight gray hair like dirty straw worn long and loose. His lips moved without sound and in his slitted eyes lay a deeper sickness than physical pain. But the pain was there; exploring with careful fingers, Borg drew a sharp wince.

He said quietly, "A couple ribs, maybe more, are busted."

Dart nodded briefly. "Pawnee Harry, old derelict Injun swamps saloons 'round Liberty for drinks. Couldn't hurt a body if he wanted."

"He is a man, a hurt man," Borg said softly.

Dart grunted, his rifle loosely trained on the vapid-looking fellow. "Ain't met you, mister."

The man phlegmily cleared his throat, muttering.

"Speak up, mister."

"Panjab Willing."

He wore a crudely sewn bearskin overcoat, and his lean arms and big rawboned hands stuck out grotesquely from the baggy sleeves. Like his pants and boots it was ingrained with filth and grease stains. He kept wetting his loose lips.

"Hide hunter, eh?"

Willing found his wheezy voice. "Goddamit, I 'uz just—look, you ain't gonna take 'er on the peck cuz I 'uz havin' fun with this goddam ol' siwash—"

Dart spat sidelong in his gentle way. "Best you hyper along, Mr. Willing."

The buffalo hunter rubbed his palms once on his greasy pants, then swung with a gangling movement into his saddle. Staring at Borg and the Indian, he almost spoke again, but then wheeled and put his horse up a near slope, quartering northeast.

Borg said thickly, "The man should be shot."

Dart's rifle butt thumped on the ground. "For a whiskey-bellied old Injun? 'Round here any Injun's life's worth a cur dog's, only less."

"He needs help." Borg squinted up at the scout. "Do I help him alone, Mr. Dart?"

"Slack off, Mr. Vikstrom. Lived with Injuns, had a half-Apach' woman down in the Tonto Rim country. Good woman." Nathan Dart paused gently. "It's how things are, son."

They went to the grove and packed up the old man's scanty camp gear, and then, Borg holding him erect ahead of his saddle, rode slowly back toward the wagon camp. It was well after dark when they rode into the compound. Most of the people were bedded down, but a few late-stayers looked on staring as they eased Pawnee Harry gently down to the ground in the saffron firelight. The old man simply folded out on his back, one scrawny hand pressed over his side. He had endured the agony of the ride without a murmur; his seamed face was expressionless, expecting nothing, asking nothing.

From Lars' wagon came a baby's thin wail.

"Borg—" Sigrid had struggled out of her sheepskin robe spread under their wagon. Half-risen she stopped, brushing back the pale fall of her unbound hair, her blue eyes wide. He went over to her and tiredly knelt, taking her by the shoulders.

"Helga?"

"Well. The baby too. But—"

"If a piece of that sheet you tore is clean, bring it. Hurry now."

She was fully dressed, and now she quickly pulled on her shoes and climbed into their wagon. Kjersti made a sleepy complaint and was sharply hushed.

24

Beneath the wagon Magnus grunted slowly awake and rolled over in his robe, staring out. "What is it?"

Borg didn't answer, tramping back to where Dart knelt opening the Indian's shirt. His quick expert hands confirmed that two left ribs were broken. "Won't be movin' a spell. You bought yourself a problem, hoss."

"So?" Borg growled. "Already I have a few."

"That's my meanin'."

The soft gasping cries of the baby continued, and Inga's low husky voice was crooning to it. Some of the men wandered over to ask questions; Borg gave curt short answers. Sigrid hurried up with the strip of sheet and while Borg held the old man upright, Dart folded the cloth and bound it tightly around his brown flesh-less torso.

Sigrid said, "I will get a blanket," and returning with it, brushed Borg impatiently aside; she and Dart carefully lifted the old man onto it and covered him. While she fussily tugged the blanket smooth, Borg glanced about at the quiet creaking of Lars' wagon. Inga had stepped down, softly crooning to a swaddled bundle she held.

He went over to peer at the red tiny face in the bundle, wrinkled in newborn sobbing discomfort, then gave his sister-in-law a foolish grin. *"Der ar en pojke,"* she murmured with a strange deep softness he had never heard.

"A boy," Borg said, adding dryly, "Now the Lord be praised. Women enough in this household."

"Oh shut up," Inga whispered without her usual

25

acerbic edge. Studying her dark handsome face, Borg realized with a sudden pity what the coming of the baby meant to her. Turned downward, her bitter and brooding gaze was softened to a misty shine.

"He's named?"

"Not yet."

"A fine boy needs a good Norwegian name. What about Lisj-Per—the Little Peter? How does it sound?"

"It's not bad, considering the source." She tried the name on her tongue, "Lisj-Per," and nodded.

Borg smiled. "Of course you will ask Helga first."

"Yes, yes," she said irritably.

Wondering if Inga had begun to cruelly deceive herself, Borg said almost sharply, "It is Helga's, *mor* Inga."

"Who said it wasn't?" Her eyes hated him; again her voice would etch glass. But their relation had always been friendly, and after a moment she gave a shrug and her bitter smile. "You're right too often, for such a squarehead." Her dark gaze flicked toward the old Indian, and with sardonic mockery then: "A girl with child and no husband. A hurt old Indian. Vikstrom loves lost little strays; he takes them all in. What a softhearted fool."

"We are two fools, Inga."

"And you're the biggest." She turned away, gently rocking the baby in her strong arms. A slight sound drew Borg's glance to Lars, rolled in his blankets under the wagon. The fireglow sallowed his face and his eyes were open, staring straight upward. Borg sighed and moved away.

Dart was spreading out his bedroll nearby, and Sigrid stood waiting by their wagon. She looked gravely at her husband and then at old Pawnee Harry, but if she felt any reproach for this new burden, she hid it well.

"Let the telling wait till tomorrow, *litagod;* we're all tired and out of sorts."

"Mr. Dart told me already, *ja?*" Her grave eyes held on his face, and smiling she shook her head slowly from side to side. "You great good *dumskalle.*"

CHAPTER THREE

THE ENTIRE TRAIN ROUSED OUT BEFORE DAWN, BUSTLING with the excited knowledge that the last stop lay a few miles farther. And a new beginning, for all had varied strong reasons for tearing up old roots to find a fresh life for themselves and their families. It was with highly mixed emotions that they pushed their plodding oxen down the last long slope onto the bottomlands at high noon.

A temporary camp was set up and the men unloaded some of the furniture and boxes of household goods from the wagons while the women prepared the *middag* meal. Afterward they ate and joked with high spirits. Then at Nathan Dart's request, Borg called the men of the party together. When they were assembled, Dart suggested that he and Borg go into Liberty this afternoon and sound out Mr. Haggard, who would drive a very sharp bargain. Let Vikstrom whittle Hag-

27

gard down to a fair price per acre for them all, and once an agreement was reached, let the others make their individual deals with Haggard. A ripple of murmurs and nods followed the suggestion, and then big stolid Olof Holmgaard raised his voice:

"Mr. Dart is right. Borg Vikstrom will do good by all. Let him talk for us."

There was general nodded assent, broken by Syvert Hultgren's loud surly objection. "I talk for myself." Somebody hooted sarcastically, but Borg raised his hand, saying quietly, "Syvert?"

Young Hultgren elbowed himself roughly ahead of the others to face Borg. He was a dark second-generation Swede, lean as a whip, fidgeting with the high-strung energy that was part of him. His eyes flashed like agates in his axblade of a face, and he kept impatiently tossing back the long black cowlick that fell over his brow.

"Syvert," Borg said with a faint smile, "you don't trust me?"

A startled flush mounted to Syvert's face. "Ain't that," he muttered, shifting his feet. "Why you say that?"

"Bargaining's for cool heads. You're a good sharp boy; no one's said you ain't, eh?" Borg gave him a friendly slap on the shoulder. "But you got a cool head, Syvert?"

There were a few chuckles, and Syvert grinned sheepishly. "Nah. I'm mean as a catamount. Touch off like Chinese firecrackers. Ah, sure, you make the deal, Borg. For me an' Arne."

The men broke up in good humor, and Borg stood with hands on hips, shaking his head.

"Look like your stick's floating upstream, hoss."

"There's a thing I can't put my hand on, Nathan. Look, it was the understanding I'd lead the people on the journey. But that now is ended."

Dart spat mildly. "Not by a whoop and a holler." He paused reflectively. "Don't know how to put it exactly. 'Member a fella I sojered under in Georgia, kid general name of Custer, friend of ol' Billy-hell Sherman's. This lad had the look an' feel of command. Born leader, kind his men'd foller into hell. The breed's a seldom sort; body can smell 'em out a mile away upwind on a March day." Dart's gray smile flickered. "Boy, I smelt it in you first time we met, an' strong lye soap don't wash it out. Like it or not, these is all your people."

Borg gave him a frowning regard. He'd straw-bossed a few logging crews, but had thought little of the ease with which he handled gangs of tough lumberjacks. His real trade was farming, and he'd always held down his small farmstead alone.

Dart said, "They like and trust you, sure. But these people is used to standing on their own. Poke a Swede, you kick a mule. Careful folk and stubborn, distrustful of authority. Don't foller a man lightly; particular a hothead like that young Hultgren don't. Think it over, Borg." He turned on his heel and walked away to fetch his horse. Borg, standing bemused, realized then that Dart had used his first name for the first time.

He hunted up Magnus, found him walking by the

river with Greta Holmgaard, quite indifferent to the idea of a ride to town. A little nettled, Borg returned to his wagon. It was unloaded now, and the canvas top removed. He'd abandoned the oxen yoke and harness and rigged up the two-horse hitch. He teamed up their mare and a borrowed animal, because Hans, ungelded in his head, was also exclusive about his saddle use.

Lars did not want to come along of course, and Inga was busy tending Helga and the baby. Inga, Borg reflected, seemed to have taken both Helga and her infant son under her wing, so perhaps his cautioning words to her last night were unnecessary. Or maybe to her mind, both were lost waifs needing her fiercely tender protection.

After checking on Pawnee Harry, who was resting comfortably, Borg clucked the team off at a brisk clip. He and Sigrid sat on the seat with Kjersti sandwiched between them, and Dart rode alongside the wagon. In the excitement of journey's end, Sigrid seemed to have shed, for now at least, her fears and misgivings; she chatted away quite cheerily.

"We should buy some things in town, mister, and maybe Mr. Dart will help us. He will know what we need most in Kansas."

Borg grinned. "Of course Nathan will help. And tomorrow he'll show us how to build a sod house."

Nathan Dart said only, "Sure," and jogged along for a time in brooding silence. Curious, Borg was about to speak when Dart said suddenly, "Reckon I'll be pushin' on afterward."

"Whoa!" Borg shouted. Bringing the team to a halt

he turned on the seat, scowling at the little scout. "What's this, you'll be pushing on? You don't like our company?"

A little jolted, Dart said, "Sure . . . yeah. Only my job's done. Aside from seeing you-all snug for the winter, ain't a sight more I'm good for."

Sigrid protested, "But you must stay, Mr. Dart. You now are one of the family, *ja?*"

"No, ma'am—what I mean—"

"Nathan is a Texas man, old woman. He don't want to be a dirt farmer."

"Now hold on!" Dart's mild voice rose. He chewed his mustache reflectively. "Had me a fiddle-foot forty years, since I was sixteen, and that's too long for any man. She's wore pretty thin, I tell you." He paused. "Told you about my half-Apach' woman. Her other half was Mexican. But we was married proper, even if it was in the Injun way. Had five good years before the pox took her off. Best years of my life. Too old and ugly for any woman now, but I'd fancy bein' a settled man again. Still got enough rawhide I can push a plow."

Sigrid sent her husband an oblique glance. "Gurina Helgeson, *ja?*"

Gurina was a robust widow in her early forties who had driven her own wagon all the way. "The very one. Farmers are family men, Nathan."

"Now hold on—" Dart began, but Borg started up the team with a cheerful, "Leave it to us."

Guiding the wagon up the long hill that formed the east flank of the river divide, Borg mentally charted its contour for the future road that would connect Liberty with their farms. When they topped the rise, Nathan Dart signaled him to halt, then pointed out the gray sprawl of buildings that was Liberty on the flat below. Next they followed his pointing hand off left toward the cattle grazing on the bottomlands where the buffalo grass still lay lush and green. There was a camp near the bedgrounds, and they could make out wagons and men and a cavvy of horses.

"My guess that's the first herd to hit town for the fall season. See a sight more in a few weeks. Town'll be busting red-eyed and wide open with cowmen, stock buyers, an' railroaders."

Toward midafternoon they rode down the main street of Liberty, and the Vikstroms were amazed at its dusty width. They took in the vast maze of stockyards and loading pens and the long rail siding on the south side of the Kansas & Colorado tracks. By contrast the town itself, except for its generous main stem, seemed cramped with its narrow cross streets and twenty-foot lots with their small establishments shouldered together. There was a blacksmith shop, a feed company, a livery stable, and numerous saloons. A good-sized professional building covered two lots, and the Stockman's Hotel was an edifice of crude grandeur—biggest hostelry west of Kansas City, Dart allowed.

They put in at the hitch rail fronting the professional building, and while Borg swung Sigrid to the ground, Dart tied up the animals and said: "Ma'am, we'll be makin' pretty dry medicine with Mr. Haggard. You might be more at home in the general store sizin' up possibles. Join you later."

Sigrid, lifting Kjersti off the seat, gave him a grateful smile. "Thank you, Mr. Dart."

She quartered north across the street, holding Kjersti's hand. Borg had started to follow Dart onto the boardwalk when a sudden pandemonium from the south end of town drew his glance. A dusty bunch of strung-out riders poured down the main street, wildly yelling, pushing their shaggy ponies at an all-out gallop. A pistol went off in the air, and Borg caught the rebel yell he'd heard at Chickamauga, Shiloh, and other places— *"Yip-yip-yeeowee!"*

Dart chuckled, "Drovers from the herd we seen. Primed for white lightnin' and pure deviltry."

But Borg's concerned glance shot toward Sigrid and Kjersti. He shouted a warning to Sigrid, she being a shade on the deaf side, but she'd already halted and turned in mid-street, frozen with surprise. Borg left the boardwalk in a lunging run and reached them well ahead of the riders, pulling them both back as the lead rider careened his mount to a stop. Touched his hat to Sigrid as a wide grin flashed in his sun-boiled face.

"Don't be fussed, ma'am; Texican don't ride over ladies." Next his gaze passed carefully over Borg, coldly narrowed then. Abruptly he said, "I make you a clodhoppin' pig farmer, mister. I can smell pig ten mile off," and wheeled his horse away.

Borg's hand became a fist at his side, but Sigrid caught his arm tightly. "It's nothing. Mr. Vikstrom, it is nothing."

He let out his breath. "No."

Sigrid murmured as Dart joined them, *"Himmel,* I have thought that all Texas men were like Mr. Dart."

The scout's leathery face crinkled. "Ma'am, don't you whitewash us Texans. I was a younker, I was all bull 'gator an' wild mustang." He added soberly, "Should of mentioned a cowman's feelin' about farmers. Purely hate the breed. Don't let it throw you. Two, three years from now the drovers'll be done with Liberty and she'll go tame as a lady's lap dog."

"They got wild horsies," Kjersti said, clinging wide-eyed to her mother's hand. The riders were piling off their horses by the saloons, and now again one whooped exuberantly and shot off his pistol; broken glass jangled as a store window collapsed.

A man who had been leaning quietly in a store entrance across the way stepped swiftly off the walk and crossed the street. He was a tall man in his shirt-sleeves with a body narrow as a snake's and something snakelike in his long gliding movements. A flat-crowned black Stetson rode his lean head, and his light curling hair was worn long, brushing his collar. Long silky mustaches divided his bony upper face from a clean-shaven chin; even at this distance his eyes were flecks of bleached ice. His neatly buttoned vest and trousers were of black broadcloth against which his black shellbelt and holstered gun lay almost invisible; on the vest a badge glinted.

He stopped by the rider's stirrup, saying in a passionless way, "Get off that horse."

The Texan was about eighteen, with a cocksure grin that slowly faded. He eyed the speaker over thoughtfully, then turned his head and spat at the sidewalk.

"Once more. Get down."

Aware of his friends watching this, the boy gave his cocky grin. "Not for no goddam Yankee marshal I don't."

The man with the badge shot up a hand and caught his belt, dumping him sideways from his saddle and stepping smoothly backward as the boy sprawled in the dirt. With the same fluid motion his gun blurred out of its holster, covering the Texas men. Then, as the boy scrambled up cursing, he slashed the long barrel across his head and struck viciously again as he went down.

A surge of movement among the standing or mounted men, and the marshal's voice whip-lashed across it. "Usual rules. You men know them. Keep your guns in your belts. No riding horses into saloons. No brawling inside; do your fighting on the street. Jail and fines for any damaged property." He paused, his lip curling off his teeth. "And leave any decent women you see alone."

It was a calculated insult, as needless as his second striking of the young rider. There was a stir of muttering and a couple of blistering curses, but an elderly rider with the look of authority squelched it with a few words. Sullenly the men began filing into a saloon. The leader went over to the marshal and the talk between them was sharp and brief. The old man tramped in after his crew, his face heated with anger. The boy, blood streaking his face, had climbed dazedly to his hands and knees. Prodding him onto his feet, the marshal pushed him stumbling toward the frame jail.

Kjersti whimpered softly, and Sigrid picked her up and held her, eying her husband almost accusingly. Borg knew a first sinking doubt: To what kind of a country had he brought them?

"That was Tiger Jack Tetlow in action," Nathan Dart observed. "Killer for hire if there ever was. Seen him in Abilene last year. They hired him as marshal for three days, killed two men and crippled two more before they run him out. See how he buffaloed that kid? Soon pistolwhip a man as give him time of day." He wagged his head in disgust. "So the law's come to Liberty. Eb Haggard's like to gone dotty, hirin' a man like that to police his town."

Sigrid said nothing. She set Kjersti down, took her hand and marched off toward the general store. Borg sighed deeply. "All right, Nathan, lead on."

Entering the building, the two men went up a rickety staircase and down a narrow hallway. Dart paused by an open door. Inside a man was leaning by a window, looking down at the street. He turned at Nathan Dart's low cough, and with a wide smile came around the desk to grasp his hand.

"Nate, you tamed old tornado—damn' fine to see you."

"Howdy, Eb. Get my letter?"

"I did, weeks ago, and you could have knocked me over with a short breath. So you took my casual remark about bringing in settlers to heart and corraled me twenty-some families back in Wisconsin! . . . Nate,

I don't know what to say except thanks. And you brought them with you?"

"Surest thing you know. Borg Vikstrom—Eb Haggard."

Haggard extended a big-knuckled hand and Borg took it, feeling the restless, magnetic impact of the man without quite identifying its reason. Except for his deeply weathered face, Eben Haggard might have been a staid preacher or the lawyer Dart had named him. He stood a few inches shorter than Borg, seeming taller than his height because of his rawboned spareness. His long face was gaunt and hollow-cheeked with melancholy deepset eyes, and his rumpled black hair, unlike his spade beard, was shaggy and untrimmed. Physically he went with his sober dark suit and tie.

Borg saw that Eben Haggard was taking his measure with equal intentness; the man's eyes, irised like shiny tar, were as careful as his smile was warm. "Nate, you needn't have said a word. I know Mr. Vikstrom at once from a one-line description in your letter."

He motioned them to the two chairs beside his desk and sank into his swivel chair, saying pleasantly, "How wet do you gentlemen whistle?" as he opened a drawer and produced a bottle and three glasses.

"About three fingers worth," Nathan Dart said. "She's one dusty day."

Borg took his whiskey in a swallow, and Haggard pursed his lips approvingly. "Mr. Vikstrom, I've heard it said that it takes a good Scandinavian to show a Yankee how to drink his own liquor. Now I believe it."

They all laughed, and having set a genial atmos-

37

phere, Haggard grinned, "Let's quit beating the brush and get to business." He leaned his elbows on his desk, steepling his fingers. "Have you and your people decided exactly where you'll sink your stakes?"

"I have." Borg hesitated. "It is not easy to say—"

"Here," Haggard interrupted, coming to his feet, "you can show me on the chart." Borg joined him by the two maps tacked to one bare wall. One, Haggard explained, was of the square mile that comprised the town proper. The lots were marked off with colored lines, and those in red, he indicated with a bony finger, were still unsold, belonging to him as townsite owner. Some of these squares were blank, but Borg noted that others were filled with the names of businesses, and those printed in red—mostly saloons—were all owned by Eben Haggard.

The other map showed all the prairie land southwest of the town that Haggard claimed. Some of it he'd bought from the handful of original squatters, dirt-cheap as he frankly admitted, and the rest had been deeded to him by the railroad, which had bought up the government land in this river valley for that purpose, as part of the package deal in which they extended their track to Liberty.

The meandering line of the Cherokee bisected the map plainly, and in one deep crook of it Borg pointed out the choice acreage of his selection. They roughed it out as one hundred and sixty acres, and then Haggard returned to his chair, crossed his legs and folded his hands on his belly, thumbs toying with his watch chain. He eyed Borg with a faint shrewd smile.

"And what is your idea of a fair price per acre, Mr. Vikstrom?"

"Ten dollars," Borg said without hesitation.

Haggard's somber eyes twinkled. "You're joking, of course."

"I joke only till you say your price, Mr. Haggard."

Haggard gave his booming laugh, and they settled down to a hard, stubborn seller-buyer exchange.

An hour later, with both sides satisfied and the loose ends tied together, Eben Haggard poured another round of drinks and the three men clicked glasses. Borg drank and smacked his lips, mildly studying his host. "We Norskies all are good Republicans, Mr. Haggard."

"So I've been told."

"You've been told too, maybe, that you look like Abe Lincoln?"

"Oh, about a thousand times. Why?"

Borg shook his head sadly. "He was a very fair man."

Haggard roared again. He fumbled out a silk handkerchief and blew his nose, still chuckling. "Your wife came in with you, didn't you say?"

"And the little girl. They will be at the store."

"Good. I'd like to meet them. Then I'd like all of you, Nate too, to join me at my house for dinner."

Both Borg and Dart politely protested, but Haggard firmly waved off their objections. As the three of them left the building for the dust and glare of the street, Dart nudged Borg. He followed the scout's watchful gaze to the buffalo hunter, Panjab Willing, slacked in a barrel chair on the hotel veranda. He turned a glance of naked hate on them, then furtively lowered his eyes and wiped his mouth with a hand. He was too stupid and trifling to return whatever injury he felt his due, Borg thought, and dismissed him.

The store, one of Haggard's own businesses, was big and spacious but so crowded with counters of goods supplementing the heaped shelves that a man had to edge awkwardly between them. The smell of leather and new cloth and foodstuffs was pleasant; Borg paused to take it in before moving on to join Sigrid, arguing with her frugal quiet stubbornness about the price of flour to a harassed-looking clerk.

"My wife, Mr. Haggard," Borg said, and Haggard doffed his hat with a smile. "*Hur mar du,* Mrs. Vikstrom?"

Sigrid replied with surprised pleasure at being addressed in her native tongue. "I know 'hello' and 'goodbye' in Swedish," Haggard twinkled. He turned to Kjersti who was sitting on a counter and drumming her heels while she eyed the candy display, won her over at once by giving her a bag of licorice. With the help of Nathan Dart and Haggard, they began their careful buying.

Sigrid murmured as she and Borg inspected some shovels in the hardware section, "Sixteen dollars for an acre, this you call a good price?"

"You should have been there to hear his first offers," Borg said dryly. "It's not a bad price."

"But only five thousand we got for the farm in Wisconsin."

"It wasn't much of a farm. Anyway, old woman, we have the money—more than half yet—for a plow and other tools and to keep us in food till we sell our first crop next year."

She compressed her lips. "We must have a stove, a tub for washing, some furniture and beds. We could have brought these things if you had not taken so much room in the wagon for your wonderful sacks of seed."

"That seed is our future," Borg said grimly. "A table, benches, and bunks like we had in the logging camps I can make with my hands. We'll buy some lumber now."

"It is very costly. I asked the clerk."

Ignoring that, Borg went on, "And some of the seed I plan to sell to the others. Some brought their own—"

"But most did not have faith in your plan."

"It wasn't that," he said irritably. "They weren't thinking. Too many came for other reasons than to farm."

"That is so." She patted his arm. "You think of them all, when they don't think for their own. Otherwise I would not like you."

He gave a sarcastic grunt, and they made their final purchases. Borg brought the wagon from across the street and the men loaded it. Sigrid, hand on hip and tapping her foot, studied the heap of assorted goods in the wagon bed and gave it a brisk nod.

"Now you can drive it over to my house," Haggard told Borg. "Nate'll show the way. I have a little business . . . Second thought, I'd better go with you. My wife is apt to be put out at preparing dinner for four extra people at the last moment."

Borg and Sigrid exchanged surprised glances; their family way was a warmly proud concern with them, and until now Eben Haggard had not even mentioned a wife.

Sigrid began, "We must not put your wife out—"

"Nonsense," Haggard said shortly, then smiled. "Margaret won't really mind. She's a Texas girl from Austin—her father was big in state politics before the war—and all her ties are there. She's had a lonely time here, the men of Liberty still outnumbering the women—mostly saloon riff-raff, I'm sorry to say—by about fifteen to one. You can imagine how pleased she'll be to meet you, Mrs. Vikstrom."

CHAPTER FOUR

BISON STREET, WHICH CROSSED MAIN AT ITS NORTH END, was obviously the lone part of Liberty that could qualify as residential. Eben Haggard explained that the few merchants and their families lived here. The houses were plain and rather small, but clap-boarded and whitewashed; considering the paucity of lumber trees here, any good frame dwelling was impressive. Haggard's own house was the most grand by far, two stories high with a roofed and pillared veranda. In front was a patch of lawn and a row of cottonwood saplings.

As they entered the parlor, Sigrid exclaimed at the

expensive, yet quietly tasteful, furnishings that Haggard had freighted in. His wife entered the room now, a slender and quite beautiful woman in her late twenties. She wore a calico dress with the same queenly grace she might have worn the silks and crinoline to which she was doubtless more accustomed. Her rich darkly auburn hair was done in a simple but immaculate coif, and her complexion was smooth ivory untouched by prairie sun. There was something Chinese—or-i-en-tal, Borg mentally fumbled—to the fine planes and hollows of her slim face. Her full lips were almost primly firm, her gray eyes calm and level—and he had the baffled feeling that such self-collected perfection could not be real.

She replied to the introductions with quiet reserve, the Southern softness of her voice a cool refinement to the ear. And then as her gaze touched Kjersti, a dancing warmth lighted her face. She bent down to take the child's hand. "Kjersti," she said softly. "Hello, Kjersti."

Sigrid murmured, "You must say hello to the lady, *flicka*."

"Hel-lo. You smell nice."

"That's verbena—perfume." Margaret Haggard laughed. "Come along, Kjersti, and I'll give you a little dab—yes? Oh, and you come too, Mrs. Vikstrom . . . Excuse us, gentlemen."

"Such a pretty parlor," Sigrid said as they went up the stairway, then Haggard called, "Juanita!" Slippers slap-slapped the floor, and a stout Mexican woman appeared in the entrance to the dining room. Haggard gave her directions for the meal, then told the men to sit, afterward offering a box of long pale brown Havanas. Borg and Dart had wiped their boots and slapped the dust from their clothes before entering the house, but both were uncomfortable, sitting gingerly on the edge of the sofa. Haggard sank at ease into a well-worn leather chair, puffing fragrant clouds of smoke.

"I'd offer a drink, but those were pretty stiff ones we had in the office, eh? . . . Now, Mr. Vikstrom, I'd like to hear more about your plans."

He listened for a minute as Borg talked, then cut in with mild interest, "Winter wheat, eh?" He leaned sideways to tap ash into an earthenware tray. "Interesting. Something new out here, that's certain. You'll pardon my ignorance of husbandry matters and sundry, but I'd wondered how you Midwestern farmers meant to deal with the vagaries of Kansas weather."

Borg explained that in the old country winter wheat was planted in the fall, the summer being too short for a good seasonal crop. The wheat had to sprout before the first stiff cold set in, but once it had a start, neither snow nor cold would damage it. In fact the snow cover kept the ground warm and watered the young plants during the spring thaw. Plenty of moisture was important, and he guessed that the summers in Kansas were hot and sometimes very dry.

Haggard nodded, and Borg went on, "Now the wheat's got an early start, eh? That bottomland I have bought of you will stay wetter as the summer comes than higher land. By June, maybe July, the wheat is ready to cut. Now the soil is very good there; I figure thirty-five to maybe forty bushels an acre—"

Haggard laughed and slapped his knee. "By the Lord Harry, and I almost felt guilty about the way I hedged you up from ten dollars. Vikstrom, you know how to set your sights. Hardheaded enterprise combined with farsighted shrewdness and a gambler's nerve. I like that. It's the way I came up from a cramped shyster's stall by Boston Common to . . . all this." He made an expansive gesture that included house and town and prairie.

Borg leaned forward, set his elbows on knees and laced his big callused hands together, wanting to convey more and not knowing the words. "This is something I have thought about for a long time."

"Interesting." Haggard blew smoke, idly inspecting the tip of his cigar. Borg leaned back, feeling a faint nudge of disappointment. Well, as the man said, he was no farmer; he could not be expected to feel this thing in the same way. Yet . . . you'd think that a man with the large foresight of Eben Haggard would see the larger vision of this country. For Borg had his dream, the sort of long-cherished obsession that got a man restless nights, deep moods, and the concern of a puzzled wife.

Of course there were clever and long-headed men to whom success was a totally personal thing, involving only money and prestige. And Borg would not lay judgment on another's way. Surely Eben Haggard's way would help many, if only incidentally. No doubt he'd reap a quick fortune from the cattle railhead he had established, then leave for greener fields. But the town he'd built was legacy to the many who would come; Liberty and its railroad would be their lifeblood. Johnny-come-latelies, but they would be the stayers and the builders; the country would grow, and the town, and then it would belong to the people, towns-folk and farmers. People and the land. . . .

Borg grinned at himself, lunging a deep drag on his cigar. A dream. But a damned solid one.

The women returned from the upstairs, and Sigrid and Mrs. Haggard went out to the kitchen while Kjersti romped from Borg to Nathan, holding up her hands for them to sample the nice smell. Haggard swung the talk in other channels, discussing with Dart the new prosperity of impoverished Texas since McCoy had started Abilene and the Chisholm Trail drives; Borg listened with interest.

Margaret Haggard listened too as she set the dining-room table, and when her husband paused to snuff out his cigar, she said, "About that fever quarantine on Texas longhorns east of here, Eben—did I tell you that Dad mentioned in one of his letters that—"

"Margaret, this is man's talk." Haggard spoke casu-ally, not looking at her. After a moment she bent her head and resumed her placing of the silverware. As Haggard talked on, Borg studied him without expres-sion. A woman had her place, and a man had his, but the division was also a giving and sharing toward a common thing. A man did not cut his wife in such a way. Minded now of other details in Haggard's whole attitude, Borg thought wonderingly, *Why, to him she is nothing at all.*

Dinner was a pleasant affair of much talk and laughter, for Haggard was a deft and jovial host who plainly enjoyed his role. The prime roast was excellent, and so were the dark fiery cordials of French brandy. But Sigrid grew silent toward the end of the meal, and Borg knew the sign of something weighing on her mind.

In the pause as the men lighted up their post-brandial cigars, she said firmly, "Mr. Haggard, there is a point that troubles me."

"Ma'am?"

"There are a number of children in our party, *ja?* They will need to have teaching. I did not see a school in Liberty. Nor," she added severely, "a church. We are good Lutherans."

Haggard leaned back, exhaling smoke with a wry smile. "Some of the amenities of civilization will be a while catching up here. Though your point is well-taken." He squinted thoughtfully at the ceiling. "Two of my business associates have children of school age, but sent them to boarding school in Kansas City. Of course now you've brought a large number of kids, we'll have to work out something locally. In fact I believe we can kill two birds with one stone."

Sigrid raised her eyebrows, and he went on, "There's a young fellow came here a month back, from Salt Lake City. He was raised in the Mormon Church, sent back East for his missionary turn, then left the Latter-Day Saints to preach the word at large, as I understand.

47

However, he's a schoolteacher by trade."

Sigrid frowned. "You have a man who is teacher and preacher, but no school or church?"

"And no kids till now." Haggard chuckled. "Brother Jevers says that his concern is saving sinners, not filling pews. He came to Liberty specifically because he'd heard it was a sinkhole of iniquity. Told me he's holding off pulpiteering till he's through personally wrestling Satan. Sits in a different saloon every evening resisting the dual temptations of red-eye and the scarlet Jezebels. Says he can't preach in good faith till he's proven his own."

"Why, he is the very man we need!"

"I don't know," Haggard demurred. "Abel Jevers is an old potato any way you cut him—hate to find I'd sold you a pig in a poke. He's obviously intelligent and educated—told me he attended Harvard for two years, so no doubting his qualifications as a teacher—but can you imagine a man like that swamping in a livery stable, as he's now doing? Nor is he ordained in any denomination—in fact says he's dead set against Christians splitting into sects."

"I think that is not important. A young man so sincere as to humble such gifts, and himself too, before he shows others how to live—such a man we need." Sigrid laid a hand on her husband's arm. "Isn't that so?"

Borg, with good food and brandy in his belly and a fine cigar in his hand, nodded agreeably, and she said briskly, "Good! Now you will go find this Mr. Jevers and tell him why he must come home with us."

Borg coughed, opened his mouth and closed it with a resigned nod. Haggard said with a broad grin, "Jevers'll be finishing up at the stable about now. I'll go along, Borg—perhaps help break the ice."

"I will be thankful," Borg said dryly.

"I'll mosey 'long," Dart said. Leaving the women to clear the table, they stepped out into the early evening; despite its coolness, full daylight still held. As they passed onto Main Street, whoops and laughter drifted from the saloons.

Dart said: "She'll be one ory-eyed night in Liberty."

"Our first herd of the season," Haggard observed contentedly. "Two thousand head for Chicago. Nate, you may hear raucous trailhands—I hear money jingling in the till."

"Sound won't be so sweet, you get a town-treein'."

Haggard laughed. "Liberty was wide open this spring, but that's over. We have a town badge-toter now."

"Tiger Jack Tetlow, eh? You bought yourself a sidewinder, Eb."

Haggard waved his cigar deprecatingly. "I know Tiger Jack's reputation; that's why I hired him. In a few years no doubt a pot-bellied old peace officer with a palsied gunhand will be able to keep order, but now . . . Don't forget that every cowherd that hits town this season'll be expecting to find it wide open. In this case the end justifies the means."

"Word'll spread down the trail fast enough, don't worry. The boys know that skull-splittin' bastard from way back."

Haggard frowned. "Tetlow is a little overzealous with his gun barrel, but a few lumps on thick Texan heads is better than a wrecked town and frightened citizens."

"That wasn't all my meanin'," Nathan Dart said significantly.

"He'll keep things in line, that's all that concerns me," Haggard said shortly.

They turned into the front archway of the livery barn. It was deserted except for two men, one sleeping off a drunk in a stall, the other standing in the runway with his back to them, forking down hay into a stall. He turned as they came up, tilting back the round-crowned black hat he wore.

"Good evening, Eben."

"Abel, like you to meet Mr. Vikstrom and Mr. Dart."

Abel Jevers was a banty-sized youth of perhaps twenty-two, no taller than Nathan Dart and just as wiry-seeming; his handshake confirmed it. Under a close-cropped shock of stiff black hair, his thin tanned face held a sensitive strength tempered by gentle humor. His light eyes contained a sparkling intensity that caught the attention.

Haggard explained their purpose, and Abel Jevers thoughtfully dropped the tines of his pitchfork to the clay floor, leaned lightly on it and rubbed his beardless chin. "You and your people have a need, Mr. Vikstrom, and no denying it. But the men of Liberty have a worse need. That is my call here, and when I feel that I'm ready—"

"Abel," Haggard broke in, "what's to prevent you

from teaching their children days and holding a service each Sunday while you go on holding your private nocturnal seminary in our emporiums of evil?"

"Nothing," Abel Jevers said, "except I wonder if you don't hope I'll get tired of making the ride in."

"I have gotten complaints that you make the customers nervous," Haggard agreed humorously. "And of course you like pitching manure."

"Hate it," Jevers said frankly. "That's why I took this job."

"More of your self-immolation, eh? But how about 'suffer the little children,' Abel?"

Jevers smiled. "It would be great to get back to . . . even if the schoolhouse is a sod one."

"You may as well say yes, Mr. Jevers, since my wife will not hear no." Borg said dryly.

"Ah," Jevers said, and laughed. "But I can't very well impose—"

"Listen, I have already"—Borg counted on his fingers—"a wife, a son, a daughter, a brother, his wife, an old Indian named Pawnee Harry—"

"I know him. But how come you've taken him in?"

Borg told him, and Jevers said, "I'm sorry to hear the old man is hurt. He needs help of another sort too. Any one else?"

"Yes, a young girl, Helga Krans, and her baby," Borg said slowly, and paused. "She has no husband."

"I see."

"She has been hurt, Mr. Jevers. A wrong word said could hurt her more."

It was a test, and Abel Jevers perceived this at once.

"I understand. Look, Mr. Vikstrom, I'm concerned with saving souls, not consigning them to hellfire. I'll work alongside your people, get to know them. That comes first. Then to give help when it's asked for, not meddle—that's the trick."

Borg, who as a boy had been basted to a turn in righteous brimstone, felt surprised approval. "You look like a boy, Abel, but I think the look is wrong."

"And I think that a man who takes in a husbandless girl and her baby and an old hurt Indian needs no sermons from me, Mr. Vikstrom."

"Not me," Borg said stolidly. "But others."

"I thought so. You impress me as a self-contained man who carries his religion about with him and has little use for formal worship."

"I know the feelin'," Nathan Dart observed mildly. "Preachin' and prayin', wagh."

Jevers grinned and stabbed him lightly on the chest with a finger. "On *you,* Mr. Dart, I may work." He leaned the pitchfork against a stall. "I'll go back to the office, give Mr. Harmody my resignation, get what's owed me, get my bedroll and things out of the loft, and I'm set to join the household, Mr. Vikstrom."

The squat, wasted-looking man who had been snoring in the straw, now got clumsily to his feet, watching with a bleary stare till Abel returned with the sack of his possibles. Then he shuffled over, dragging a stiff right leg. His voice rasped like a rusty saw. "That right what you say, Abel? You leavin'?"

"Not far, Lutey. I'll be around time to time."

The man snuffled and dug his hands in his pockets,

staring at the floor. "You reckon 'fore you leave, man might be good for one last bait?"

"No, Lutey," Abel said kindly. "If you'd buy a good meal . . . but all your baits are fluid."

Lutey nodded vaguely. "No blame to you, boy. Know your call." His watery eyes shifted to Eben Haggard. "How 'bout you, Haggard? How much you figger you owe Lutey Barnes?"

Haggard had not even looked at the man, and he didn't now. "Not a cent. I paid you for that section you'd squatted on."

"Thirty dollar an' a bottle o' whiskey," Lutey rasped shrilly. "Fer a whole passel of two-by-four lots you sold fer two thousand dollar apiece!"

Haggard flicked his cigar butt to the floor, ground it underfoot and lifted his glance with a distant, easy contempt. "Don't come whining to me, man. You made your own bed. If you need money, get off your sodden face and ask Harmody for Abel's job."

Lutey snuffled again, his eyes brimming with self-pity. "Man takes a busted leg fightin' for his country, no fault o' his, an' ever'one stomps him like a dog. Ain't fair."

Haggard reached in his pocket and flipped a silver dollar to the ground, saying softly, "You want a drink?"

Lutey stared at him, bent painfully and picked up the coin, then shuffled out. The easy ruthlessness of Haggard's gesture was a cold finger on Borg's spine; did any man—or woman—cease to be in his eyes when they became of no use to him?

And now Haggard said with his warm smile, "Let's go, gentlemen."

As they moved out of the archway, a wild rebel whoop shattered the muted street sounds. Then a burly bearded Texan raced his mustang down the street from its north end. He fired his pistol off three times, raising high a long bolt of bright red cloth which flapped out behind him. Panic rushed over the street; horses screamed and reared, tearing at their halters or harness. Several tied animals broke free and bolted. A woman shrieked; Lutey Barnes, scrambling out of the way, was bowled over.

Men poured from the buildings as the rider hauled up near the south end roaring his laughter. He rammed the gun in his belt and dug a flask from his saddlebag. Yanked the cork with his teeth, spat it out and tilted the flask, his thick red throat working as he drained it. Then Tiger Jack Tetlow moved onto the street, a slim, dark, and deadly figure in the fading light.

The marshal halted a few yards from the Texan, who wiped a hairy hand over his mouth, squinting at him. Tetlow snapped his fingers and made a motion.

The Texan pitched the flask away, lifting his reins. "Ain't gettin' down fer you, you bluebelly sonof-abitch. Bufflered three of our boys awready, one of 'em after you took his gun. Ain't usin' that hogleg on ol' Bill Chaney, nossir."

Tiger Jack's voice stung like a whip. "I can use it any way you want it, fellow. Get down!"

The Texan sent him a crooked grin. "Shoot a man

clean from his hull jis' like that, eh, you snakey li'l bastard?"

"Just like that, fellow."

Chaney shrugged his lifted hands in defeat, then swung down off-side to Tetlow. At the same time Chaney furtively slipped the Walker Colt from his belt, a gesture hidden to the marshal, then wheeled about swinging up the gun from under his horse's neck.

Tetlow's dragoon pistol was already out; it bloomed flame twice, and the Texan spun about, dropping his gun to grab at his belly. He lurched a long step, his other hand settling his leaning weight against his horse. The animal shied away, and when he started to fall, Tiger Jack fired a third time. Chaney's burly frame jerked as the slug, through his open mouth, burst the rear of his head. He went over on his side and then slumped on his face, his legs twitching.

Borg, watching this with a sense of numb shock, saw the Texans start to move off the sidewalks in a concerted ominous movement. Tetlow calmly faced them with his gun leveled. Haggard said curtly, "I'd better side him against these mongrels . . . excuse me, gentlemen."

He went over to Tetlow at a long whipping stride, and now Abel Jevers moved too, but toward the fallen Texan. He knelt by the dead man and bowed his head, his lips moving soundlessly.

"Nathan," Borg said stiffly, "is this a lawful killing?"

"You askin' could a dead shot like Tetlow wing a likkered man from three yard away 'stead of shootin' him in the belly and head? You seen it, son; you name it."

Haggard spoke for a minute with the gray-haired trail boss; it took the old man longer to break the seething tension of his men to where they broke up and dispersed, carrying the dead man. Afterward the four men walked in silence back to the Haggard house.

There Sigrid met Abel Jevers and was at once pleased with him. Then the good nights were said, Kjersti gave her "nice-smelling lady" a goodbye hug and kiss, and they climbed into the loaded wagon; Dart mounted his horse and Abel rode perched on the heap of supplies.

As they moved onto the open prairie, with sunset a red-gold dye staining the last blue patch of western sky and gray still dusk creeping over the grassland, Sigrid, who had been chatting with Abel grew silent. Borg knew that his own heavy silence was the give-away—but the telling would come easier later, when they were alone.

Glancing at her as she sat with hands folded in her lap, studying the empty vastness of prairie unfolding on every side, he knew that her feeling went far deeper than immediate concern. Yet the difference that lay between them was almost tangible in its strength. Sigrid had never said as much directly; she would follow where her man led because she sensed his need, but he knew what the sacrifice had cost her. Though he could hardly put it into words, Borg knew that it was more than the difference between a man's outlook and a woman's.

Quite simply he was an American and she was not; she had her citizenship, but this was another thing. Borg's own parents had been among those first Norwegian-American immigrants who had followed Cleng Peerson from Stavanger, Norway, in 1825. Borg had been reared in the old-country culture in Koshkonong, and had spoken only Norwegian until he was fifteen. Yet he was a born American citizen, with his whole root feeling for this country and its destiny.

Sigrid had been sixteen when her father and mother left Sweden, had spoken hardly a word of English when Borg took her as a bride. First steeped in the native ties of Sweden, then thrown in young womanhood into a new land, it had been a brave struggle for her to adapt, for she had a keen, aware pride of tradition. Woman-like, her entire world was bound in that tradition, in her woman's world of husband, children, and the little farm that had been home for nineteen years.

And now, Borg thought bleakly, he'd torn her up again from adjusted soil, brought her to an unsettled and violent country. Driven by a man's dream, he couldn't have done otherwise—but he'd known Sigrid's thoughts behind her dry-eyed mask on the day they'd left their Wisconsin farm forever. The farm where their three children, the two boys and a girl born between Magnus and Kjersti, all dead in the way of one typhus epidemic, lay buried in a little flowered plot. A home which held stronger memories for both than for most of those families who had followed them West.

We must talk, Borg thought heavily; always before when there were troubles, we could talk and it was better. But the time wasn't yet right, he knew leadenly; not when he felt so strongly in his own shaken guilt from what he'd just witnessed in town. Sigrid . . . Magnus . . . Kjersti . . . to what kind of a land had he brought them, and what would it do to them?

Now Sigrid spoke quietly, as though wishing to divert his thoughts: "It's not so good between them. They are two unhappy people. Yes, Mr. Haggard too, though he doesn't see it yet."

Borg nodded; it was like his wife to be concerned about the lack in others of what she and he had so strongly together. The indefinable unhappiness he'd felt behind Margaret Haggard's composure was now clear; she had wedded a man to whom people were pawns to an end, who shrugged them aside when their use was gone. *How would he be to us if his town did not need our good will?*

"I guess Haggard is too full of himself, of his own business. No room left for anyone else, eh?"

Abel Jevers murmured, "That, Mr. Vikstrom, is one of the things we must try to understand and forgive in others."

From his jogging shrunken shadow in the dusk, Nathan Dart's voice came still and dry: "Maybe. Only allowin' Eb Haggard's a solid man in some ways, allowin' what you say, Brother Abel, there's worse'n a lack in a man treats a woman like dirt. Man who looks through his woman like she wasn't there is worse'n a wife-beater. You can forgive an empty man like Lutey, even a cold-crazy one like Tiger Jack. Mean man who turns his meanness off an' on is somethin' else."

CHAPTER FIVE

NEXT MORNING BORG ROUSED THE WHOLE FAMILY OUT at dawn. As they squatted shivering in the thin chill sunlight, wolfing their hot porridge, he said sternly, "Now listen all of you to what Nathan says. You all will help, except Kjersti and Helga and the old man. You help too, Lars; and Magnus, there will be no mooning after Greta today. We all work."

Sigrid expressed her emphatic doubts about living in "a hole in the ground," but Dart was forceful. "Ma'am, I grew up in a soddy down in the Caprock country. Where there's no timber, there's no finer make-do'n a soddy. She holds the heat in winter, stays cool in summer. Prairie fire or cyclone comes through, she won't burn and won't smash to flinders, may save your life too. Easy to build, and she don't cost a cent but in sweat salt. Lone man wants to pull up stakes, all he's got to do is put out the fire and whistle up the dog. You can raise truck or stake out a lamp on the roof, and the jackrabbits 'n' coyotes'll stay clean off. Fella builds his permanent home, he keeps his soddy for a root 'n' storm cellar. And ladies, you want to brighten 'er up, you can plant flowers on every wall."

"They must be very damp places to live, *ja?*" Sigrid said severely. "The children will come down with the croup. The roof will fall in my food. And the *dirt!*"

The word was anathema to a tidy Scandinavian house-wife.

Dart scratched his head. "Body can only allow for drawbacks, Miz Vikstrom. Later we might plaster up the walls if you've a mind, though it's a sight of bother. Get a hold of a little whip-sawed lumber or some puncheons, we can even floor her. For now we can cross cottonwood poles for the roof, lay canvas over 'em and the sod over that. It'll help some."

Borg set aside his bowl and said impatiently, "Let's go to work."

He and Dart had already chosen a likely site: a hill-side just off the river flats, one with a southern expo-sure. Dart said that the Injuns built a type of low-down soddy not worthy of the name; you simply dug a pit on flat prairie and laid brush and sod for a roof. Snug as toast, but a man as lief wake up in a cistern after the first heavy rain. Trick was to build on a slope to drain off rain and snowmelt, well above the lower gullies which marked the routes of flash floods.

Dart and Abel and Magnus set to spading out a deep rectangular wedge of hillside while Sigrid and Inga dipped out loose earth with pans. Borg hitched up two span of oxen to the turning plow, then grimly beck-oned to Lars who sat by the fire nursing his coffee. Lars picked up his crutches and heaved to his feet, his scowl deepening as though he even resented the ease with which he'd come to get around on the crotched staffs.

"As I turn over the sod, cut it into slabs three feet square," Borg instructed his brother. "This a man can

60

do sitting down. The shovels all are in use, so here's the ax."

He thrust it out handle first, and when Lars hesitated, said bitingly, "You want Helga to do the job? The old man? Maybe the baby?"

He nodded toward the wagon where Helga sat against a sideboard nursing Lisj-Per. Pawnee Harry lay half-upright on a bundle, watching the builders with wrinkled-face stoicism and thinking perhaps of the buffalo herds and the untrammeled prairie that had been.

Lars curled his lips and took the ax without a word. Borg hoorawed the team and started it moving. But there was no thrill in watching the black virgin earth turning behind the thrusting plowblade. . . .

How long could a man go on making amends for an ancient hurt, a thing only partly Borg's fault? Yet, because he was Lars' older brother, he alone had been saddled with a lifetime cross of guilt. For a single playful joke that had wrecked Lars' and Inga's life together before it had begun. . . .

"No couple can be warmly bedded till they are shivareed," had roared Sven Nyblad, Lars' best friend, on Lars' wedding night a dozen years ago. And six other friends and Borg, all warmed by too many skoals of potent *glogg,* had echoed him. A moonlight ride would lay the stage for further developments, they had drunkenly opined as they set the protesting couple on a spring wagon and whipped the team to a wild run. As the wagon careened around a sharp bend, Lars fighting to halt the terrified horses, it had canted to a high tilt and crashed over on its occupants. Inga was only bruised, but both of Lars' legs were broken.

He had screamed curses and damnation on them all as they carried him to the doctor's. And maybe he had never stopped doing so in his own mind. From boyhood there had been a weakness in Lars that made him run wailing to Mama with a little cut. And on this night that weakness was shaped into his whole future. For after the broken bones had healed and every doctor consulted and pronounced him sound, Lars could neither walk a step nor stand without aid. Also he was impotent, as Inga had once revealed in a vitriolic tongue-lashing of him. As her girlish sweetness had been strong, so was her deepening bitterness over the years. Only she had not directed it at Borg, as had Lars, but at the world in general.

All that Borg could do was take them into his household, numbly accepting the entire burden of fault and living with it in the constant reminder of Lars' crippled presence. Sigrid had tried equally to share this great continuing mar in their lives, and for this more than anything, he was grateful.

But if here was a time to begin wholly anew, it must be now. Borg had grimly resolved that for Lars' own good, he'd bear what share of the work he could. Now, with a rising sun against his back, gripping the plow handles and digging his boots against the loam, feeling the warm sweat clinging his shirt and the good ache in shoulders and arms too long away from this work, Borg felt the slow lift of his spirits.

He turned sod for a steady hour, and only then

stopped, sleeved the sweatband of his hat and glanced back at his brother. Lars was hunkered by a furrow trimming a square, whacking at it with dogged strokes; Borg felt startled pleasure at his solidly contented look. Not a lasting sign, but it would do for a start. Borg grinned to himself as he hoorawed up the team again. . . .

At the end of this exhausting day, all except Borg rolled into their blankets early. He went out to tramp about the camp and chat with the families who had returned from town. All were excited about the deals they had made with Haggard, showing him their deeds and describing their choices of quarter, half, or full sections; all approved the price that Borg had wangled per acre. They had already inspected the work on the Vikstrom soddy, and all vied for Nathan Dart's advice. Borg good-naturedly agreed to let them have Nathan tomorrow, and they could draw straws for first service.

The deep wide trench in the hill was almost squared away as Borg had marked it out, and the next day they began bricking up the front and half-sides. The sod squares were loaded on a sledge and oxen-drawn to the site. It required many haulings, for Borg had planned ambitiously, to insure both elbow room and a little privacy. He and Dart had lined ropes with the North Star to stake out the walls and corners compass-true. Three big rooms would run adjacent, the largest comprising kitchen and parlor and dining room. The second would be for sleeping and the third would be a joint stable and tool shed.

Two wagonloads of cottonwood poles were cut and

brought from the riverbank grove. The roof was built pitched toward the hills so that rain cascading off the hillside could be troughed away around the sides; otherwise the roof would waterlog and fall in. They ditched around the entire structure and channeled downhill to carry off as much water as possible. The three rooms were partitioned by yard-thick sod. The floor was leveled by covering it with water, marking the level, bailing out the water and raking and tampering it even.

Some of the lumber bought in town made door and window frames. The common room was fronted by two windows and a doorway. Borg and Dart spent a day fashioning a front door and hanging it by wooden pins. The latch was a string which hung outside through a hole; it was "locked" from the inside by pulling the string through the hole.

The floors were so dank that they slept under the stars for several cold fall nights till the two-high tiers of crude bunks were finished. The men also made two long benches of sawed lumber and a puncheon table of split straight cottonwood logs. They drove pegs into the sod walls and laid plank shelves for storing food, cooking gear, and possibles. The women sewed thick woven plats of grass inside sackcloth for mattresses. They rounded up enough jute-sacks to make a drape for the doorway between common room and sleeping quarters, another to separate the latter into men's and women's quarters. With these basic preparations complete and a lean-to sod privy set up nearby, they could add refinements at odd times. Dart, quite satisfied with the job, said they had a dwelling that would last a man's three-score-and-ten, allowing for settling of the walls and roof.

The next day being Sunday, Brother Jevers preached his first sermon on a sunny hill above the river. Hardly a dozen came to hear, but that was only to be expected, for the people were old-country and inflexible in their creed; Jevers was not even of their faith. The few came mostly out of curiosity.

All the Vikstroms, except for Lars and Inga who had not attended a service in years, were there—Sigrid saw to that. Nathan Dart joined them, allowing wryly that Brother Abel had the medicine tongue. For Jevers had sounded out every settler, and had at least totally abolished any general rancor toward him. Jevers' boyish grin lighted up his whole pug-nosed face; it was impossible to meet him and not like him, difficult to refuse him.

Standing bare-headed on the hill above them wearing his stained and dusty workclothes, Abel opened the service with a very short prayer, then launched into his sermon by quoting Martin Luther to the effect that a Christian should laugh and sing and pleasure himself. His poker-faced congregation relaxed a little, and he went on cheerfully, "Of course a man who takes to himself a wife should settle down. And we Mormons, as you know, believe very strongly in marriage. In fact, as I told Brother Brigham Young when he tried to dissuade me from leaving the fold, we're a shade too zealous thereof."

The aging Mormon leader and his famous "harem"

were a nationwide source of humor, and there were chuckles and smiling nods. Abel had them now, and he went on to speak seriously of the destiny of the nation, warmly of their own part in braving a harsh new country. "Our differences, even as to worship, are our greatest strength as Americans, for differences in men make freedom necessarily cherished, and out of tolerance comes brotherhood."

The words stirred Borg strongly; also, though he was too independent of mind to be caught up by Abel's manner, he sensed its effect on the others. As a preacher the boy had power and magnetism, and might someday be a great one. Such a gift could be turned to good or harm, but to Borg's mind Abel had dispelled any lingering doubt that morning.

After conferring with Borg, he had gently said to Helga Krans, "Sister, will you come to meeting today?" Her grave eyes looked a question at Borg, and when he'd translated, she had hugged Lisj-Per tighter and murmured in Swedish. "She says she cannot come now," Borg had told Abel, who had somehow conveyed his understanding to the girl without a word, only a nod and look. But Helga had smiled before returning her attention to her baby. . . .

They had a good teacher for the children, a good preacher for all, Borg decided.

Abel closed the service with a well-known hymn which could be sung in English or Swedish, a moment of silent prayer, and a benediction. It was stolid Olof Holmgaard who then went first to shake his hand, saying gruffly, "It was fine as snuff. More will come

66

next Sunday." As meeting broke up, Borg caught muttered comments and one disapproving note: "Religion is a very serious thing, and this young man is too lighthearted," a woman said, and then added: "*Ja,* but he *is* a very young man."

Their first Sunday dinner in the new house was good and hearty fare (marred only as Borg jokingly said, by Sigrid's perpetual *sill och potatis,* to which she retorted, "Boiled potatoes is what makes Swedes so strong. Eat!") and Sigrid made radiantly proud over her fine young preacher, loading his plate with the biggest portions and patting his shoulder—"*Gad valingne def* . . . God bless you, mister."

But her smile became a frown when Borg, fretting to plunge into the real work of putting his acres to the plow, announced that he would begin today. "*Gud bevara,* Herr Vikstrom, on the Sabbath—"

"Now let Mr. Jevers handle the Lord's work, and Vikstrom will do his, eh?" Borg said firmly, and tramped out. He looked around for Magnus, who had excused himself from the table five minutes before, and could not find him.

Irritably Borg tramped around the hillside and came up on the boy, finding him sitting with a piece of stiff pasteboard propped on one updrawn knee, drawing. Hearing Borg's step, Magnus hastily wadded the pasteboard and crammed it and a pencil into his pocket before coming to his feet. But not before Borg caught a glimpse over his shoulder of the sketch Magnus had made of the river and hills. He must have done it in a few minutes, but the drawing was a fine one—as fine,

Borg realized, as Magnus' strong slender hands.

Before this he had noted their nimble dexterity when Magnus had played Borg's old fiddle at dances, wondering with puzzled pride at his son's playing when, like his father, he'd had no formal training in music. Yet oddly, he had never looked at those hands closely, and only now did he realize that they belonged not to a farmer or a woodsman. Maybe to a craftsman, but more likely to a musician or artist. . . .

Conscious of his father's regard, Magnus shoved his hands in his pockets and stood hipshot, a trace of sullen defiance in the stance. And Borg faintly scowled, trying to find the words that would never come. How could he reach out to the boy with understanding when he wasn't certain that he understood at all?

He had one slender clue, if it meant anything, and now he slowly pondered it for the ten thousandth time. Once when Magnus was eleven he had taken the boy hunting on one of the great salt-grass marshes near their farm. As the geese took flight, Borg had brought one down with quick accuracy, but Magnus had not fired. His lifted face was almost radiant as he said, "I couldn't, *For*—I couldn't shoot one. They are too lovely." And strangely Borg, to whom hunting was a lifelong joy, had understood—"I know, sonny." There had been between them a shared closeness, in that lonely marsh with the geese veed in honking flight against a gray sky, a cold wind and the smell of marsh grass and coming rain in their faces. A warmth they had never found again.

Of these thoughts Borg said nothing now, nor did he summon Magnus to help him, as he'd intended. Only said gruffly, "I saw you and Greta talk after the service. You have plans, maybe, for today?"

Magnus relaxed with his sardonic grin. "Thought we might spend the afternoon together. Been sort of a busy week."

That came close to sass, Borg decided, but he passed it over; he was becoming accustomed to Magnus' subtle defiance, sensing that it was rebellious and not malicious, a part of being caught between boyhood and manhood, and especially in this strange boy of his.

"Well, you done good this week, and it's the Sabbath. Run along."

"OK, Pa. *Tack.*" Magnus sauntered away, whistling.

OK! Looking after him, Borg snorted gently; even the language of young Americans was becoming insolent. Still, because it had the taste of something lively and vital, he rather liked it. Some of Borg's good humor was restored as he fetched the oxen; he had to feel things out in his careful way before he and Magnus talked seriously, but there was plenty of time.

When Dart and Jevers came out to offer their help with the spare plow, Borg stolidly beat down their arguments. "Nathan has done enough for ten men this week, and because I break the Sabbath is more reason for our preaching man not to. Nathan, you said there are catfish by that bend downstream where the water is slow and deep. Abel, you converted him yet, eh?"

"He's a tough one to crack," Abel grinned. "But he likes to argue."

"Good. And a man likes to fish. Ask Sigrid to show you where my tackle is, and you both be off."

It was good to again put his full muscle into a long straight furrow behind his own plow, into the pleasure of old work on his new land, before the ache and sweat would melt into a daily grind. There was much to be done while the fall season held early. He plowed a half-acre that afternoon without pausing to rest, running the furrows up the whole north boundary of his land. Finally he halted for a break and, scanning with satisfaction the bare long furrows of black earth against the buff prairie, tramped back to a lone big cottonwood on the slope where he'd left his water jug. He lifted it and drank deeply, letting cool dribbles run down his neck and chest and cut dark stipples on his dusty shirt. Boiled river water, even, was good when a man had earned his thirst . . . Nathan had said that tomorrow he could begin sinking their first well. Tapping water here should be no problem.

Slowly Borg lowered the jug, his eye corners etching to fine wrinkles with his far squint . . . bawling cattle were lumbering up over a rise from the south. Another herd for Eben Haggard's stockpens. Only one other had been sighted in the last week, but soon the drovers should swarm north in full force. Borg seated himself in the shade, and rested, watching the shape of the strung-out crescent grow nearer. A big bunch, maybe two thousand head. He could make out the riders hazing at point, and he pitied the poor devils in the drag . . . even a Texan could not want so much grit in his craw. The herders were pushing hard these last miles, with Liberty town almost in sight.

Borg's squint turned to a frown, studying the track of the route which was taking them parallel to the river, also across the east limits of some of the settlers' marked-off acres. Though this was as yet a small matter; let them divert their routes later when the land was obviously under plow. . . .

The left flank of the herd made a deep swing down a draw. Abruptly now Borg came to his feet, seeing that they would pass directly over the end of his today's plowing. Perhaps they had not yet seen. . . . And then he caught the faintly drifting laugh of a point rider as he swung the tip of the crescent across the plowed ground, trampling the furrowed earth.

Borg's fists knotted and all his muscles tightened. He took two steps and halted. Feeling the rage beat and swell in his temples and neck, and knowing he must not face any man like this. His temper made rare showing and came slowly as a rule, which was fortunate because once as a schoolboy he had almost killed a classmate with his bare fists. He had not needed the fierce licking his father had dealt to warn him to control his strength afterward—and he had been only thirteen then. Even the time he'd fought Emil Klitgaard for the privilege of seeing Sigrid Hansdatter, his future wife, home from a dance, he had carefully pulled his punches.

Now he let his rage boil back to a simmer and did some careful thinking. Bare-fisted anger would be nothing to armed Texan riders who, Dart had told him, disliked fighting with their fists. A cool head behind a good rifle would deal better with this sort of thing when it came again. Next time he would be ready.

CHAPTER SIX

DURING THE NEXT WEEK THEY SAW ONLY THREE HERDS, two of which bypassed the Scandinavian settlement by coming up the opposite bank of the Cherokee and fording it at a shallow crossing just below Liberty. The third came from an easterly route that took a wide skirt around a range of obstructing hills, thus missing their fields entirely. But eventually some drovers would try the lower river flats on this side, Borg knew, and he grimly watched and waited.

Meantime the people built their soddies and settled into their daily routines. On a rough half-moon swath of five thousand acres arcing back from the riverbank, every prominent hill boasted a smoking stovepipe and a sod-bricked side that fronted a dwelling; the flats and slopes had abandoned their tawny cover for raw black furrows as the oxen and horses plodded steadily before the plows.

Nathan Dart and Abel Jevers chose a central hill, gutted it and soddied up a schoolroom. Some of the men pitched in at spare moments with elbow grease and odds and ends of lumber, and they had benches and a desk for Jevers. Dart found time to dig a well by the Vikstrom soddy, and the water was plenty and pure. Borg and Magnus kept their shoulders to the plows, and Borg looked forward with pleasure to the time of sowing his precious wheat seed.

By Saturday the plowing was well advanced, and at midday Borg and Magnus were sitting under the big cottonwood eating their meal of cheese and rye *flat-brod,* when they heard the now-familiar sound of a longhorn herd passing beyond a rise toward the east. They could not see it, but it was close. Borg chewed his food slowly, listening.

"Sounds like they're passing over by Eric Slogvig's place," Magnus observed.

Borg merely nodded, coming up off his haunches then. Hans was ground-haltered by the tree in readiness, and Borg threw on the saddle in a hurry. He checked his Spencer .54 and rammed it into the boot, then swung astride, looking down at Magnus.

"When you finish the eating, get your plow moving."

"Look, Pa—

"Do like I say," Borg told him harshly, and wheeled away toward the long rise at a lope, cutting across the fresh furrows. As he crested it, he saw the small bunch of gaunt longhorns pushing across the east flank of Slogvig's freshly plowed acres.

Just below him now a man came stumbling up the slope. Borg rode down to him and dismounted, catching Eric Slogvig about the shoulders as he almost fell. Eric, a slowwitted young householder, met Borg's look with a kind of dazed incomprehension. Blood trickled down the side of his wide face.

"I tell them, keep off Eric Slogvig's fields, you don't drive your cows over a man's fields. This one dark man laugh, hit me with his gun. And they push the cows over my plowing." He paused, scowling over his slow thoughts. "So, you have a gun, Borg. I take it and kill that Injun bastard."

"You stay here and shut up."

Borg eased him down to the ground, swung back into his saddle. Nathan Dart now came around the long hill, goading his roan to a run with flap-legged kicks. He hauled up by Borg, jerking his head backward. "Was witchin' up water with a willow fork over by Holmgaard's, thought them beeves sounded damn' close." He nodded at Eric sitting on the ground rubbing his head. "So the ruckus is due."

"There will be no ruckus, Nate. That we maybe head off, eh?"

They quartered off at a wide angle to get ahead of the moving tight bunch of longhorns, there halted and sat their horses waiting.

"Bunch of strays these boys was herdin' up," Dart observed. "Only three riders with 'em." He squinted off to the southeast. "There's the main herd . . . pass us by with plenty of room."

Borg said softly, grimly, "Even so, Nate. They would have to be faced. Three or thirty."

"Reckon so." Dart rubbed his chin, with a thoughtful glance at Borg's mule-stubborn look. "I make us lucky, then."

One man bellowed an order and the bunch was milled to a stop. Borg and Dart had unbooted their rifles, and now they paced their horses forward. Two of the riders flanked the bunched longhorns, sitting their horses at a silent watchful slouch as the third man ranged up by Nathan Dart.

He was a square bull-built man of perhaps thirty-four with hard merry eyes of twinkling blue. He wore soiled range clothes with one startling incongruity: a hard derby pushed jauntily back on his sandy hair. The sun glanced full on his broad red face and chalky grin, from which a dead cigar projected brashly.

"Divil a man but it's himsilf, Nathan Dart, an' turned clodhopper." He thrust out a meaty hand. "An' hev the saints frowned on your heathen hide, Nathan, that I find ye in such company?"

"I name it a smile, Denny. Meet Borg Vikstrom. Borg, Dennis O'Hea, *segundo* for the Singlebit outfit down in East Texas."

"Linus Quincannon's Singlebit, biggest outfit in the Sabine country," O'Hea enlarged placidly, reaching his hand across the neck of Dart's horse. Borg took it, and O'Hea tried the hand game; Borg gave back enough grip to make him break it off. O'Hea settled back in his saddle and twisted his mouth comically around the cigar stub, brashly measuring Borg.

"Shades Quincannon a mite, don't he?" Nathan Dart offered dryly.

"Mebbe, mebbe. Size don't tell all the broth of a man, Nathan. Still you're a hefty divil, Swede, and no mistake."

"Norskie."

"So ye'd be Norwegian; I'll call ye Swede anyways. There was a sight of snorkies around in Chicago where I growed up." He continued to size Borg shrewdly.

"And would ye be Aaron to his Moses, Nathan?"

"Reckon Borg'll do his own talkin'."

O'Hea's merry grin hardened. "Aye, and precious small difference that'll—"

Borg cut softly and deliberately across his speech, saying, "No talk then. You can turn your cows around and get them and your men and yourself the hell off this field, Mr. O'Hea."

The thin dark-faced rider reined his horse a little forward, setting his hand to the butt of his pistol. He wore it in a low-thonged holster. Borg had already noted the pistol shoved in O'Hea's brass-studded belt, and the other rider had no handgun; his booted rifle looked ready to hand.

Dart watched him and O'Hea, and Borg slightly tilted his rifle to bear on the dark man's chest. This man wore a Texas-creased hat, but there was an alien and dandified air to his embroidered brown vest and tight trousers. His fine bay horse wore a cruel-looking spade bit and his spurs were the size of silver dollars. His face was coffee-brown with black, turgid eyes. They contained a wickedness in leash, and his lips were fluted contemptuously around a dead cigarette.

"Snorky," he murmured, as if savoring the word. "You say it so? Snorky."

Borg said gently, "Like mick or greaser—a man can be dead from saying it too much, mister."

"Now Pete, now lad, none o' that." O'Hea's grin at Borg was almost friendly. "Were ye by chance in the war, Mr. Vikstrom?"

"The 15th Wisconsin," Borg said shortly.

"Ah, the famed Scandinavian regiment! The lads who gave the gray all that hell at Chickamauga in the late '63. Aye, fighting damnyanks they were. I rode with the Texas Brigade mesilf. It would be a pretty thing if ye're also a follower of the divil heretic Luther."

"Does all this matter, to Americans?"

"No, no," O'Hea said cheerfully. "I'm but stokin' the fire, Swede. As it's no grudge I bear ye, there'll be a certain zest to breakin' your head knownin' you're a sodbuster, a Yank, and an inimy of the true faith all rolled together." He stepped to the ground and tossed his reins to Dart, moved off a few steps on his short rolling legs, pulled out his gun and laid it and his derby on the ground, pitched his cigar butt away, spat elaborately into his palms and rubbed them together. "Now it's fair warnin', Swenska, that I prize-fought a bit in me palmy days."

Borg said slowly, "This better settle something," as he swung down off Hans.

"Why, only whether Singlebit herds'll trail across your dirt fields or not from this day; ain't this better than messy bullets flyin' about?"

Borg sheathed his rifle, then squared off facing the squat Irishman. The Mexican's cartwheel rowels jingled to a movement and O'Hea said without looking at him, "Robles, ye keep that hogleg in leather, hear?" He wiped his hands on his pants and moved in with mincing steps, sparring lightly at the air. Borg slowly raised his fists, seeing the way of this and irritated by it.

O'Hea began flicking tentative left jabs at his head, holding his right hand cocked. Impatiently Borg swiped at his arm and O'Hea's left jolted his chin; Borg turned his shoulder to catch a follow-up right, but O'Hea merely feinted that hand and hooked another hard left to his face. It hurt enough for Borg to feel a sting of anger, and he told himself, *Easy now, easy, for God's sake.*

O'Hea broke away and began circling him, his short powerful body sunk in a crouch, and Borg turned with him, watched his sweating red face rather than his hands. A flickering squint of decision warned him and he blocked a sudden flurry of left and right crosses, took a swing at O'Hea that found only air, and dropped his guard enough for O'Hea to land a light jab high on his face. It was only a feint to bring Borg's guard up, and now O'Hea sank a battering ram of a right into his belly. Borg merely grunted and stepped back, clamping down on his anger; a startled look fleetingly touched O'Hea's broad face, and his grin began to fade.

He danced carefully around Borg, keeping out of close quarters, obviously chagrined that Borg wouldn't carry the attack. Borg knew that the man meant to drag it out and break his wind and he stolidly refused to rise to the bait. He parried most of O'Hea's blows and kept turning to meet his sparring offensive. Getting nettled, O'Hea landed a hard one on his cheek and Borg countered with a solid clout on the neck.

"Agh!" It burst wrathfully from O'Hea's lungs; he fired a wild blow which Borg brushed aside, and thus goaded, O'Hea started to close. Relentlessly now Borg began to advance, and as he did so, blocked one wicked hook and took another on the chest. Too late O'Hea tried to retreat, and Borg uncocked his waiting right. O'Hea's head snapped back on his neck, and he simply folded to the ground. He sat there and hung his head, gingerly feeling of his jaw.

Borg said evenly, "I will call that good for Eric Slogvig's hurt," briefly meeting Pete Robles' murky stare. Then he bent and caught O'Hea by the arm, effortlessly pulling him to his feet. The Irishman took a weaving step backward, got his balance, and rolled his eyes to focus. A grin broke his wide mouth.

"By all the saints, and I'd make you the reincarnation of Cuculain of Ulster himself, heathen notion that it is! All's against it, but dammit, I like ye, Swede. A bargain's a bargain, and here's my hand on it."

Watching the three riders push the bunch off east toward the big herd, Borg wryly winced, touching a cut above his eyes. "Does he talk for the big boss?"

"Linus Quincannon's a hard man, some says a mean one. Denny there, he's the one man alive holds Quincannon's ear. Reckon the bargain'll be kept, and a damn' lucky thing."

Borg eyed a question at him, and Nathan Dart smiled. "You just whipped the tough *segundo* of the toughest cattleman in Texas, made a deal with him to boot. Word'll spread down the trail, and others'll take it to heart. You drove your stakes about a mile deep today, Borg."

CHAPTER SEVEN

IN THIS FALL OF 1868, LINUS QUINCANNON WAS THIRTY-five and he looked fifty-five. The deception was not apparent in the giant virility of his six-foot-five of height; his big-shouldered frame had the pared hips of a horseman and was whittled to the tough spareness of rawhide. His face, with its lean-featured regularity that might have been handsome once, told another story. It was weathered and scarred to brown granite, with a nose like a twisted beak, and whatever humanity or gentleness it might have contained was burned out. His hair, once black and curly, lay like a close cap of grizzled iron-gray on his heavy head which was hunched forward on a short, muscular neck, lending a truculent, almost brutal, thrust to the sharp chin. His eyes were cold flint, colorless as fog, showing nothing of his thoughts.

The black flat-crowned Spanish hat with its band of silver conches was fairly new; the rest of his clothes and gear matched those of his sorriest crewman. His empty right sleeve was rolled up and pinned above the shoulder stump.

Quincannon sat his big yellow mustang now with a centaur-like ease, reins gathered in his left hand, shuttling his colorless stare over the bedgrounds where his crew had halted the thirty-five hundred trail-gaunt longhorns. It had been a long trail and a hard one. Where the blazing sun had not turned the trail into a dust-choked kiln, the rains had made it a river of greasy mud.

They had lost nearly forty head crossing the flood-swollen Canadian. On their first night in the Cherokee Strip, jayhawkers had run off two hundred head. Near the border of the Nations a band of half-starved Choctaws had been driven off, but not before they'd stampeded the herd and killed two nighthawks. Altogether, well over twelve hundred head had been lost between the lower Sabine and the Kansas border.

Quincannon, regarding himself second to no man at any job, bossed his own drives. No point doing a thing well or better when it could be done best. He had brought thirty-five hundred cattle seven hundred miles against grueling odds and would turn a good profit. Where another man might feel a flicker of buoyant pride, to Linus Quincannon this trouble-plagued drive merely dovetailed into his whole foul run of luck.

His stony glance now passed on to the camp where the chuckwagon and a canvased linchpin stacked with the crew's warbags were drawn up. The men were wolfing their supper with an occasional cough or curse against the smoke furling off the cook's fire, which had some green wood in it. Dennis O'Hea, having assigned the night watch, came over to Quincannon at his jaunty rolling walk. He took off his derby, sleeved his broad ruddy forehead, and squinted at the crew.

"Eh, the dear lads'll look to see the elephant tonight."

"That'll wait. We might still push on to Abilene, and I'll not be waiting to pamper broken heads."

O'Hea clamped on his derby at a droll angle. "So ye still think there may be a joker in Mr. Haggard's deck? Word down the trail is, he's fair-dealin' despite his sharp Yankee ways."

"By all accounts he's a Boston man and surely Protestant," Quincannon snapped. "For a professional Irishman, you have a short memory; when's a Boston Protestant missed a chance to do an Irishman dirt? I drove to Liberty as it's nearer, but let him try to sharp me and I'll make direct for Abilene."

"And have the men further blessin' your name?"

"Let 'em gripe. Or quit. If they want their pay bad enough, they'll stick."

O'Hea sighed, studying him reflectively. "Ye push hard even for a man so hard, Linus."

"As you've said often enough. When it gets too hard, Denny, a man can always quit, even you."

"Aye," O'Hea said dryly, and spat. "That'll be the day, cap'n dear."

"And leave off calling me captain," Quincannon said roughly. "El Capitan is dead. I buried him in Mexico with my damned arm."

O'Hea said mildly, "An' how does a man lay a legend to rest?" He shrugged then. "It's always as ye say, Linus."

Quincannon gave a dour grunt; he'd have taken a hint that he was running away from himself off no man but O'Hea. Denny's was the only friendship to survive the cold brutalizing of the man Quincannon had been; it would stand no matter how sorely Dennis O'Hea felt put on at times, and it could not be otherwise. During

82

a lifetime together through thick and thin, they had been nearer than any two brothers, and always O'Hea had cheerfully followed Linus Quincannon's lead.

Throughout their boyhood as a pair of street urchins in the Chicago slums, Denny had followed Linus out of one scrape and into another. When Linus' father, a burly roistering wheelwright, had gone to the Texas plains to hew out a cattle empire by sheer spit and drive, thirteen-year-old Denny had run away from home to follow his chum Linus West. They had eaten dust together on that first trail drive to New Orleans; later while old Bill Quincannon was dining at the governor's house in Austin, his son and Denny were out scandalizing high society with wining and wenching.

They had fought side by side for Texas, both getting their first honorable wounds at Brown's Ferry; after the war both had ridden with Jo Shelby on his ill-fated Mexican campaign. Now with Bill Quincannon dead and Linus heir to his cattle empire, no man but Dennis O'Hea could be his right-hand man.

Even in his gray bitterness Linus knew he wouldn't trade Denny for the return of his own good right hand, though he'd have cut out his tongue before saying so. His voice held cold and dry now with his nod at O'Hea's bruised face: "Are ye ready to tell me about that?"

O'Hea touched a bruise and winced, then explained in a few reluctant phrases. Quincannon snorted softly. "That I'd see the day when you let a snorky sodbuster stomp you!"

"Man," O'Hea protested, "he's your own size and

broader. Could I have handled it otherwise without that gunhappy Robles killin' a man?"

"And Nathan Dart," Quincannon mused. "Aye, he was a scout with Shelby. A Texan who fought with the damn yanks, now a cowman turned sodbuster. A born turncoat."

"That's harsh on the little man; I've a sense that he's bigger than he looks."

Ignoring that, Quincannon went on coldly, "And where do ye get off, speaking up for me? I'll drive my cattle where I please, across all the damned snorky fields in creation if I please."

O'Hea grinned placidly. "Go on, break the bargain."

"That I won't, and you know it. But you take too much on yourself, Denny. If I run into that clodhopping squarehead, it won't be Quincannon left holding the short end."

"Ah, we'll likely never see him again," O'Hea said cheerfully, and smacked his lips. "And now we'll ride into Liberty and wet our dries over a deal for these ugly *ladinos* of yours."

"I will," Quincannon corrected him curtly. "You'll stay and keep all these thirsts in check—and your own."

After turning his tired mustang into the cavvy and cutting out a short-coupled paint from his own string, Quincannon rode up from the green bottomlands onto the higher flats. Here he drew rein, seeing the sun make a tawny richness of the upper grasslands, against which the town, a mile distant, looked ramshackle and tawdry. A far cry and a long trail from his own

drought-ridden spread to this cowman's paradise—
and a railroad too. Every turn of his thought seemed to
heighten his sour mood as he rode on.

Low dusk had touched the prairie as he rode into
Liberty, and a few lighted windows threw soft yellow
squares onto the dust of the street. Quincannon bought
one drink and a few words of information at a saloon.

Afterward he walked to the professional building,
mounted the stairs and groped down a murky corridor
to the last door. In his present mood and keyed for a
warm session with a Yankee sharper, he didn't trouble
to knock. Simply went in and closed the door behind
him.

A lamp burned on the desk and the gaunt man in
dark broadcloth glanced up from some papers, not at
all perturbed by the rude entrance. He removed his
steel-rimmed glasses, his face and voice genial: "And
what might your business be, sir?"

"You'd be Haggard? I'm Linus Quincannon."

Quincannon, not impressed by either Haggard's firm
handshake or his fine smile, took a chair, stretched out
his long legs and crossed them while he let his pale
arrogant stare circle the office and come back to Eben
Haggard's smile.

"I've heard of you, of course, and I'm honored that
you chose to make Liberty your shipping point this
season—"

"Trailed to Abilene before, heard your town was
nearer," Linus interrupted. "I've thirty-five hundred on
the hoof."

"At current prices, about eighty thousand dollars on

the hoof," Haggard said approvingly, and when there was no reply, cleared his throat. "You'll deal through the stock buyers, of course."

"Come now, Mr. Haggard, are you telling me you've no thumb in a plum as juicy as the cattle trade on which your town depends?"

Haggard smiled. "Two, actually. Some of my establishments will clear a very tidy profit from your crew's . . . recreation. Also I have an agreement with the railroad whereby I get five dollars for every carload of freight shipped from Liberty. But—"

"My cattle are this moment grazing on riverbottom graze that I understand belongs to you. They'll want fattening."

"Of course," Haggard nodded. "On lush grass your steers should add a hundred pounds apiece in little more than a week. However, hold them there as long as you please." He smiled faintly. "For which there will be no charge, Mr. Quincannon."

Linus merely grunted, though this was the point on which he'd meant to satisfy himself, and Eben Haggard had turned his evident hostility neatly back on him. Again Haggard's faint smile: "You know, Mr. Quincannon, I've got in the habit of flinching whenever I meet an Irishman without a Mason's ring."

"Have ye now," Linus murmured, frosting it with the brunt of his chill stare. "And do you know, Mr. Haggard, that as a Boston schoolboy, my father was whipped for not reciting a Protestant prayer?"

Haggard picked up a pencil and gently frowned at it. "Bigots, sir, generally come in the handful everywhere, though all the Irish seem inclined to think that Boston is Bigot Mecca. It's barely possible that among the mixed reasons why some men come West, one is to escape such civilized niceties as bigotry. And the graze is still at your disposal, free of charge."

A very pleasant man, Linus thought, saying only the right things with the finest of emphasis. A pity there still remained something about this grand lad that a man had to distrust: call it if you would an Irishman's bigotry in reverse; still . . .

Having to honestly concede the atmosphere cleared, he accepted the drink that Haggard poured and gave the man civil answers to his pleasant questions. No, it had not been a good year; there was drought on his range, and this drive had been plagued with trouble. Haggard could draw a man out neatly, and Linus found himself griping about the way that Texas, for all its new prosperity, was going to the dogs from high taxes and damnyankee carpetbaggers.

"I know the breed," Haggard nodded somberly. "And Phil Sheridan's so-called reconstruction policy as occupation commander there has been more than any decent man can stomach."

"Plague on the Irish," Linus murmured sardonically.

"And you'd think the Yankee Army would clean out that riff-raff border scum, ex-redlegs and jayhawkers, that prey on your drovers," Haggard countered with an undaunted grin. He folded his hands on the desk and leaned earnestly forward. "Tell me, sir—have you ever contemplated a move from Texas, a fresh start elsewhere?"

This very consideration had been revolving through Linus Quincannon's mind for some time, though he hadn't mentioned the bitter and angry memories that Texas held which had largely motivated it. Now he replied shortly that his father had built up the great Singlebit ranch from a shoestring, and his roots were there. But presently he found himself standing by the wall map designating all the land owned by Haggard, listening to the man's quiet, persuasive words. Fine a parcel of graze as you can find north of the Nations . . . free of buffalo migration . . . town and railroad handy.

A half hour later, Linus Quincannon made his decision. And for another hour they thrashed out the details. What about those snorkies and their sod farms and their damned fields?

"Don't trouble yourself about those fools, sir; future of Kansas'll be grass and graze as God intended, not crops. The land itself'll break them, drive them out inside a year or so. Regrettably, I have to unload this land fast, and they were the first comers. Anyway they'll serve as a good example to others, so it really works out for the best."

Studying the map, Linus said idly, "And this Vikstrom lad—he's the head fool?"

"Oh, Vikstrom. He's a resourceful fellow in his way, I suppose. But limited. He has a fool notion about wheat—" Haggard laughed. "Not worth discussing. Have you met him?"

"No, my *segundo* O'Hea did," Linus said dryly, and abruptly then: "It's settled. That parcel of five thousand acres east of the snorkies at twenty dollars an acre—and as I'll be a spell clearing up my affairs in Texas and converting my properties into cash, I'll next see you early in the spring."

"Fine," Haggard said warmly, and after the papers were drawn up and signed, he poured them a pair of stiff ones. Linus took his in a swallow, feeling the heady lift of his spirits. Damn, he felt almost fine about the world again. A new start, far from the old memories. A small and prospering spread, shorn of the too-many irons his old man had left in the fire, would give him leeway to experiment with his personal dream of cattle-breeding. A thing to welcomely occupy a man's attention. . . .

He did not turn from the map as the door opened. Then Haggard said irritably, "Well, Margaret?"

"You didn't come home for supper, Eben, so I wondered . . ."

Her soft voice trailed. And for Linus time stood still in the long moment that he slowly turned. Whatever a man might see in her face was muted by sallow lamplight and shadow.

"Mr. Quincannon, may I present my wife?" A faint note of irritation shaded Haggard's pleasantry now. "Some paperwork kept me, Margaret—then Quincannon here came on business, and we concluded another matter. He'll be almost our new neighbor, by the way. Plans to develop a ranch on that remaining acreage over east of the Scandinavians . . ."

"How nice," she murmured, lowering her gaze. Linus thought obscurely that she had always had a fine gift for composure.

"See here, Quincannon, why not join us for dinner—"

"Ye'll pardon me, but I ate back in camp," Linus lied. He went to the desk and picked up his hat with a curt nod. "See you again before I leave . . . servant, ma'am."

Out on the street Quincannon quartered across toward the nearest saloon, walking fast, feeling the seething bitterness sear his mind with a worse fever than on that night two years ago when he'd come to his senses in a foul adobe hut to find his right arm gone.

When he heard her call "Linus" he halted on the boardwalk in the dense shadow of a building. Her quick half-running steps came up behind him and paused, and he came around to face her.

"Maggie Danaher," he said softly, brutally. "Margaret Haggard, is it?"

She only looked at him saying nothing, with dim light glowing along the curve of her cheek, and then he looked away. "Say it and be done with it."

"I waited," she said almost inaudibly. "And you knew that I would—"

"For what!" He drove his left fist against the stump of his arm. "Haven't you eyes, woman!"

"Ah, Linus! Linus, you proud dear fool, and that was all?"

"All! I'll bring a woman a whole man, or nothing!"

He had learned how a man could cover a lot with raging bluster, but had forgotten how he could hide nothing from Maggie Danaher, the girl to whom he had poured out another side of himself, one that even

Denny O'Hea didn't know, in one long magic evening on the veranda after they had met at her father's house in Austin . . . was it seven years, or an age, ago?

While inside their fathers had talked about the war into which that damned Lincoln was dragging the country. When a few days later it had begun, he rode off with his head full of an exchange of bright promises. It had sustained him through four years of the bloodshed men called right and honor and valor. And when it was done, how could a man explain that his own part in a war where he could see nothing but a blind chaos of right and wrong on both sides, had left a sickness in him that could only be wiped out by finding an ideal for which he could fight and believe? But Maggie had understood his need to bring her a full and fulfilled man, and again the parting. When Linus had marched off to Mexico with Jo Shelby, it was with no sympathy toward Shelby's grandiose scheme of enlisting enough Confederate sympathizers to revive the beaten South to bloody new struggle.

The civil war in Mexico was only ferment for Shelby's yeast, though neither Juárez nor Maximilian wanted him. But for Linus, the issues had the alluring clean-cut shine of a saber: Juárez was the embattled underdog fighting to free his people from the tyranny of Maximilian and his French troops. After deserting Shelby, Linus and O'Hea had gathered a band of half-naked peons and organized them into an efficient guerrilla force, striking, harassing, retreating, striking again. A ghostlike undercover army led by a gringo called El Capitan. A thorn in Maximilian's side broken finally by a chance Minié ball. His men had borne Linus to a friendly peon's hut; a mestizo medic was summoned and gave his swift verdict. Linus had come out of hell's own delirium to find his arm amputated.

To a man who had taken less pride in his size and strength, who had not needed a fullness of physical pride to match his ideals, a surgeon's knife would have cut far less deep. But after his return to his father's ranch, the black brooding began like a cancer in his mind, and he could not return to Maggie.

And she had waited, she told him, until a year ago when Eben Haggard, who had dealings with her father, had first won her father over, and through him Margaret herself. She had recognized that Eben was a secretive man who did nothing without a reason, yet at the time he was gentle and attentive and would surely be a good husband, and she had learned that a woman who expected too much could only find hurt.

"Perhaps I should have come to you, Linus," she whispered, "but I am not a forward woman, and I knew when you did not answer my letters that you had made your decision. I had my own stupid pride, you see."

He looked above her head. "How much did you know?"

"About El Capitan—everything. Oh yes, you became quite famous—the newspapers were full of you, the daring, half-legendary secret weapon of Juárez. All I heard after that was that you were wounded and had returned to Texas." He felt the deep hurt in her low words. "Only to Texas, Linus."

His eyes lowered to her face, seeing there everything that he had ever wanted, and with the full wrenching knowledge at last of what he had thrown away, knowing that all the foolish damned pride had never mattered.

Except that he had learned too late.

She took a step toward him and her hand lifted. He moved back before it could touch his scarred face. He fitted his stony stare over his thoughts and said quietly, "How have you been otherwise, Maggie?"

A sob broke in her throat. "Linus—Linus! You could never pretend to me!"

He stood for a long time after her running steps died away. An explosion of laughter from the saloon roused him then, and he went through the batwing doors, letting the din deaden his insides a little more as he moved to the bar and lifted a finger for whiskey.

When it was brought, he only stared into it and slowly scrubbed the back of his neck with a palm. Well, and what now; go to Haggard and tell him he was chucking up the deal? Could a man live so close to what had been? Suddenly his knotted thoughts, driven to a reaction he had not expected, turned outward angrily. He took the whiskey in a gulp, letting its raw sting burn out the ghosts he'd lived with for two years.

O'Hea had inferred it, and by all the saints, he was right—Linus Quincannon had been running from himself too long, and for a man nothing could be worse. In the end, no man could run that far. He'd come back to Kansas next spring and build his new ranch. And face whatever came of it.

CHAPTER EIGHT

THE MORNING WAS BRIGHT AND WARM AS MAGNUS Vikstrom and Arne Hultgren set their horses to a brisk clip across the low range of hills toward Liberty. The sky was a scoured blue and against it a lone chicken hawk dipped and wheeled; the sun already hot against their right sides turned the rolling monotony of grassland to a drab golden-brown. It was the long lazy sort of Indian summer day when the blood of a young man paced sluggish to work, but restless, to thoughts of a cool dip in the river, a card game, a chilled beer—anything to relieve boredom.

Arne softly whistled "Marching Through Georgia," and now and then rubbed his fingers gently over the converted Walker Colt in its worn old handmade holster at his hip. His brother Syvert had killed two Rebs with that gun at Chickamauga, or so he claimed, and he'd given it to Arne for the trip West. An honest-to-God talisman for Arne, Magnus sardonically thought.

Arne drew the gun and set a careless bead on a prairie dog village off to their right. He pulled trigger and laughed as dust geysered and a brown head popped back from view.

"Stick to what you can hit," Magnus dryly advised him.

Arne grimaced, now glancing off toward the river bottoms on the far left. Quincannon and his drovers had been camped there a week, letting their herd graze and fatten. Arne, extending his gun to arm's length, squinted along its sights at the distant cattle. "All the big game I seen 'round these parts is cows." He arced the gun to line on the drover camp. "Maybe Rebs too."

Magnus cocked a sardonic eyebrow. "Now how good you hear, Arne?"

Irritably Arne let his arm fall and jeered, "Daddy's little boy."

Magnus gave him a steady sidelong regard. "You want to step down, we can argue that better."

Arne, being mostly impulse and temper like his brother, flared, "Don't get smart 'cause you licked me when we was kids!"

"Licked you a month ago for saying a wrong thing to Greta, too."

"Sure, when I was likkered up."

"You're not likkered now," Magnus said thinly. "I asked how's your hearing. Pa said we should shy off trouble with the Texans even if they push it."

"Don't recall anyone electin' your old man the big mucky-muck. He ain't my nursemaid!" Arne paused, his eyes narrowing. "Maybe that's why you're ridin' with me.

"Maybe. Pa's got enough troubles. He don't have time to watch one hothead Hultgren, let alone two. You don't want me watching you, then watch yourself."

Arne's hot stare fell away; with a soft, vicious, "Ahhh—!" he slapped the gun into its holster.

A silent hostility lay between them as they rode down the last shelving thrust of hills above Liberty.

Magnus was coolly aware that he had his father's ability to stare down anyone who crossed him, but it meant nothing . . . it was a trait useful only if you wanted to play Joshua and lead the people.

Magnus felt a quiet backwash of shame, knowing the unfairness of this judgment of his father's way. He had no false humility about his own keen and sensitive mind; as a boy he had felt bitterly alienated from his playmates, then his parents, silently infuriated by their hopelessly simple acceptance of life. Only of late had he come to accept his mother's narrow, trusting simplicity of outlook as part of her real goodness, to be loved and not forgiven. But from his father he wanted more, feeling Borg's troubled fumbling toward a common ground where they might meet man to man. For all their awkward apartness, that common feeling remained, so strongly that at times the impulse to tell his father how he had always loved and respected him made an aching cry in Magnus. But his tongue was numb to words that would not come, only the covering mockery which widened the breach.

On that middle ground his father might have understood the restless furies goading him. Otherwise how could a stolid, toil-rough farmer ever understand a son who wanted—what? Magnus was not really sure. But he had read voraciously of places he'd never seen, and faraway France had become a lodestar in his mind. He had been dazzled by Zola's morbid *Thérèse Raquin* and stirred by reading of Pasteur's untiring research; in Paris he could paint and study and mingle with kindred minds. He was sure of one thing: the limited horizons of his life had become unbearable. . . .

Only Greta Holmgaard understood. Her family was not from Koshkonong; Olof Holmgaard had joined the wagon party at Prairie du Chien, and for that purpose had brought his family clear from northern Minnesota on word of mouth. There had been many girls in Magnus' young life, for he had an easy way with them. Now there was only Greta, lovely and quick and sensitive; the right girl for whom a young man looked and rarely found.

Could he simply leave and take Greta with him? She, hardly turned seventeen and very much in love, would go. Only the finality of such a break, of leaving too much unsettled behind him, held Magnus. The fact irritated him to defiance: *I might do it anyway.*

He shook his head with a baffled sigh; he was still groping for the answers. Behind his restlessness, the fact of growing up had jarred home the knowledge that a strong head alone did not make a man. He needed to think over his responsibilities to his parents and Greta and himself, and he needed to make plans. He even, hating the self-admission, needed help and advice. With nobody to turn to but a father with whom he could never find the right words.

Sunk in his dour brooding, he hardly noticed when he and Arne rode past the loading pens that marked the south end of Liberty. Arne let out a whoop and spurred down the street, pivoting to a dusty stop by Lavery's Saloon; Magnus followed sedately. He and Arne were of like age, but their restless young instincts followed different channels, and feeling had always stretched thin between them. Still, on a Saturday morning when Pa had given you the day off and your girl was busy helping her mother, what was there to do but head for town?

As Magnus dismounted and tied up Hans, he felt a tight wariness, running his eye over the racked saddle horses. Two wild-looking mustangs bore Quincannon's brand. Arne, standing hipshot by the tie rail, said with a faint jeer. "You scared of a couple big hats?"

"Don't be a kid," Magnus said coldly.

"What's that mean?"

"What I said."

Arne laughed derisively and elbowed through the batwing doors. So did Magnus, after a brief hesitation. A musty coolness clung to the high-beamed room, and the smells of stale whiskey and smoke. At a nearby table, caught in a hazy sunshaft from the half-frosted front window, two men in range clothes were calculating their poker hands. Magnus moved up to the bar by Arne, and the bald apron had a jaundiced stare for their youth as he poured the drinks.

The slick whisper of cards went on behind them, and one player drawled, "See y'all, Pete, and raise you ten—" The other man swore quietly in Spanish, and now Magnus twisted a curious glance over his shoulder.

The man looked lean and sinuous in his tight jacket and trousers, and his profile was dark and sharp and hungry. A wheatstraw cigarette hung in a corner of his mouth, and he squinted against the smoke as he slapped down a card. Then, feeling Magnus' glance,

98

he lifted a stare like black lightning.

Uneasily Magnus turned back to his drink: Pa had had little to say of his clash with three Singlebit herders a week ago, but at supper that night Nathan Dart had told it in his dry droll way. If the Mexican-looking man at the table was Pete Robles, this was no place to drink.

He said softly, nudging Arne, "Let's move on."

Arne said irritably, "Hell, I just got here," then swallowed his drink and banged his glass on the bar. He looked back at the two trailhands and made a soft profane sound with his tongue and teeth. Robles' hands stilled on his cards as he looked up, gently revolving his cigarette between his lips.

"Come on, Pete, let's play," the Texan drawled mildly.

Robles' murky stare slid back to his card hand. For a time there was only the creak of chairs and the light slap of cards. With a disgusted oath Robles flung his cards down and scraped back his chair. His big silver rowels chinked to his stalking tread to the end of the bar; he raised two fingers. From the corner of his eye Magnus watched Robles almost delicately sip his drink, leaning one bent arm on the bar.

Roughly Magnus jogged Arne. "Let's go."

"Go to hell," Arne murmured, motioning to the bald man for a refill.

Robles took the rest of his drink in a swallow and said, "Whoof," gently waving a finger in front of his nose. "All this pigsmell in here. A man can cut her, it's that thick."

Arne swiveled a flushed face toward the bartender. "What you got here, a nigger place?"

"Pete. Hey, Pete," said the Texan, "let's doan' have trouble."

"Man, it's this gringo pigsmell. It is a black vomit."

Arne swung around, slamming down his empty glass, and Magnus took an instinctive backward step. With a sense of dismal urgency he caught at Arne's arm and Arne batted his hand away, not looking at him. "You see any pigs here?"

Robles' spurs lightly chinked with his lazy half-turn. "Only two," he murmured, "from where I stand."

"You stinking greaser bastard!"

"Talk is cheap."

"All right, you got a gun."

"And I am not a large clumsy farmer of pigs."

"I know what you farm, peppergut."

Calmly Robles slacked an elbow against the bar, tugging his ear. "What's in your guts, boy? I think a lot of wind."

"You can find out!"

"Say, look," said the bald apron in alarm.

"Show all that belly you talk, boy. Now. Or crawl out on it." Robles did not stir a muscle, his smile wicked and waiting.

Arne opened his mouth and closed it. His face changed with some blind realization, and now he pushed away from the bar. Robles' words came with a sibilant flatness: "Not that way!" Arne stopped. "You leave now, you go on your belly. Down on it."

Arne opened his mouth again, and only now looked

at Magnus with a fumbling and frightened bewilderment. Tears shone in his eyes. Magnus started to put out his hand, and then Robles spoke a quiet obscenity, turning it off his tongue with a wicked softness. Arne spun toward him, goaded now past fear and even desperation, clawing for his gun.

BORG TRAMPED ALONG the black turned furrows with the seed bag slung over his shoulder, sifting down the pale yellow kernels from his hand, again knowing the serene excitement that had gripped him during the early plowing. Today, though plowing was not finished, he had begun to sow. He thought that the time was right, but he would mark these acres off from those to be sowed later. This first season would be experimental; next summer's ripened crop would tell the full story.

He paused to gently juggle a handful of slippery kernels, feeling almost a shame at the sense of overwhelming goodness that always took hold of him at the first sowing. This was no ritual but a function of manual work, and as Sigrid had severely observed, it was how a man should feel in church, not at his daily labor. Yet a man's religion must lie in his true feeling, not in the manners he assumed for the Sabbath. He could understand why his Norse forebears, peasants of the soil, had worshiped their red-bearded Thor, with his coarse, earthy good-nature and his hammer Mjolner which flung bursts of thunder and lightning and presaged the life-giving rain. To Borg there was something mystic in the unknown chemistry by which these inert hard seeds would reach from the moist blackness for sunlight and life. He was the tool of a process far beyond him, awed by its unfolding.

The kernels seemed to warm his palm with a meaning of their own; he felt their latent life and knew the smooth soundness of each. For under his watchful eye the entire family had sat about the table every evening, carefully sorting the seed into small heaps on white cloth. It must be clean of shrunken or damaged kernels. He opened his hand and watched the kernels glow against the sunlight, and grinning then at his foolishness, gave them to the waiting soil.

The hoof thud of coming horses reached his ear, and he looked up squinting against the sun, now seeing Magnus come down a north slope over the raw, newly sowed ground. A quick frown darkened Borg's face as he started to wave him off, but his words died unvoiced and slowly his hand fell. A limp burden jogged loosely across the back of a horse Magnus led.

Borg shed the feed bag with a twist of his shoulder. He loped up the slope at a long trot, meeting Magnus halfway. His son's face held a residue of blank shock, and he made a meaningless mute gesture. Borg knew, before he turned Arne's head sideward and saw his face.

"Pete Robles," Magnus said thinly.

"Tell it," Borg said harshly, and as Magnus talked, rested his big hand lightly on the mane of Arne's horse, watching the fingers flex and open. *Be steady now.* The thought glided like cool water over his gathering rage; one hothead to die was enough.

Borg rubbed a palm over his sweaty forehead.

Arne's death might be the spark to trigger off his people's slow but dogged tempers, already tensed against freewheeling Texas insolence. Though the bypassing drovers now avoided the plowed fields, for that lesson had taken well, their pungent insults carried clearly to the men behind the plows; minor clashes in town had further fueled a mounting hostility. Now, Magnus had said, Marshal Tetlow called Arne's slaying justifiable self-defense . . . Robles would not be held for trial.

But worse, there was spark-blooded Syvert, who, restless with workaday drudgery, had ridden off south two days ago for some hunting. It was Syvert's way to go off alone when his vicious tensions built too high and he felt his thin restraints slipping, which they usually would anyway. But Syvert would be back soon, and when he went after his brother's killer, one of them would die—a second killing could only explode into larger retaliations.

Yet there had to be justice for Arne Hultgren. Remembering his one meeting with the gun-ready Robles and his weighing of the man, Borg made his cold judgment: *This was murder, and there is no law to help.* There must be justice, but only a calm head could deliver it without causing this situation to flower into worse, and there was only one way. He let the decision settle like a massive ridgepole beam dropping into place, and then he did not think about it.

"Get down."

Magnus dismounted and Borg took the reins and stepped into the saddle. He untied the lead rope and handed it down. "Take him home."

"To Hultgren's?"

"No. Take him to our place. Tell our family what happened—no one else."

"Pa, let me—"

"You hear what I say, sonny, do it."

Borg turned Hans on a tight rein and rode to a nearby stand of scrub oak where he had cached his rifle against emergency. He got the weapon and checked its load. Afterward he lifted Hans into a long lope, heading for Liberty.

CHAPTER NINE

BEFORE HE CAME OFF THE LAST SLOPE ABOVE TOWN, Borg pulled up and shaded his eyes, lining his gaze along the flats below. A small party of riders had quartered off the river bottoms toward town: drovers coming in to "see the elephant," perhaps more of Quincannon's men. Borg waited till they reached the outskirts of Liberty, then nudged Hans downslope.

He did not head for the south entrance of Main Street, instead made a wide swing around the maze of stockpens and came up back of the hotel. He got down and ground-tethered Hans, then slipped his Spencer from its scabbard and tramped up the areaway between the hotel and Lavery's Saloon. He flattened his back against the hotel wall by its corner where he could obtain a broad view of the street and not be seen.

There were eight saddle ponies tied in front of

Lavery's, where Arne had been killed. There would be more than only Robles and his friend to face if he went in to confront the Mexican now. Sunlight shafted hotly against his chest and face, and Borg moved back into shadow. He sank down on his heels and laid the sun-warmed rifle across his knees, a cold patience in him. A man could wait.

As he watched the lazy currents of life along the street, Dennis O'Hea pushed out of Lavery's, paused to bite off the end of a cigar and spit it out. But it was the big one-armed man stepping out behind O'Hea who caught his attention. Though he hadn't seen him before, Borg knew that this was Quincannon, and he wondered now, *Could a man talk to him?*

Quincannon took off his hat and ran a bandanna around the sweatband. His face, under a thatch of grizzled iron-gray, held a look of granite, and Borg saw nothing of it but a kind of unfeeling self-certainty that edged on arrogance. O'Hea spoke, and Quincannon gave a curt nod; the two walked on and turned into the China Cafe.

Borg held his vigil. The sun, mounting against a blue-brassy sky, wiped back his meager patch of shadow. He felt sweat glide down his ribs and pool in his boots. Shifting his cramped body, he took off his hat to sleeve his forehead, and then a creak of batwing doors pulled him alert.

Pete Robles had left the saloon, jauntily carrying his weight on the balls of his feet, and Borg knew a cold pleasure that he was not drunk. He had never faced a man this way, not on the battlefield of war, and had wondered how it would be with him, and now seeing his man, felt only a deep wicked certainty.

Robles ducked under the tie rail and caught up his reins. Borg clamped on his hat and took three long steps out into the street. As Robles swung astride his horse in an easy motion, the sharp levering of the Spencer sent its cold metallic sound across the midday stillness. Robles, wheeling his mount out sideways, stiffened. His black glance found Borg and he drew gently on his cigarette, carefully lifting a hand to take it from his lips.

"You are a fool, man."

"Get down," Borg said thinly, "or take it like you are."

Robles' laugh was a dry and sibilant whisper. "I think I take you either way. Even a big *chingado* can die fast."

"Not so fast there won't be a bullet for you."

"The boy had a big mouth that got him killed."

"You wanted him to crawl. How good you crawl, mister?"

"I do not crawl." Robles' restless black eyes, gauging his chances, coldly hardened now and he pitched his cigarette away. "I feel ver' sorry for you, señor."

He swung his horse on a quick tight rein to baffle Borg's aim while his free hand dipped to his gun. Borg, aiming by instinct, let his rifle arc smoothly up to chest-level and the instant it hung steady, he shot. Robles was driven sideways by the bullet's impact, and his horse reared as the line of buildings flung back a thin flurry of shot echoes. Robles' body, jolting limply free, fell in a splayed arch across the tie rail; the dry wood split with a flat crack like a pistol shot. Robles hit the dust and lay like a broken doll, one arm flung out.

Borg let his breath sigh away and his gun slack into the crook of his arm. He started across the street, halting midway as the Texas men crowded out through the batwings. People began to converge along the walk. There was a hush of arrested traffic, broken when an aroused dog somewhere downstreet set up a frenzied barking. Standing high and stolid in the dusty heat, Borg was the cynosure of a town's angry curiosity and he ignored it all, waiting.

The crowd broke into restless mutters as Tiger Jack Tetlow came angling across from his office at his long brisk stride. He bent above Robles, straightened up shoving the dead man's gun into his belt. He turned toward Vikstrom with a snap of his fingers.

"I'll take yours too, fellow."

"I think you will not."

Tetlow slightly hunched his shoulders, but did not move. He watched Borg's face carefully. "Why did you kill him?"

"You know why, mister. I did your job for you."

"Don't read me the law, fellow! That boy's killing was self-defense."

"Then, I would say this was." Borg made a gesture at the bystanders. "Ask any man."

Tetlow turned and pointed at one of the Texans. "You. Did you see it?"

The Texan was a long leathery man in his late fifties and a hard-won wisdom lay behind his bleached eyes. "End of it, anyways. Pete went for his gun. This fella's rifle wa'n't pointed. I make it even. Reckon, all told, Pete asked for it."

"That he did." Dennis O'Hea had moved up through the crowd, and now he stood hands on hips, eying the dead man with a wry shake of his head. "Seen it from the cafe. Ah, saints. And so the world goes."

"Where's Quincannon?" Tetlow snapped.

"Mr. Quincannon is drinkin' his coffee, Marshal dear."

Tetlow said frostily, "You tell him the law will handle this," and looked back at Borg. "Once more. Give me your—"

O'Hea cut dryly across his speech. "Tell him yourself," and the crowd broke apart as Quincannon left the cafe. Close up, Borg guessed that the giant Irishman's gaunt, easy grace of movement belied a considerable strength, also that he was younger than he looked.

It was Borg's shrewd observation that a man who fell back on gestures was a man basically flawed, and Quincannon's dallying over his coffee had been a gesture. Yet seeing past this casual arrogance, Borg thought, *This is a man,* and was baffled, for what need did a man have of stage gestures? He wondered about this, and about the man's missing arm.

Quincannon, halting now, settled a passing glance on the body of Robles, afterward flicking cold and colorless eyes at Borg in brief assessment. Then he took a few steps forward and sideways, this placing him between Borg and the marshal.

Tetlow said with flat warning, "I'll handle this!"

O'Hea showed Tiger Jack his brash grin, and Quincannon ignored him. Tetlow stared at the rancher's broad back, but did not move, and the crowd fell into an uneasy silence, matters easily accounted for by Quincannon's hard reputation and his crew backing him here. Borg stood alone, facing the thing out as he had started it.

Still he had the abrupt conviction that the situation had narrowed down to himself and Quincannon, two big men of backgrounds poles apart in America of this time. Even discounting the bitter clashes of their nationalities and creeds in this country, there had also been a war whose wounds still lay raw and open—and now a head-on hostility concerning the land and its use. A couple yards of dusty street separated the two men, and they could not have stood farther apart. Borg sensed that a stubborn and uncompromising strength was all that he shared in common with Linus Quincannon, and curiously now, he wondered whether this might not be enough.

"You'd be Vikstrom, of course." When Borg nodded, Quincannon gave a backward nod toward the dead Robles. "Can a man ask why?"

"He killed a boy. It was murder."

"Your word, murder?"

"My word."

"And this was any affair of yours?"

"I made it mine, maybe."

Quincannon slightly nodded, his voice hard and even. "I can understand that; I stand by my men too."

Borg shifted his feet, feeling the crawl of sweat between his shirt and back. "Good. But here was a matter of justice."

"An eye for an eye?" Quincannon frowned. "But Robles was my man; you could have come to me."

"And if I had, how would it go?"

"Probably not to your liking."

"That is why." Borg laid down his words hard and flat. "I don't know what you see here, Mr. Quincannon, but I see justice done. This I will not argue."

He said it with a finality honed by a quickening tension; Quincannon's cold and measuring stare told a man nothing. Still when the rancher spoke, his words implied respect without a jot of yielding. "I know how Robles was. It's an even score. I've no quarrel with you, Vikstrom."

Tiger Jack Tetlow's shifting body betrayed his uneasy anger, but no one else moved. Borg gave a curt nod, then backed slowly toward the alleyway, not lifting his gun but giving none of them his back.

Once in the alleyway and cut off from the street, he faded swiftly back to where Hans waited. Again he made a broad circuit of the stockpens, not breathing easier till he achieved the first lift of grassy slope beyond Liberty. He assessed his feelings as to Robles' death and felt nothing; maybe it would come later. As he neared the brow of the slope, a rider came on over it at a hard lope. It was Nathan Dart, and Borg felt a swift rough warmth toward the gray scout.

Dart hauled in his blowing roan. "Make it I'm too late."

"There was no need, Nate, but thanks."

They swung into pace heading for home, as Borg related what had happened. Dart said afterward, "You done smart, handlin' it alone. Hard sayin' why, 'less you know Quincannon."

"Now maybe I do, a little. A strange man."

Dart spat dryly. "Yeah. Like decidin' to sell out in Texas and movin' up here."

That startled Borg. "This I had not heard."

"Was helpin' Holmgaard's boys sink their second well this mornin'. One of 'em, Sven-Eric, heard it in town last night. Seems Eb Haggard sold Quincannon them five thousand acres east of us. El Capitan'll be back to stay, come spring."

Borg, scowling over the news, muttered, "To ranch."

"Could be a right unneighborly neighbor."

Borg knew a swift feral anger then. "What the hell is Haggard trying to bring off on us?"

"Reckon that's no matter to him, where there's a profit involved."

Borg swore feelingly. Today, by deliberately crowding a situation full of explosive friction, he'd shown the Texas crowd that any pressure on his people would bring hard and decisive retaliation. Had it been for nothing? A hardhead like Quincannon running cattle close by could cause the uneasy stalemate to snowball into real trouble.

It could only be faced in its time; now came a more urgent concern: heading off Syvert Hultgren when he returned. He spoke the thought aloud, and Dart said grimly, "You best hyper then. Syvert's back."

Borg said quickly, "When?"

"More'n an hour ago anyways. Passed the Hultgren place when I come back from Holmgaard's. Chimley stack was smokin' and Syvert's horse was in."

"I'll leave you here, Nate. Ride on to our place—get Arne's body and bring it home. I will have finished talking to Syvert when you get there."

When Borg reached the Hultgren soddy an hour later, Syvert was leading his saddled horse out of the small brush corral. His set scowl barely relaxed as he answered Borg's nod.

"Can't palaver now," Syvert said, and stepped into his saddle. "Got to find my fool brother. His horse was gone when I come back this mornin', and he ain't come home. Likely in town with his face in a glass, and all them east acres to be plowed. Damn lazy kid."

"Syvert . . ." Borg reined Hans up alongside him, and young Hultgren's scowl deepened with a chafing impatience. "There is no need, Syvert. I am sorry."

"What?"

Borg told him, seeing the shock and grief and rage chase uncontrollably across Syvert's thin face. He broke off in midspeech as Hultgren suddenly slashed his horse with the reins, lunging the animal away.

"Syvert!"

Hultgren iron-handed his mount to a wheeling halt, his face working with a pale and murderous passion. "Don't try to stop me—I'm warnin' you, Borg!"

"There's nothing to fight over, you young fool!

112

Listen to what I say. Arne's killer is dead!" Borg's voice dropped, holding low and even. "I killed him. It is finished."

"Not by a long ways! It wasn't your place, Vikstrom—Arne was my brother! Them goddam Texas—"

Choking with fury he started again to rein his horse away, and froze then with lifted reins at the sharp levering of Borg's Spencer. His hot glassy stare fell to the leveled rifle.

"No, Syvert," Borg said gently. "There is too much riding at stake to let one man blow it up. You think I won't shoot to stop that, eh?"

Syvert swayed like a drunken man before his saddle creaked to the slow settling of his tense weight.

"Now get down," Borg said, "you damned hothead, and hear me out."

CHAPTER TEN

As suddenly as it had come, the golden spell of Indian summer ended. There followed blustery days of overcast skies and raw winds from the north. Linus Quincannon sold his herd and headed back for Texas. The two last trail herds of the season straggled in, and the drovers were forced to meet a cutthroat price of eleven dollars a head from the departing cattle buyers. These rib-gaunt cattle were shipped out immediately, to be fattened up later at the stockyards in Kansas City or Chicago.

For the settlers it was a time of seeing their planting finished up and their households made snug for the winter. Food staples must be bought or prepared and stored up, and feed for the stock. In this near-woodless country, fuel was the main concern, and the settlers exhausted every resource. All the dead brush and buffalo chips available were scoured up; bundles of grass and weeds were gathered, and the youngsters spent most of their idle time knotting these into tight hanks.

On November third the first snowfall came, rather a slushy mixture of snow and sleet which later froze like a nubby glaze across the stone-hard soil. The next morning Borg, muffled in his heavy sheepskin, tramped out alone across his fields. Snow fell in thin, stinging gusts, driven against his face by a cutting wind, and he breathed deeply and felt strangely exhilarated. Let the enemy elements do their worst; the germinal life of his sprouting wheat was safe, six inches beneath the frozen topsoil.

There were pleasant evenings in the big common room of the sod house. While outside the wind howled bitterly at the eaves, a pot-bellied stove fanned its aura of warmth over the room. They were lucky to have the stove as well as the usual fireplace of plastered clay, and instead of candles or a lard-burning "Betty lamp," a big coal-oil lamp on the table shed a good light, while the cheery blaze of the fireplace played tawny patterns across the old-country picture cloths that adorned two walls.

Magnus spent his idle hours painting intricate *rosemaling* designs on plain platters, trays, and bowls.

Like their Scandinavian forebears, the Vikstroms were not demonstrative parents; only when Magnus wasn't present were they quick to point out to visitors that, untutored, his skill in the old-country craft of rose-painting matched that of a trained craftsman. Opportunity for such boasting was frequent, for Magnus spent most of his evenings at Holmgaard's, with Greta.

Pleased that his son had settled his attentions to one girl, Borg wondered if after all Magnus would steady down without his offering parental advice. His manner had lately become more subdued and polite, which pleased Sigrid. Yet Borg was uneasy. Often he caught Magnus daydreaming over his *rosemaling*, his hands idle. Else he would pick up a book Magnus had been reading, always books by foreign authors about foreign places. *We must talk*, Borg resolved to himself, but continued to put it off.

Syvert Hultgren's state of mind was another worrisome detail. Borg had clamped a brutal check on Syvert's rash impulse to further revenge his brother, but afterward it was as though Syvert had gone dead inside. He had not turned a furrow of earth on his fields since that day. He became more morose and solitary than before, letting a black gnawing grief eat out his insides. Borg had been over to see him twice, found him drunk and maudlin the first time. The second time Syvert was lying dead drunk outside in subzero cold, and would have frozen if Borg hadn't arrived to pack him into the house.

In a way Borg did not condemn him. The job of raising young Arne after their parents died had fallen wholly on Syvert, and though he had infected Arne with his own unbridled wildness which led to his brother's death, there was no denying that he had always worked hard to see that Arne had lacked for nothing. His father, a ne'er-do-well, had left many debts, and Syvert had paid them all. Syvert had never had time in his youth for anything but his occasional wild sprees—no time to make friends or meet a good girl and settle down. There had been only Arne, and for Syvert, as for many high-strung men, such a reversal in his life left in him nothing but a despondent and purposeless lethargy.

Borg wondered whether he might have contributed to Syvert's state by roughly deadlocking him in his fresh grief, and it left him with a nagging sense of guilt. He'd mentioned the feeling only to Nathan Dart, whose spare reply was, "Hoss, no good one man tryin' to carry all the world's worries on his shoulders."

Dart, with his blunt shrewdness, had probably summed it up. But leadership, as Borg had found, was the loneliest burden a man could bear. It made him sensitive to details of life he had once passed over lightly. It made him try to dig for understanding into the character of Linus Quincannon, since their very future here would be at stake when that hard-nosed cattleman returned in the spring. But his one brief, almost enigmatic, meeting with the man yielded little clue, except that he respected a firm stand. For Borg, this remained the most worrisome problem of all.

Yet the long, pleasant winter evenings allowed a man breathing space to push troubling thoughts into the future that no man could read. The baby Lisj-Per, fat and healthy and cooing, was the center of attention, and all the women, including little Kjersti, vied to fuss over him. Helga seemed happy in her quiet way, doing more than her share of the common work.

It was Abel Jevers' suggestion that he teach her English, and it became an evening ritual for them to sit at the table over a child's primer. Now and then came Helga's soft laughter at her own ineptness, and it was good to hear; Borg liked the sense of vital youth these young people brought to his household, and was glad that half of his "family" was young: it was like a good omen in this young and unbroken land.

Better yet was the way young and old had become as one under his roof, the different threads of their lives weaving together in a strange completeness. Even Lars and Inga, though having long ago lost whatever they felt for each other, were drawn into the unity. Inga, with the baby to fuss over, seemed happier than she had been in years. Lars, though still subject to moods of surly self-pity, had found a way to busy himself usefully. He had always spent much idle time whittling on odd pieces of wood, covering every bedpost, table leg, and cabinet face with ornate designs. It chanced that no other in the settlement was skilled in the intricate wood designing dear to Scandinavians and Lars did wonders with whatever wooden pieces they had; his services were wanted by every household, with payment promised after the first crop.

The ancient outcast Pawnee Harry, too, had found a home. After his brittle old bones healed, he spent most of his time out prowling the prairie and frozen river. He snared jackrabbits and caught fish through the ice, which, dressed and salted, were no mean contribution to a larder always stretched to feed this large household. Pawnee Harry had his straw pallet in the isolation of the utility shed, but stole in many an evening to squat down and watch with brighteyed fascination Borg's and Dart's poker games.

"Injuns're hellfire for games of chance," Dart explained, whereupon Borg set out to teach him the game. The white man's gambling was the only thing about his alien world that made any sense to Pawnee Harry. "White man goddam fool," he told Borg placidly. "Injun gettem grub, robes, stuff makem all he need from buffalo. White man killem buffalo, raise cow, sellem for money, buy what he need. Huh. Alla same, but too much work. Vikstrom too much work, diggem ground, plantem wheat, sellem, buy same stuff." He patted Borg's shoulder gently. "Good man, Vikstrom, but damn fool."

Life gained a solid feel when an oddly assorted group of people began to shape their lives anew together, bringing their distinctive rituals of living to one hearth. Still a pleasant pattern could grow monotonous through long days and nights on the winterlocked prairie, and everyone looked forward to the Christmas season. It was a time to renew the Yule traditions of old in a way that gave an added substance and meaning to the present.

For Sigrid especially these were happy days as she busily prepared for the Christmas Eve celebration. The whole household knew a relaxing of her Spartan frugality in the luxury of cinnamon and melted butter on their porridge for a week. She had Borg drive her to town and there selected small gifts with frowning care, seeing that no one was neglected. Borg followed her lead with humorous resignation, except for one inspired suggestion.

"*Gud bevara!* The cost, Herr Vikstrom."

"Ah, why not, it's Christmas. And it might do Lars a lot of good, not just the gift, but getting."

She tapped her foot, frowning thoughtfully. "*Ja,* I think so. All right."

Borg, casually pressing the moment, added, "And we had better buy some little things for the Holmgaards. I invited them over Christmas Eve."

She stared at him. "Oh? *Tack sa mycket!*"

"Now, *litagod,* they may be family soon. To know them better is worth a little extra bother, eh? Besides Olof told me that he had invited Magnus over for Christmas—"

Sigrid gasped. "But the family must all be together at Christmas!"

"—and I knew you would not like that," Borg added placidly. "So I invite all them to come, and we can keep Magnus home."

The last few days before Christmas Eve were a bustle of activity. The women made *knakkebrod, krumkakke* cakes, and plum sauce. The men butchered a yearling steer for the traditional meatballs and *rullepolse.*

The Holmgaards, father and mother, two hulking

twin boys, and a daughter, arrived in the afternoon. Except for quiet-eyed Greta, they were a boisterous crew, and the mixture with Borg's ordinarily quiet household was about right. They had brought gifts and, rather to Sigrid's dismay, a large quantity of food; she should not have prepared so much. Big Olof had also brought a couple of jugs, and he gathered the men together in the stable. The gala effects could be heard clear to the common room where the women were preparing the feast. Inga commented, referring to the old-country Holy Roller sect, that they sounded like a lot of crazy Lestadianers, to which Sigrid said tartly, "Ha! Our men should have so much religion."

Nathan Dart arrived with Gurina Helgeson, whom Sigrid had invited, afterward slyly urging Dart to fetch her over. Dart, as they entered, looked completely ill-at-ease. He had added a rusty clawhammer coat to his usual frayed homespuns, and the effect was slightly ludicrous. Also he stood several inches shorter than the statuesque Gurina. She was rather horse-faced, but a pretty good figure of a woman, Borg thought approvingly; also healthy and strong, which was important. At the moment she was blushing rose-red, and Nathan, shy as a schoolboy, looked nervous and a shade pale.

"Gurina, what a pretty dress you wear," Sigrid greeted her. "And what have you brought in the bowl?"

"Fruktsoppa," Gurina smiled awkwardly. "It is not much of a fruit soup. I make it with dried apples, prunes, raisins."

Olof, in his big bear-friendly way, dropped an arm

over Dart's shoulder. "Come on, Nate. There is something in the stable I want to show you."

Sigrid drew her husband urgently aside. "Listen, you go and see he does not get Mr. Dart drunk. I will not have it! Here I have invited Gurina—"

Borg, feeling very good and mellow, said, "Ah, there are times when a man should get drunk." But Sigrid propelled him out the door, scolding. "Don't you have any more," which had the effect of his joining Olof and Nathan in passing the jug. Some of Dart's color had come back when they returned to the noisy confusion of the common room. Borg, a little unsteady, sat down as Olof roared, "A dance! Magnus!"

Magnus, talking quietly in the corner with Greta, looked up with a grin.

"Where's your fiddle? Give us a dance!"

Magnus fetched his father's violin from the bunkroom while Olof and his sons pulled the table to the wall, clearing off a space. "A polka," roared Olof, seizing his wife Ingrid about the waist, but she objected, "Stop, you dumb *Tronder!* I must help with supper." Nathan Dart stepped to where Gurina sat and gave her a grave bow, to which she laughed and stood up.

"Come on, Magnus!" Borg shouted, and clapped his hands in time as his son struck up a lively polka. Gurina was a fine dancer, and Dart made up what he lacked in experience with an unexpected agility. Everyone laughed and clapped, and then Olof firmly pulled his wife onto the floor. One of the clowning twins swung out his brother, and Abel Jevers, who had hung back from the drinking, picked up Kjersti for a mock-dance, to her delight. Lisj-Per, looking on from his mother's lap, laughed and kicked his small strong legs in approval.

Nobody paid much attention as Greta Holmgaard quietly stood, slipped on her coat and went outside. Unlike her boisterous family, she was not overly fond of visiting or merrymaking. It was Sigrid's opinion (confided to her husband) that all the Holmgaards were a little crazy in one way or another. Borg, wanting a chance to talk alone with the girl who might be his daughter-in-law, made an excuse about stepping outside to clear his head, shrugged into his sheepskin and went out.

He paused to fill his lungs with the biting clean air. The sky was bright blue, and the full sunlight shed a sparkling glaze over a fresh snowfall. It mantled the vast sweep of prairie with a pristine white brilliance that dazzled the eye. Greta stood off from the house, her back turned. A breath of wind toiled with her skirt, and the sunlight made a pale blaze of her uncovered hair.

Borg hesitated, for the girl was usually quiet to reserve and cryptic when she did speak. After a moment he tramped over to her, and she glanced at him with a faint smile. Her cheeks were flushed with cold, and her large gray eyes, wide-spaced in her fine sensitive face, were grave and still.

Borg smiled back. "Answer me something, eh, Greta?"

"If I can."

122

"Why does the prettiest girl in the settlement walk out on a party?"

His tone held a friendly banter, and now her eyes smiled too. "Is that a question, Mr. Vikstrom, or flattery?"

"I always flatter a pretty girl."

She laughed and threw out her arms. "Oh, I like it out here, the cold and the snow. It makes me feel so alive. I guess I like nature better than people." She eyed him warily askance. "Does that sound very terrible?"

"Not so much. I feel that way a lot of times." His gaze was humorous. "You got to live with them, Greta."

"I like people who are individuals," she said seriously, and lowered her eyes. "That's why I like Magnus. Other boys his age are so alike. And they're concerned with such unimportant things." The color deepened in her cheeks. "I don't know why I tell you this."

"Why not?"

"Magnus—" She bit her lip.

"Ah, I don't understand Magnus, eh?" He sighed. "Well, that's right, Greta."

"I didn't mean—" she began, then amended frankly, "Yes, I did too. Magnus tells me everything." She hesitated. "I don't think you've ever given each other a chance."

"You're a smart little girl, Greta, and you see through a big dumb farmer."

Her grave eyes met his with the merciless candor of

the young. "I think you're a very fine man, Mr. Vikstrom."

"Nah, a pretty clumsy man, pretty sneaky too. Trying to get you to say what Magnus thinks of having a pa who is a big dumb farmer."

She quickly laid a hand on his sleeve. "Oh no. You're wrong, Mr. Vikstrom—so wrong about what he thinks!"

He waited, but again the girl retreated behind her soft reserve, and her smile was shy and brief as she turned away then, walking back toward the house.

Borg stood a bemused moment, looking after her. Sigrid thought she was an odd, moony little thing. She was a strange one for sure, but more thoughtful and perceptive than most; probably she knew Magnus better than he. Frowning over the little riddle she had left with him, Borg tramped back into the house.

A waltz was in full swing as he stamped the snow from his boots and shucked off his coat, sniffing appreciatively the warm delicious odors of cooking. Sigrid lifted her voice to say that the food was ready, and the exhausted dancers broke off with lusty laughter, sore from bumping one another in the cramped space. The table was pulled back into place and extended by laying some boards across piled boxes. Sigrid laid out her fine linen tablecloth, and proudly, her family silverware.

As the women set an impressive array of food, Olof boomed that by God, it was almost *a smörgasbord,* slapping Borg on the shoulder with one hand and with the other adroitly lifting a slice of pungent *ost* from a tray as Inga carried it past.

"Not bad," Borg joked gravely, "but—Christmas and no *lutefisk?*"

"For you we should import special *lutefisk* from Norway," Inga said tartly as she set down the tray.

Olof roared as Borg clamped a bearhug on her and gave her a funning kiss on the mouth. He was totally unprepared for the look of her as she drew slowly back then, somewhat pale, one hand lifting halfway to her lips. She turned away quickly.

Borg swept an uncomfortable glance around the room; in the general chatter and gaiety, nobody had noticed Inga's reaction. Olof was gulping his filched slice of cheese and exclaiming over its savor. For Borg the jocular pleasure of the occasion was ended, leaving a great heaviness in him. Small things in his sister-in-law's behavior toward him seemed to take on a meaning he had been too thickheaded to consider. During the meal he mechanically joined the talk and laughter, but afterward, when the gifts were brought out and Lars could only sit and stare at the fine chest of wood-carving tools he had received, trying not to show how deeply the present affected him, Borg knew only a weary dejection.

He had reckoned rightly that the gift given at this time would go far toward melting the cold barrier Lars had built between himself and the world. But for many days to come, Borg Vikstrom would bear the tired, baffled conviction of a new worry.

CHAPTER ELEVEN

WITH THE LOOSENING OF WINTER'S ICY CLUTCH CAME the thaw, turning the Cherokee's lazy flow to a turgid sullen yellow which overflowed its banks and lapped at the back doors of Liberty. The main street was an oozing mire, trampled to potholes and deep ruts by an increasing traffic of boots and wheels. To Eben Haggard, looking down from his office window at a bustle of creaking Murphy freighters and cursing teamsters, the walks thronged with cattle buyers, drummers, and cowmen, it added up to the most prosperous season yet.

"Eben, please listen to me."

Ignoring the soft voice of his wife behind him, Haggard leaned an elbow on the window frame and scrubbed his forehead with his palm, frowning thoughtfully down at his town, his key to the future and fortune. Maybe he was picking at trifles, letting Minifee's cryptic telegram get under his skin this way. Things could hardly be going better; Linus Quincannon had returned to close the deal on the five thousand acres. Moreover all the building material, supplies, and breeding stock that Quincannon needed to develop his new ranch were being brought in through Liberty—another good stroke of business, and Quincannon would be a steady customer thereafter. And the new cattle season was off to a fine start, with the first two herds driven across the swollen Cherokee only yesterday and the cattle buyers vying with big offers from their packing houses in Kansas City and Chicago.

Yet the telegram from Minifee three days ago had left a keen edge of worry in Haggard. The wording had been spare, crisp, and urgent, telling him nothing definite. But the matter had to be important to cause Jason Minifee, president of the Kansas & Colorado, to leave his comfortable offices in St. Louis for the discomfort of one of his own railway carriages, clear to Liberty. Minifee would arrive today. Staring at the street, Haggard worried his lower lip and wondered. . . .

"Eben."

He swung irritably around. "All right, Margaret, what is it?"

"I want a divorce."

He regarded her an expressionless moment, then went to his swivel chair and slacked into it, dropping one hand on the desk and gently drumming his fingers. He eyed her speculatively. "Your latest mood, eh? Last time it was the poor neglected wife. Very well, bring me up to date. What's this latest nonsense?"

She stood near the door, nervously kneading her small handbag in one hand. She was wearing a dress of rich maroon silk which she hadn't worn since coming to Liberty, and a matching tricorn hat was perched on the dark auburn coils of her hair. Her face had been flushed with the chill of this early April morning, but now she looked pale and was biting her lip, her face lowered.

"That's all," she murmured. "I just want a divorce—

any kind of settlement that suits you, but—"

"I know, I know, you want a divorce!" He picked up a pencil and slammed it down. "Go on, what is it? Get it out of your system."

"I'm sorry, Eben—you're a busy man. Time is money."

He smiled patronizingly and leaned back, crossing his hands on his stomach. "We're going to make a game of it, are we? All right, go ahead. Your move."

"You know why, Eben." The soft and musing bitterness of her tone did not change. "You're a cold and hard man, but you're not stupid."

"Life too hard for Mr. Danaher's baby?" he gibed. "Want to run home to Papa?"

"If that were all," she said quietly. "If it only were . . . but no woman could live as I've been living, with a man—"

Abruptly Haggard stood with an irritable, "Oh, come on, Margaret," ramming his hands in his hip pockets and pacing a restless half-circle. His face held more of a weary contempt than anger. "I know you've led the sort of sheltered existence that results in a plethora of romantic illusions, but you're a big girl now. Romantic love is a lot of empty deadrot that wears off; two people can't build a married life on that. I thought we had a clear understanding when we married; certainly I never deceived—"

"Oh, you didn't. You told me quite frankly that the marriage would be a mutually beneficial association, an affair of convenience. That for a while you'd be unable to support me in the style to which I was accustomed, but that would come in time. I never doubted it; you were clever and ambitious enough to become whatever you wanted." Her voice, no longer subdued, rose on a brittle note. "What I didn't see was that your ambition was a fever—a disease."

A corner of Haggard's mouth lifted in a crooked grin. He folded his arms and leaned back against his desk. "Always wondered if there was any Irish spirit behind that red hair. Disease, eh? Very good. Likely accurate, too. All right, and I needed a wife who'd help further my disease, a cultured and gracious lady." He bowed slightly, ironically. "I, at least, have no complaints, and damned if I can see why you feel cheated. What else did I promise you?"

"Nothing . . . what I took for granted, I suppose."

"And what was that?"

"A little kindness. Call it consideration for me as a person. Being treated as something other than a stick of household furniture." She lifted her face, her eyes bright with tears. "Any woman has a right to expect that much, Eben!"

He nodded imperturbably. "Anything else?"

"Yes. One thing I believed of you—that you were a big man, as big as your ideas. I've found you're able to let honor, decency, everything, go by the board where money is concerned!"

"Oh, good Lord," he said mildly, throwing up his hands with a baffled impatience. "Grow up, Margaret, will you? Honor and decency are Platonic values that man himself sticks up in the blue yonder as yardsticks for his social posturing. Nothing but convenient points for platitudinizing to cover the very real world we all live in—" He shrugged. "Call that viewpoint cutthroat and unscrupulous if you like—more relative terms. Personally I'm a realist, and I accept things as they are. Also I'm a businessman, and what you think of as low, dastardly scheming is simply business to me."

"I know."

He eyed her calmly. "And you want a divorce."

"Yes."

Haggard heaved his shoulders with a serene high. "Have you considered exactly what that will entail for you? Impractical a fool as you are, my dear, you'd better look at the facts. I've met your family and your friends. In your little circle, a divorce is social death. A miserable situation for you even if your father would take you back. Where else can you go—and what, pray, can you do? Beyond the social graces, you're versed in exactly nothing. There are few trade demands for a woman's skills"—he chuckled mildly—"beyond some rather basic services which wouldn't be exactly to your taste." He paused before adding with a soft and pointed brutality, "Go on home, Margaret."

When she was gone, he swung briskly to his desk and sat, put on his spectacles and got out some letter stationery. But then only sat with pen in hand, staring unseeingly at the blank sheet. Abruptly he cursed, snapping the pen in half between his fingers. He crumpled the sheet, balled it and flung it across the room. He clasped his hands together on the desktop, staring at them numbly. It was a mood that came on him rarely, then with an intensity that took him savagely by the throat.

Everything goes by the board where money is concerned, Margaret had said. Not really: he had his needs, but next to the driving and ruthless demon in him, nothing else meant a damn. He had been a sensitive boy, and the yesterdays of that boyhood still played before his eye with a bitter and frightening immediacy. The sights and stenches of a city slum were vivid in his memory; so was his father, a whaling seaman crippled for life, drowning himself in drink and self-pity. A taciturn drudge of a mother who had coughed constantly, her lungs rotted by consumption. A sister prostituted at fourteen. An older brother whose last breath was cut off by a hangman's noose. He remembered it well, the disease and filth and poverty, so well that these many years later it still framed the most pressing reality of his life, a terrible and goading fear that never left him.

He ran his hands through his hair, bringing himself out of it with a disciplined wrench. He saw that his hands were shaking, and he yanked open the drawer and got out the bottle. After a long pull at it, and the explosion of false warmth, the mood became sluggish and softened away. Every so often . . . then it was past and done, and again his mind functioned with cool precision. He slapped the cork home with the flat of his palm, put the bottle away.

He breathed deeply, passed a hand over his hair, and consulted his watch. Almost noon, and the train carrying Minifee should pull in more or less on time. He

131

adjusted his tie, put on his hat, and left for the street. The heightening sun had hardly touched the frosty chill of this spring morning. The air was like cold wine, and a wind off the prairie bore the smell of earth and thawing life. These things, and the rough jostling of passersby, barely registered along the surface of his mind, sunk in its brooding worry. He slogged through the trampled mud to cross upper Main Street, head bent, paying no attention to a big freighter wheeling narrowly past him or its teamster's blistering curse.

Haggard swung past the stockyards and tramped up the cinder apron by the siding, hauled up on the platform and stood glumly, his hands shoved in his pockets. Shortly the distant whistle of the locomotive drifted across the prairie flats, its funneled stack belching a black smudge against the clean blue of the sun-drenched sky. He watched it come, giving a bare curt nod to the agent's "Mornin', Eben," as the old man stepped tiredly from the small station building and stood hipshot alongside him.

When the train with its mixed cars hissed and coupling-crashed to a stop, Haggard sauntered over by the single passenger car and waited—no president's coach for the Kansas & Colorado, which had borrowed heavily to get its first feet under it. The brakeman descended from the forward car, gave the agent a perfunctory greeting, and set down pieces of luggage as they were handed out. A sick-looking drummer in a cheap checked suit got off clutching his sample case, then Jason Minifee stepped down, passing friendly conversation with the man behind him.

"'Lo, Haggard." Minifee extended a well-fleshed hand, pumped Haggard's once, and restored his cigar to his mouth. He pursed his lips around it luxuriously, as if inhaling the smoke of an exotic drug. He was a fleshy man who'd once been burly and hadn't gone entirely to fat. His thick face was scarred and broken-nosed, the face of a pugilist or alley tough, and his conservative suit, expertly tailored across a heavy wedge of shoulders, did not conceal that he'd come up the hard way. His eyes were small still slits; his manner was quiet, judicious, and shrewd. Haggard felt the usual nudge of wary respect for one of his own kind who had matched or overreached him.

Minifee took the cigar from his mouth and gestured with it at his companion. "John Trevelyan, Eb Haggard."

Trevelyan was a wiry little beanpole of a man in a tweedy costume of cap, traveling coat, and a startling pair of knickerbockers. His hair was prematurely gray, and his blue eyes and round face weathered to a ruddy glow gave him the look of a friendly cherub. His handshake was surprisingly strong.

"Got talking with Mr. Minifee on the train, sir. Told me about you and your town. Damned fine show. American enterprise, eh?"

Haggard smiled mechanically. "Hope you'll stay on a while, Mr. Trevelyan. Regrettably, though quite a few Englishmen tour the colonies, they rarely settle."

Trevelyan's smile was broad and white beneath his precisely trimmed mustache. "This one might be an exception, Mr. Haggard. The country seemed a bit tame at first—hunting in Africa and India spoils a chap for new vistas, I fear—but Gadfrey, I like it! As little as I could see from a train window, I'm enthralled. Limitless country, buffalo, red Indians—damned fine show."

Haggard nodded, instinctively alert to an easy mark. "If you're at loose ends for a while, Mr. Trevelyan, why not be my guest? Plenty of country right around here—and good hunting too."

"I say, damned decent of you. Can't accept such generosity, of course—"

"Western hospitality allows no objections, sir; you'll be my guest. And now, gentlemen, I suggest we attach your luggage and move on to my house . . ."

A half-hour later, when Haggard's guests had deposited their bags in the spare room and washed up, they sat about the parlor over Haggard's cigars and brandy, and Haggard drew the Englishman out further. When his father had died last year, the entire estate had gone by law to Trevelyan's older brother. Because of an old unsettled quarrel, this left Trevelyan barred for good from his ancestral home. It had been something of a blow, for his habit of rootless wandering had worn thin.

"Galls a chap my age to have no place he can call home because of a bally ass of a brother, but fortunately I've plenty of money to speculate with. Simply following my nose now, as y' might say, till I find a place with good prospects that suits me."

Haggard, downwind of a likely scent, was eager to follow it up. But he was also anxious to learn Minifee's business with him, and a covert study of the heavy-set railroad president, slacked at calm ease on the divan sipping his brandy and puffing his cigar, had told him nothing. .

Margaret came to the dining-room entrance and announced that the noon meal was ready, and the men snuffed out their cigars and went in. Trevelyan, with quick gallantry, held Margaret's chair for her, and she smiled her pleasure. Her face was pale but composed, and Haggard decided that his acid rebuttal of her rebellious mood had taken its effect. Perhaps he'd taken her too much for granted; she was a valuable pawn in his game, after all. That fact was newly enlarged for him as during the meal she listened with unfeigned interest to Trevelyan's tales of society abroad. This was her element, and she had been too long away from it; she was a poised and lovely woman of lively intelligence to whom any man would warm, and the Englishman was no exception.

Minifee, looking faintly bored, took little part in the conversation, and Haggard adroitly withdrew from the talk. He let his wife and Trevelyan chat animatedly on for a while, then casually suggested that he and Minifee go to his office for their talk. Minifee nodded, complimented Margaret on the meal, and the two men left the house. The Kansas & Colorado president puffed his cigar in silence during the walk downtown, and Haggard did not attempt to draw him out.

In the office, Minifee took a chair, refused a drink, and said bluntly, "Let's get down to cases, Haggard. The railroad has decided to cancel its agreement with you."

Haggard halted in the act of pouring a drink for himself, set the bottle carefully down. Prepared for anything by this time, he was able to cover with a smile of cool confidence. "You've come too far to make idle jokes, Jason."

"Right," Minifee said curtly. "It would take too long to have this out by letter, so I came personally; we've wasted enough time—and money—on your little venture already."

Haggard stared at him. "You've wasted—on four thousand carloads of cattle I've shipped on your rails since last year!"

"Wasted, hell; we've *lost* money. Cattle are a damned poor bet as freight. They have to be tended all the way; they damage the cars. We've averaged a three-dollar loss on every carload shipped out of Liberty."

Haggard, feeling a nudge of real panic, reached out a hand and toyed with his glass. He noticed the hand was trembling, and he dropped it back to his knee with an idle gesture, saying coolly, pointedly, "That's a little hard to swallow—unless some party's cutting too big a wedge of the pie."

Minifee grinned thinly. "Someone is. You. That five-dollar fee you charge per carload of freight shipped from your town. It adds to a damn' steep overhead, and the company just can't meet the gaff and pay its shareholders too."

"Hell, raise your freight rates!"

Minifee shook his head. "The meat packers and commission houses wouldn't go for that. Anyway the rates are fixed by contract."

"I have a contract with you too, a signed agreement—or have you forgot?"

"Contracts can be canceled."

"And railroads can be sued!"

"File your suit any time," Minifee said agreeably, firing up another cigar. "We can make it as rough as you want it, boy."

Haggard waited, hardly breathing.

"You see, we need the packers and commission boys as much as they need us—we're in no position to dicker rates with them. On the other hand, you need us and we can shed you any time. It'd be a minor inconvenience to build another depot east of your town . . ."

"And lose all your business in Liberty?"

"Don't play cute, mister. You own the stockyards and right of way here, but it's not worth it to the merchants here for 'em to kick up a row about wagon-freighting their goods a few miles from our new depot." He paused mildly. "Other hand, no law saying we have to carry freight for any business owned by you."

Haggard did not reply, his lips twitching.

Minifee exhaled a negligent smoke ring and perforated it with a gentle puff. "Start your think-box ticking, boy. Why cut each other's throats? You call off your notion about a suit, we'll call off the new depot. Your businesses will continue to thrive—"

"But the five-dollar fee is out," Haggard said tightly.

"Right." Minifee yawned, uncrossed his thick legs and stood, stabbing out his cigar in a tray on the desk.

"Train's not worth a damn for sleep. I'm gonna catch up in that room you thoughtfully provided, take the next train out." At the door he turned with a thinly veiled amusement in his heavy face. "Maybe you can con that Limey into making up the difference. Worth a try, eh?" He touched his hat. "Always good to do business with you, boy."

After Minifee had gone, Haggard sat with his elbows on the desk, rubbing his hands over his face. Even a slight setback in the way of his obsessive ambition could upset him, and this one was a severe blow. With iron self-insistence he'd set in his mind a sum to be realized before he left this town with the necessary capital to back a more ambitious project. Knowing that the bulk of his profit must be taken from Liberty in its early stage, he had sunk all he had into building the town and buying up the choicest land nearby. All that acreage had now been sold, except for the river-bottom strip where the drovers fattened their beeves. And Liberty had seen its flush days as a drover rail-point; the railroads were pushing deeper West—the new shipping pens at Emporia, Kansas, would save the drovers a week or more on the trail. With the dwindling of the drover trade, Haggard's personal profit would decline to a steady dribble. That five-dollar fee on the cattle carloads had been his ace in the hole, a free and clear source of profit, and he could not meet the gaff without it.

And he could not wait.

His life was a timetable with every stage planned toward a day that would see him a not-old millionaire (beyond that day he never dared to think). He was thirty-eight; consciousness of passing time laid an invisible pressure against his brain, almost at times with a physical pain. Now, head throbbing with an insistent ache, he pressed his knuckles against his forehead and groaned aloud. He poured a long slug of whiskey and downed it, and a second one, and the near-panic retreated into the back of his mind and settled there like a silent, gibing goad.

He returned to the neglected letter he had put off earlier, a query to an Eastern broker on some prospective investments. This and other paperwork occupied him till early dusk, then he locked up the office and went home.

Juanita was preparing supper, and she told him that the señora had retired to her room with a headache, and that Minifee was still napping. The Englishman, however, exuberantly unwearied by a journey across continent in the jolting discomfort of a day coach, had said that he would rent a horse and ride out to inspect the country. That was hours ago. "The *Ingles is* a crazy man," Juanita declared flatly. "*Por Dios,* what is to see but empty prairie and nothing? *Nada!*" With a cross emphasis she banged down a skillet on the range.

Haggard grunted and lifted the lid of the cookie jar, peering inside. He selected a cookie and bit into it thoughtfully. Trevelyan might be a shade eccentric, but as Minifee had suggested, there could be possibilities there . . .

Trevelyan returned within the hour, bright-eyed and jovial. His boots and knickerbockers were spattered with dried mud, and he beat them clean on the steps while Haggard inquired about his ride.

"Gadfrey, man, this is country! Sense of bigness, y' know; damned fine feeling, gets a man where he lives. Best grass I've ever seen, along that east side of the river. Thinking of buying up a piece of it. Perhaps raise cattle, eh? Saw a good many grazing there. Need a bigger stretch, though. I say, happen to know who owns all that?"

Inside of a minute he was ensconced in Haggard's favorite chair with brandy and a cigar. Tentatively Haggard mentioned price, and when Trevelyan offhandedly tossed off a sum of twenty thousand pounds, Haggard did some silent arithmetic and swallowed hard. It was an effort to keep his voice steady and his words casual:

"And how many acres did you have in mind?"

"Hum." Trevelyan drew on his cigar and frowned at the glowing tip. "I know a bit about ranching. Lived with my cousin for a time on his ranch in Zululand—South Africa, y'know. Veldt, nothing like this of course, but the notion got into my blood there." He grinned suddenly, boyishly. "But your West is the place for me. Feel of bigness, what? By Gadfrey, I'll settle for nothing on a petty scale. Say ten thousand acres, at the least."

Haggard's face was a mask as he finished his drink and set the glass down. "That creates a problem, I'm afraid," he said slowly. "That strip you saw along the Cherokee, between Liberty and that range of hills to the south, is owned by me—but it doesn't cover three thousand acres. Now beyond those hills is more river-bottom graze every bit as good, but most of it's been sold."

"I say, sorry to hear it. Assumed the lower bottoms would be as choice, but didn't realize they were taken up." Trevelyan's shoulders lifted and fell in a spare shrug. "Really—too bad, that."

"You wouldn't settle for less?"

It became apparent that he wouldn't. A bulldog facet of British stubbornness tinged Trevelyan's pleasant tone with clipped precision as he reiterated his terms. *These damned empire-builders,* Haggard wordlessly seethed, and again his frantic frustration welled high—he had been downwind of the key to his dilemma, and it was slipping from his gyp.

The solution was plain: if Borg Vikstrom and his people were gone, the prairie they had plowed would revert to its original state—he assumed, knowing little of land and grass cover. Their land, taken with what he already had, would turn the trick . . . but they would not sell out, not when they had come so far to put down roots and not with Vikstrom's dream of winter wheat becoming a solid reality.

Could they be driven off? Instantly Haggard's thoughts veered to Linus Quincannon, and a drastic idea sparked in his mind; he let his feverish excitement triggered by Trevelyan's offer fan it to full-blown decision. The basic antagonism was there—now use it; play Quincannon and the farmers against each other. Any number of things might happen to explode a touchy situation into open conflict, and he would see that they did. It could be done with no one the wiser as to his part.

He had no doubt of the outcome, not with Quincannon's seasoned crew of feisty, prideful Texans against a handful of stolid, plodding farmers. Even Vikstrom, watching his dream gutted by violence, would be forced to pull up stakes. While Haggard, with expressions of regret and sympathy, would buy them all out for a pittance.

Abruptly he asked Trevelyan whether they could let the matter rest for a time, vaguely explaining that he might be able to arrange something.

The Englishman's broad white smile flashed. "Gladly, old man. I'm moving onto the mountains up north for a while anyway—heard there's bally good hunting up there. Always wanted to dust off a North American grizzly. Be back in about three months— hope you'll have good news then. Damned well serious about this, y'know. Cheers now." He gestured upward with his glass, drained it.

Haggard echoed, "Cheers," and smiled at his guest. "Well, let's go in to supper—if you're as hungry as I am."

CHAPTER TWELVE

SIGRID'S FINGERS PLIED THE NEEDLE WITH THE DEFTNESS of habit as she darned patches in some old socks. With the deep content that was part of this accustomed task, she glanced around the lamplit common room now and then, pleased that everything was in its usual order. At the table Inga was changing a soiled diaper for Lisj-Per, and Abel was quietly instructing Helga in her nightly English lesson. Over in the corner Lars whittled contentedly at a decorative wooden dish.

Her glance came back with gentle warmth to Abel Jevers—what a fine young man!—and she thought with a wistful pang of Magnus, her own son. Was it wrong to wish that he might be a little different, a little more like Abel? It would be almost a relief if his wayward behavior were of a common and understanding sort, like other young men's. But Magnus, aside from his uncommon attraction for girls, had no seeming interest in sowing wild oats. Indeed, the girls' mothers would go out of their way to tell her what a fine boy he was, broadly hinting at a prospective marriage.

Now it seemed that he had settled on Greta Holmgaard and might even marry her—he was over at Holmgaard's tonight as usual—and the fact did little to ease Sigrid's apprehensions. Greta was pretty and pleasant, obedient and a good worker, but rather strange—sometimes she would hold a long deep silence till you forgot she was present, then suddenly come out with something crazy about life and eternity. Her family, thinking she was very funny, would laugh uproariously; but she was not trying to be funny, and Sigrid was disturbed. If one mate was strange, it was best that the other be ordinary. Magnus and Greta were both too different from everyone.

Borg thought this was perfectly all right so long as they annoyed nobody, and his attitude left Sigrid fret-

143

fully indignant. Borg had recently decided that it was best to let Magnus entirely alone. She was not surprised, seeing that he had put off so long a man-to-man talk with his son. Like the time when Magnus was sixteen and she had found some pamphlets in his pocket, written by that godless lawyer Robert Ingersoll, and Borg had just grunted it off, saying that Colonel Ingersoll was a great war hero and a stanch pillar of the Republican Party and a man's beliefs were his own business. Or those wicked French novels Magnus had taken to of late, scrimping all the money he could save to send back East for them!

Yet such things were but part of a larger shadow that she had sensed between her husband and herself for a long time, and she felt it more strongly since they had come to Kansas. She thought aggrievedly that it should not be so between a man and his wife . . .

By the stove Nathan Dart sat with Kjersti on his lap, telling her a wonderful story about an Indian Princess to which she listened with rapt attention, and Sigrid smiled. How fine Nathan was with children, and how good that he would soon wed Gurina—perhaps she was not too old to give Nathan a child or two. There was Mrs. Gustafson back in Koshkoning who had borne three sons after she turned forty.

Pensively Sigrid glanced at her husband. He was relaxed in a hand-carved chair at the foot of the table, squinting over a frayed month-old copy of *Skandinaven,* the Norwegian-American newspaper posted from Chicago. He had had little enough time to relax of late, she thought compassionately. And with a soft shock now she saw the threads of gray in his blond mane, bowed against the lamplight, which hadn't been there a year ago. Why had she not noticed this before?

Perhaps because of his tremendous zest for life that made him seem ageless; it had made her almost discount the enormous burden he had carried for them all in this last year. His capacity for leadership had not surprised Sigrid; she, with a loving quiet pride, had always recognized the abilities of her man. He was no man to set by the hearth with his porridge bowl between his knees; like a Viking of old he had to match his strength and determination against the unknown horizons, pulling lesser men in his wake like a magnet. If this made an added trial for her, she could accept it as she accepted his pagan love of the land and his calling it "the body of God," because this was her man and these things were a part of him and it could not be otherwise.

Besides there was the strength of him that had sustained her so often—she could recall as though it were yesterday those eight sick, frightened weeks with her parents in the cramped steerage of a sailing ship coming over from Sweden, how the tearing up of home roots had left an emptiness in her unfilled till he entered her life. The forty acres of logged-off Wisconsin timberland that Borg had developed to a hardscrabble farm had become home because he was there. And still a difference that she couldn't grasp laid its shadowy mar between them.

The newspaper crackled as Borg folded it and laid it down, saying briskly, "Time for bed." He grinned as he stood and held out his hands, and Inga reluctantly surrendered the baby who kicked his feet and laughed. On this nightly ritual Lisj-Per insisted; he would not sleep without his lullaby. Sigrid smiled and bent to her darning to finish it up, listening to Borg's strong deep voice singing the old Norwegian lullaby their children had loved, *Ro, Ro, Krabbes Kjoer—Now We Row Us A-fishing!* Her hands stilled on the darning and her eyes became faraway till the song ended. Helga rose and took the baby, and Kjersti slid off Dart's lap.

"Why don't you sing to me any more, Dada?"

"Because you are four now, Kjersti—a big girl, eh? And you should not say Dada. That's like a baby talks."

"I'll call you *For!*" she said brightly.

"No," he said firmly. "That's Swedish, see? And you are American."

"*Mor* says I'm Swedish," Kjersti sing-songed.

Borg frowned and cleared his throat. "Maybe *Mor is* Swedish, but you are American."

Sigrid sighed audibly and lowered her eyes; such a little thing to irritate a man. It was like when after they were first married and she called herself Sigrid Hans-datter, his constantly reminding her that this was America, and she was *Missus Borg Vikstrom.*

"What should I say?" Kjersti pouted.

"Well . . ." Borg hesitated, glancing at Nathan Dart.

"Pa," Dart said. "Maybe Pap. Or Daddy."

"Daddy," Kjersti said firmly. "Daddy, Uncle Nathan."

"Good."

146

She gave her mother a good-night kiss, then said gravely to her father, "What do I call *Mor?*"

"Mama," Borg said, and swung her into the air. He carried her into the divided sleeping room, and the others followed, except for Sigrid. She and Borg now had a cubbyhole of their own, dug out at the rear of the common room, and she thought reprovingly that Lars and Inga should have one too. It was wrong that a man and his wife should sleep apart, even if it was not good between them. She had suggested as much to Inga, who had waspishly retorted that she preferred it so. Lars, overhearing them, had retreated into one of his glowering silences and offered no opinion. Sigrid had not failed to note Inga's softened glances of late at Borg, and felt more of a sad pity then resentment—she did not blame Inga, and likely it was only a passing mood.

Borg left the sleeping room, adjusted the drape over the doorway, and went outside to check the stock. *"Sov nu, sov min pojke,"* came Helga's soft voice from the sleeping room, soothing her baby to sleep, and there was a comfortable silence. Sigrid sighed gently into it, laid aside her darning, and sat back to wait for Borg. Watching the sallow flicker of the lamp, she felt the little frictions of the day ebb away on a drowsy contentment. In spite of all, at times this place was coming to seem like home.

Hearing a quick tattoo of hoofbeats in the hard-packed yard, she sat up alertly. It was not likely that Magnus, returning, would push his horse so hard—but a visitor at this time of the night! She went to the door and opened it, letting lamplight flood the yard as out of the dark Borg's voice lifted sharply:

"Who is it?"

"Oscar."

The dim shape of the rider and his blowing horse broke apart as the man dismounted and threw rein. He tramped to the doorway with a curt nod for Sigrid, as Borg followed from the near darkness. She stepped aside to let them enter, afterward closing the door.

Oscar Molnar, a short, wiry, bleach-eyed farmer from the east side of the settlement, removed his hat and ran an angry hand over his white hair. "Sorry to put you out so late, but it's a bad thing. Damn' bad, Borg."

"All right. Sit down, Oscar. Sigrid, a cup of coffee."

She went to heat the coffee, listening to Molnar's taut, furious speech: "Yust two hour ago I find them, ten of them, deep in my field eating my young wheat. Stinking longhorns!"

Borg sat down and tapped his fingers on the tabletop with a thoughtful scowl. "Maybe they stray in, Oscar. These things we must expect from time to time. I don't like it any more than you—"

"They did not stray in, they are pushed in! They are standing bunched and they were herded straight in, this I see from the trampled wheat.

"*Helvete!* What could I do? I yust drive them back over to Quincannon's range and leave them because you say we must look away from trouble. But I tell you it was in my head to shoot them." Molnar swore under his breath. "Damn crazy cowboys!"

Sigrid came to the table and set a steaming cup at his elbow. "*Kaffet,* Oscar."

"Eh, thank you." He took half the scalding black coffee in a gulp, set the cup down and shook his finger at Borg. "Listen, if they do that again, I'll butcher every damn' head that gets in my wheat. It's all right for you people over here by the river, but my place is by Quincannon's range. So is Holmgaard's—and Eric Slogvig's. We got to protect ourselves."

Borg rubbed a hand over his face, wearily. "I know, Oscar, I know. Look, I will ride over and talk to Quincannon."

Molnar eyed him starkly. "When?"

"Tomorrow."

Molnar gave a partly mollified grunt, finished his coffee, picked up his hat and stood. "All right, but it better do some good."

Borg leaned against the open doorway and watched Molnar ride off in the feeble moonlight. Sigrid came to stand by his side. "So it is come," she murmured. "What you were afraid of."

"Maybe not. There has been no trouble to now. Maybe a few of Quincannon's hands got drunk and made up some fun."

"They are wild, those Texans. Like Oscar say, crazy."

Borg snorted. "Nah, it's like this in the logging camps. Cowboys are like loggers. The men live all together in a cramped bunkhouse, work hard all the time, have damn' little. It makes a lot of steam to blow off."

149

She cocked an eyebrow. "Like you too, ha?"

He grinned. "Well, there was pretty long winters in the camps, and no wives around to watch a man."

"Ho!" She slapped him on the arm, then became quite grave. "I wish that you don't go over there alone."

"Only to see Quincannon. No call to worry. It's only the thing has to be straightened out."

"But there should be a sheriff for this."

"There's a movement at the capital to make a county here, till then a man must speak up for his own rights."

She burst out, "But why must it be you always, the one who speaks for everyone else?"

"Here now, what is it?" His hands drew her gently close and she pressed her face against the solid comfort of his shoulder, her voice coming muffled: "It's only I'm afraid. Oh, why is there so much I don't know?"

He tilted up her chin, and his eyes were gentle. "What is it now?"

She pulled slowly away and walked to the table, kneading her lower lip between her teeth. She sat and folded her hands on her lap, all the marring discontent in her deepened by Molnar's news. "I don't know. All of it maybe. Am I a fool? Why can't Kjersti call me *Mor?*"

Borg pulled up a chair by her and sat, lacing his hands together and scowling at them. "She's an American. It is all right for us, you and me, to follow the old country some, but she is young and this country will grow with the young."

"Ah, *gamla hemlandet!*" The old country—it left her like a soft sad cry. "Must it all go then? It seemed all so good."

"Sure, a lot was good. Ain't I tried to keep some of it alive for the kids? Like Abel said, not being alike is the strength of free men. Americans come from a lot of places, and keeping some of the old ways helps keep them different. But"—he hesitated, choosing his careful, stubborn words—"There has got to be a like feeling too, or it will not hold together. Good to keep the old ways inside yourself, but there is more needed to find your way with different people. Men got to talk together and be understood. If a man talks to another like a Norskie, the other says, ah, this is a foreign man. Then all the other old differences come up and make hate. Who is better than who? Europe, all the old countries, beat each other bloody asking that."

He paused, slowly shaking his head. "I only feel this thing. I don't say it good. That's why to other Americans I'm a Norskie. You see now? That's why our boy and girl must not talk like us, so people will know them good."

There was a long silence. "I don't know," Sigrid said softly. "I think I see, but how do you feel it?" She had a sudden inspiration. "Is that why you think we should let Magnus alone, maybe? Your papa would have beat your hide with a razor strop for reading that godless stuff."

Borg smiled faintly, wryly. "It's part of the same thing. That in this country a man is free to follow his own way. Even your son, even if you think he's dead wrong." He hesitated again, then earnestly: "Do you see it, *litagod?* Now?"

"I think maybe," she said cautiously. "I don't say I like it."

"Try to think on it. With time it comes easier."

"*Ja.*"

Borg reached out and turned the lamp low, and his arm around her shoulders drew her close. She sighed deeply and leaned her head against his shoulder, watching the lamp flame. She felt better, but a part of her fought against the new feeling—how comfortable it was to cling to the old, close, familiar things! But she would try for him. She thought humbly of how good God had been to give her such a man, so strong, so kind and clean. She was grateful for whatever goodness she could bring to his needs, glad that her natural plumpness was well-proportioned over a fine-boned body and that work had kept it strong and firm, not slatternly or gone to fat. She brought her lips close to his ear, a husky note to her playful words:

"Maybe, before I get too old, you would like another little American *pojke* or *flicka?*"

"Boy or girl," he amended absently, then chuckled. "Why not?"

CHAPTER THIRTEEN

FOLLOWING BREAKFAST, HIS FIRST ACT WAS TO TRAMP out to the fields and inspect his growing wheat. A faint chill still clung to the air, and the sky was sun-washed; sunlight played a transient sparkling on the river, belying its cloudy burden of silt. Borg, sweeping his glance over a landscape of pale green stalks now turning to first brown, was satisfied. He stretched and yawned, feeling the tug of spring lethargy at his mind and muscles, then bent and plucked a wheat stem and turned the husk of kernel between his fingers, liking its good fat feel.

He tramped back to the soddy. Nathan Dart was squatted on his hunkers by the front wall, fashioning a pair of pails for toting water from the well. He had cut the tops from two square five-gallon coal-oil tins and was rigging them with wire bails. Borg grinned; nothing was cast off or wasted where Dart's ingenuity could find a way.

Dart was dexterously twisting several wires into a thick bail. He looked up without ceasing his work and nodded off toward the fields. "She comin', eh?"

For answer Borg handed him the wheat stem, and Dart bit into it, tasting it judiciously. "Better'n grass. Them longhorns of Quincannon's 'ud get fat and sassy on this, give 'em a chance."

Borg said lazily, "They will not," and squatted down by Dart. He yawned again, squinting across the fields.

"It's coming good. I say forty bushels to the acre."

"When'll you cut?"

"End of June, maybe." Borg reached out and slapped him on the knee. "We got to finish your soddy up pretty quick. Here it is only four days away, your wedding."

Dart squinted along the wire bail and poked it through a hole he had bored in a tin. "Oh, I ain't in no hurry."

Borg joked, "Warm weather for cold feet."

"Longer a man's footloose, more he shies off a tandem hitch." Dart twisted the bail end into a knot to secure it, stood, and picked up a cottonwood pole leaning against the wall. "Sort of like a cold bath. Man as lief jump in, get it over. Start dabblin' his toes, he loses all his sand pretty quick." He slipped a bucket over either end of the pole, slung it across his shoulders and tramped toward the well. "Feel like a Chinee, but ought to tote your water a sight easier now."

"Better get used to it yourself."

"Hunh." Dart began filling the tins with water. "Ridin' over to see Quincannon?"

"Guess I better." Borg stood almost reluctantly and stretched. He did not feel much urgency, being sure that the chousing of cattle into Molnar's wheat had been a mere incident, but he'd promised Molnar that he would see Quincannon today.

As he saddled Hans, his mind was more occupied with sizing up the contour of land south of the soddy, where he planned to grade a road through to Liberty. He and as many of the men as he could enlist would get a good start on it before harvest. From it would branch cutoffs to every farmstead, and already Borg visualized how he would have a graceful lane curving down to the house, with a line of cottonwood saplings flanking each side. It carried his thought to a distant day when a tidy whitewashed farmhouse and a big barn and outsheds would sprawl across this flat, with a sweeping view of the river and western hills. By then those cottonwoods would be providing bounteous shade to visitors turning in, and he and Sigrid would have grown-up grandchildren to fret over.

He grinned as he batted Hans in the side to unwind him, thinking of how far ahead of himself he was getting—yet what had been only a dream nine months ago was now reality, and the rest was only a question of time. He could afford to feel confident, and anyway spring was the time for looking ahead.

A horseman coming over the east rise drew his glance, and he knew the blocky-shouldered shape of Olof Holmgaard at once. He drew his cinch tight but did not mount. As Olof swung into the yard, Borg saw the turgid wrath deepening the ruddiness of his broad face.

Olof swung down, saying, "Damn it all, Borg! Damn it all!" He threw the reins and tramped over to face Vikstrom, his big fists knotted. "Them goddam cowboys been pushing their damn' cows into my wheat. I find 'em there this morning and drive 'em off, but by God, there's a half acre of my crop ruined, an' someone better pay!"

BORG RODE UP OFF the last deep grass flats below the

shallow rise where Quincannon had built his new Sin-glebit. Short of the layout, he drew rein for a brief, curious inspection. This was his first view of the ranch headquarters—he had not seen Quincannon since their short meeting last fall.

He had built impressively and well. The rambling main house was set off midway on the well-grassed slope above the working part of the ranch. This was a maze of barns and outsheds and corrals, with a big combination bunkhouse and cookshack connected by a covered runway. Borg thought, sniffing the pitchy smell of green boards as he put Hans up the lower slope, that freighting in all that cut lumber must have cost Quincannon a pretty penny. No doubt he had plenty to speculate with, after selling out all the interest his father had built up in Texas. Strange to think that a big man like Quincannon, too, had suc-cumbed to the urge to pull up stakes and try his for-tunes elsewhere. But poor or rich, a man had his rea-sons, which a lot of times did not conform to real necessity.

As Borg rode past a barn and into view of the bunkhouse and horse corral, several punchers lounging about at minor tasks paused to give him a neutral, watchful regard. A faint apprehension tight-ened his muscles as he trotted Hans past them, across a trampled compound that lay below the house.

He had no idea of his reception here, only that after Olof's news, two minor incidents might balloon into big trouble unless they were settled now. The answer would lie with Quincannon, who remained a restless enigma in his mind. *But,* Borg thought grimly, he will listen. Olof Holmgaard was now placated for a while, and after refusing Dart's offer of company, Borg had set off with the intention of getting some straight answers to straight questions. He pressed his knee against the hard reassuring outline of his scabbarded rifle, though caution had already flagged down his first rise of temper. The good sense of diplomacy before acting was obvious to any man, but a leader, treading his lonely and sensitive tightrope, must be doubly careful.

As yet Quincannon's house had no porch, only a makeshift steps of odd lumber pieces and a couple of posts for tying horses. Borg swung down just as the rancher himself opened the door, and both men eyed each other almost guardedly. Borg felt a nudge of flat surprise, for in these few months Quincannon had changed, not toward any evident lessening of his cold arrogance. His clothes were seedy and there was a slack and surly indifference in his face. It had lost several shades of its deep weatherburn and a week's black beard slurred his sharp and truculent jaw. His eyes were bloodshot and bleary, but behind them lay a jagged edge of temper. Among other things, Borg guessed that the man had been drinking a lot lately.

"Light down," Quincannon grunted sardonically, Borg having already dismounted.

He tied up Hans and the rancher stepped aside for him to enter, afterward kicking the door shut. Though the front room had been lived in, it had a raw and unfinished look. The bare studs and sheathing were uncovered, and the plank floor was dirty and scuffed. It was unfurnished except for a rude plank table and a couple of crates which served as chairs. On the table was an open bottle of whiskey, an old bridle, a leather punch, and scattered scraps of leather.

Quincannon motioned Borg to a crate, saying surlily, "Want a drink?"

Borg nodded because talk came easier over a glass, and Quincannon left the room. He came back with a pair of tin cups, sloshed each half-full from the bottle, cleared the table of leather scraps with a sweep of his arm, and sat down. Borg took a swig of the pale whiskey and felt his belly curdle with its raw burn. It was undiluted white lightning, and seeing the faint amused malice in Quincannon's eyes, he set the cup down.

He said flatly, "Your cows have got in our wheat. I have come about this."

"Fence it," Quincannon said laconically, taking his whiskey in a swallow.

"We have not the money to build fences."

"That's your lookout."

"Yours," Borg said gently, "if your cows trespass again. A man can shoot a trespasser."

This was the kind of talk Quincannon would understand, he knew, and was silent and watchful then as the rancher refilled his own cup. He lifted it and eyed Borg thoughtfully over the rim. "I didn't move here for trouble, Vikstrom. Cows are grazing animals, they range around. What the hell you expect?"

"These cows were pushed in, some yesterday into

Oscar Molnar's wheat, last night into Olof Holm-gaard's. I expect that you tell your hands to pull their damnfool jokes someplace else."

Quincannon's eyes narrowed. "You saying I told 'em to push them in?"

"I am saying you better keep them out."

Quincannon slammed the cup down. "By God, you've more gall than a government mule!"

The crate creaked to the shift of Borg's weight. "Listen, mister. We neither of us want trouble or we could of had it last year. I don't think you know about them cows, but there will be trouble if they get in again."

"Just neighborly advice, eh?" Quincannon managed a dour smile that did not reach his eyes. "All right. You're a man-size man, Vikstrom." He took out a worn billfold. "How much for your wheat they spoiled? I'll take your word."

"I'll take fifty dollars for both Holmgaard and Molnar. But we come out here to raise wheat, not a poor fund. You talk to your boys, eh?"

"I'll talk to 'em." There was a glint of respect in Quincannon's curious stare. He thumbed off the bills and handed them to Borg, who pocketed them and stood. Quincannon, standing too, frowned as though he would say more. Then, at the sound of a hard-driven horse nearing the house, he stepped to the door and opened it.

Dennis O'Hea stamped in, his normally amiable face red with anger. Seeing Borg, the *segundo* came to a startled halt. "Don't tell me he came about the cows?"

Quincannon frowned. "What of it?"

"Nothin', so long as he pays."

"What the hell are you running on about? *I* paid him!"

O'Hea's jaw dropped. "You paid—! Are you daft?" Shaking his head, he muttered, "Maybe I am," his wrath evaporating in complete bewilderment. He went to the table and poured himself a massive slug, put it away while Quincannon bridled impatiently.

"Out with it now!"

O'Hea wiped his mouth with his palm, slacked onto a crate, and briefly told how he and one of the hands had come across the carcasses of three Singlebit beeves hard by the snorky fields. They had been shot and butchered for the hindquarters. His hard accusing stare at Borg faded as Quincannon explained Borg's mission. Afterward O'Hea took off his battered derby and scratched his head.

"Now that do beat all. Seems we've both renegades in our outfits, and I'm beggin' your pardon, Swenska."

Borg took out Quincannon's money and handed it back, saying quietly then, "That is even, but there is something funny about this."

"Maybe," Quincannon said grimly. "All I know, it's tit for tat, Vikstrom. I'll talk to my men, you talk to yours."

BORG SPENT THE REST of the day making the rounds of every family, questioning the menfolk to such dogged length that more than once he came near to provoking real anger. To a man they vehemently insisted they had shot no Singlebit cows. Borg did not suggest searching their places for the stolen meats, this being an insult none would brook, but with each man he left a veiled warning: the guilty one had done a stupid and dangerous thing of which there had better be no repeat performance. He could not believe that either Holmgaard or Molnar had committed this reprisal for their ruined wheat, then covered it with a bald-faced lie; he knew both men too well. He did not want to believe it of any of the people, and he rode home that night in a state of weary bafflement.

Next day Eric Slogvig came raging into the Vikstrom soddy shouting that during the night someone had run a large bunch of cows across a corner of his fields and trampled down an acre of his crop. Again Borg saddled up and rode to Singlebit headquarters.

He met Quincannon by the corrals and found the rancher in a near-boiling fury: he had just received news of six more slaughtered steers. "Hell, I talked to my men and none of 'em drove any cows into your goddam wheat! I know my boys to a man, and that's the straight of it!"

Borg retorted coldly, wrathfully, "And I know my people—none of 'em shot your damn cows."

They stared at each other a long hot moment, and seeing Quincannon's anger slowly fade, Borg knew they had the same thought: since neither one could afford trouble, why should either promote this savage and senseless game?

Abruptly Quincannon said, "Come have a drink,"

and led the way up to the house.

Because each was suspicious that the other might be concealing some devious trickery, the conversation was kept less than cordial, but both men cautiously shunted around an unproven accusation. Instead they speculated aloud for a time, came to no conclusion at all, then settled into an uneasy silence which Borg finally broke:

"Look, if someone is pulling something dirty on us both, maybe we can find it out. We can post some men, some of my people and some of yours, to watch along the boundary lines for a few nights . . ."

Quincannon tugged his lower lip. "That's a lot of range to cover, and they might scare off the guilty party."

They could station the men at wide-flung intervals, Borg said, laid up in good cover and keeping in touch with a prearranged set of signals. Quincannon agreed that it was worth a try, and they spent a while setting up the plan. When Borg rose to leave, he hesitated before advancing another suggestion.

"We're having a marriage Saturday. Nathan Dart and Gurina Helgeson. There will be a party and dance in Liberty Saturday night. We would like you to come, and your men."

Quincannon raised his eyebrows with a sardonic twitch that said what-the-hell-for, and ruffled Borg. He explained, keeping his voice even, "Maybe, things as they are, our people should know each other better, eh?"

Quincannon conceded that this made good sense,

adding surlily not to count on his being there.

"But you will put it up to your men?"

"Put it to 'em yourself. Just heard Cookie sound the supper triangle, and you might's well eat with us."

ABEL JEVERS SHIVERED against the chill of this May night, and at his elbow Nathan Dart said meagerly, "Gettin' buck fever, parson?"

"Just cold."

"Got your faith to keep you warm, ain't you?"

Abel chuckled wryly, knowing Dart's poker-faced chaffing was part of an eternal gadflying between them which belied a deep liking. He'd come to resignedly accept that most men thought of a preacher as different, shutting him out whenever they got together for a drink and some good men's talk, as if his manhood were vaguely suspect.

They were crouched side by side in a thicket near the brow of a hill above Slogvig's east fields. From here lay an easy view of a broad swath of uneven grass flats, over which the full moonlight spread a silvery glaze. They held the vigil with six other teams of cowboys and farmers, spread at rough intervals in good cover along a north-south perimeter. The orders were simple: no smoking and keep a strict watch for anything suspicious. Two quick shots would be a signal to converge in that direction; thus they could catch the intruder between them and cut him off.

Abel shifted his cramped legs and arms. "I suppose you're having your forthcoming union conducted in all the sanctity of a j.p. ceremony."

"Hah." Dart spat sideways. "No sky pilot in a hundred miles 'cept you, and I'm partic'lar. Besides you ain't a real preacher."

"Besides you're a real heathen."

"Like enough," Dart agreed mildly.

"Nate the apostate."

"Sounds mean, but I'll let 'er pass."

They settled into an agreeable silence, broken a few minutes later by Abel: "Where's Borg?"

"Him an' Magnus're holdin' down the south end by Holmgaard's. Olof an' one of his boys'll take over for their shift in three hours."

"And two Singlebit men'll take ours, eh?"

"Yep." Dart smothered a yawn. "Shut-eye'll look good 'round then."

"Unless something breaks before—" Abel broke off at the hard clamp of Dart's hand on his knee. Both men crouched tensely, listening.

"I don't—" Abel began, but Dart's sharp "Hssst!" hushed him. Abel heard it then, a faint brief lowing of cattle.

"Wind's carryin' it from the northeast," Dart murmured. "Watch that big rise yonder."

"Who the devil, I wonder," Abel breathed.

"Dunno, 'cept there's likely two of 'em. Borg an' me studied over some track they left pushin' over Slogvig's field last night. Watch sharp now." Dart rose to his feet, his rifle in hand.

"What—"

"Can't chance they'll make off after we give the alarm. Goin' to work in by yonder hill on foot, lay up for 'em. Soon's you catch sight of 'em, blast away."

Dart glided noiselessly out of the brush and a moment later vanished into a shadow-filled swale. Abel sat gripping his borrowed rifle in both hands, straining his eyes. He did not see Dart again; the wiry scout was swallowed by the night. Behind Abel one of the horses, ground-hitched in readiness, whickered softly.

The bawling of the cattle grew nearer and louder, and presently Abel made out a small bunch blotting darkly against the hilltop and sky, close-herded by two riders. His heart pounding, Abel pointed his rifle at the sky and quickly shot, levered and shot again. He scrambled over to his horse, caught up the rein and vaulted into the saddle, kicking into a run downslope. He could make out only dimly the cattle and riders, and then they were cut off from sight.

A rifle shot sent a crackling of brittle echoes across the hills. Abel heard two more shots as he drove his horse recklessly across the bumpy flats.

Shortly he halted near the hilltop and swung to the ground, his breathing ragged with tension. Both riders had disappeared, and now with his gun held ready Abel moved warily forward to the summit. The skittish cattle shied off at his approach; he jumped as a man's shadowed form came soundlessly past a nearby clump of brush, stepping into the open moonlight.

"Who's that!"

"Dart."

Abel let out his breath in an explosive sigh. He lowered his rifle and tramped over to the scout. "You missed them?"

"One. He was trailin' in the drag, bunch was between me an' him. Took off when I sung out, hangin' low on his hoss's side. Time I got in the clear, he'd cut down yonder arroyo an' was gone."

"The other?"

Dart led the way around the brush and clambered down the stony hillside. Halfway down Abel saw the dark form sprawled across a litter of flinty rock paled by moonlight. A horse stood by, its reins trailing. Dart knelt down and struck a match. The man's body lay at an awkward, twisted angle, his face turned up. In the orange flare Abel looked, swallowed, and looked away. The face of Lutey Barnes, the crippled town drunk he'd often staked, was hardly recognizable.

"Hoss dragged him a ways," Dart said quietly, as the match flame died on a breath of night wind. "He was on the flank of the herd by where I was laid up in the brush. Went for his saddle gun when I sung out. I give him another warnin', edge of a couple shots. Last shot was mine."

Abel, feeling sick, said thinly, "Doesn't make sense. They didn't intend to rustle these Singlebit steers—only drive them into our wheat as they did the others. But Lutey! He wasn't mean, not bad that way. Why—"

"Means he was paid. Drunk'll do anything for whiskey money."

"But who—" Abel checked his words. "What about the other?"

"Didn't catch a clear sight of him, an' Lutey won't be talkin'."

Abel nodded mechanically, looking down at the broken form of Barnes. Wind rattled the dead brush; he shivered. Poor Lutey. Sometimes the way of things seemed too senseless to accept. Later he could pray and accept, but not now.

Dart cocked his head. "Hosses comin'. That'll be the others."

"I wasn't much help."

"You didn't hold back none. Each to his own call, hoss. Why I handled this."

CHAPTER FOURTEEN

STANDING BY HIS OPEN WINDOW, EBEN HAGGARD sipped his whiskey and stared out of a brooding anger at the lighted building across the way, which spilled a gay mingling of voices and laughter out into the night. Wagons and saddle horses crowded the tie rails; the teams had been unhitched and tied to endgates so they could feed on straw in the wagonbeds, since the dance would last well into the night.

Haggard considered with a sour irony the fact that he was providing a healing agent between Singlebit and the herders, for the hall was his. During the cattle-shipping seasons it boomed with business, being stocked with light ladies and plenty of whiskey dispensed at a long bar by four busy bartenders. Not a practical operation after the drovers departed, it was then shut down. When Borg Vikstrom had come to him and requested its use for the wedding party and dance, Haggard could not gracefully refuse. In view of what had happened the other night, he had to be doubly wary against arousing suspicion.

Glass clinked behind him as Tiger Jack Tetlow poured a drink, observing dryly, "You should have shot him."

Haggard swung about with an irritable, "Who?"

"Who the hell but Vikstrom?"

"I'm in no mood for your gallows humor."

"Hired him shot, I mean. Hire everything else done, don't you?" There was an unconcerned malice in Tiger Jack's pale eyes as he slacked back into the visitor's chair, crossing his shining black boots. "The one holds these clodhoppers together, ain't he? One bullet could've saved you a passel of trouble."

Haggard regarded him with ill humor. "Your bullet?"

Tiger Jack smiled. "Bushwhacking's out of my line. Anyway since the war ended." He tongued his cheek judiciously. "Willing, now. Hates Vikstrom, Nate Dart too, for some reason, don't he? Likely he'd do it for nothing."

Haggard took another sip of whiskey and rolled it on his tongue, considering. Not long ago, thanks to the patina of semi-respectability he had acquired, the suggestion might have appalled him. He had waited two months for Quincannon to get his ranch started and his range stocked with cattle so that the plan could be put into operation. Only Vikstrom and Quincannon, realizing that a third party was behind the trouble they should have blamed on each other, had set and sprung an effective trap. Mere thought of the consequence had they taken Lutey Barnes alive left Haggard in a cold sweat.

It did not touch his insensate determination to drive out the farmers, but he must proceed more warily. Yet time was growing short, and in his harried desperation his ferreting thoughts could dredge up only a stony blank. Vikstrom was the key, as Tetlow suggested—but killing him would only dramatically martyr the man and his cause. These settlers were stubborn men, rooted in conviction, and the way to break such men was to whittle away their confidence by stages.

Again Tetlow broke the silence: "Do I keep sinking the spurs into these clodhoppers?"

"Every chance you get," Haggard said flatly. "If one of 'em gets a little drunk, if he sasses you, if he even spits on the sidewalk—haul him in. I've instructed Judge Haskell to hand out oversize fines and jail terms. I want it made so rough on 'em they'll hate the sight of this town."

Tetlow's grin lent him a death's-head look. "As long as your hands are personally clean?"

Haggard nodded coldly. "Everyone knows what you are, and you're getting paid to be hated."

"And very handsomely." Tiger Jack lifted his glass in mild salute.

Haggard turned back to the window, ramming his hands in his hip pockets. He stared bitterly at the dance hall across the way, hating the lively rhythm of fiddle and accordion as they struck up a waltz. It heightened his bleak awareness that it was not enough to goad the settlers in small ways; their solid morale must be shattered by more decisive strokes—

There was a clumping of heavy boots in the hallway, and the door opened. Panjab Willing entered, shuttling his dull stare around the door. A wad of tobacco pouched his unshaven cheek and he stood cudding it placidly.

"Shut that door," Haggard snapped, and as Willing obeyed, at once regretted his words. In spite of the evening's warmth, the hide hunter was wearing his ancient bearskin overcoat, and its reek promptly fouled the warm close air of the room.

"I told you I don't want you seen coming up here!"

Willing nodded placidly. "Suit yourse'f. Figgered you mought wanta hear 'bout yer wife."

Haggard, starting toward his desk, halted. "What about my wife?"

"I 'uz out on the prairie Way, seen 'er in a buggy headin' south. Follered 'er to Singlebit headquarters. 'Peared funny so's I got in close outa sight. Seen 'er talkin' to Quincannon by the house. Couldn't make out nothin', but they talked fer a good hour 'fore she lit out."

Haggard sank mechanically into his chair. "Go on."

"Tha's all. She come back t'town."

Haggard regarded him stonily, assessing what he knew of Willing. The man was a loner, stupid and sly and shiftless, spending most of his time prowling aimlessly about the prairie. He and Lutey Barnes had been ideal choices to handle the petty sabotage of wheat and

170

cattle that had ended in Lutey's death and Willing's narrow escape. They had come cheap. One was an impoverished boozehead; the other was a born thief and troublemaker with no bedrock in his nature except the ability to store a cheap grudge.

Willing said hopefully now, "That worth a little somethin', ay?"

"Maybe." Haggard opened a drawer, took out a canvas sack and from it a gold double-eagle. He flipped it across to the hide hunter, who snaked it deftly out of the air. Willing eyed it vacuously, bit it once out of habit, and pocketed it.

"Keep your eyes open," Haggard said. "It might be worth another of those. Understand?"

Willing nodded and turned back to the door, pausing to say almost wistfully. "Ye wouldn't want no more cows kilt er wheat tromped, uh?"

"Not just now," Haggard said patiently.

Willing grunted and went out. Tiger Jack murmured with a thin chuckle, "What else you want to know?"

"Shut your mouth," Haggard said softly. He picked up a pencil and poked absently at a sheaf of papers. Margaret and Quincannon . . . could there be anything there? He now recalled Margaret's father once mentioning his friendship with old Bill Quincannon, the cattle king. Damned strange that Margaret and Linus Quincannon should apparently meet for the first time in this office last fall, stranger still that they'd made no mention of their fathers' friendship.

Though he had sensed from the start that he was getting Margaret on the rebound from some aborted affair, he had never pressed her on the matter, and her family had refrained from any mention of it. Almost at once after Quincannon's return this spring had come Margaret's sudden desire to divorce and leave him. It was also common gossip that Quincannon was losing his grip, that Dennis O'Hea was practically running his ranch singlehanded. Maybe it all added up—two people caught in a common misery from which ordinary scruples allowed no escape. Likely Quincannon's scruples, for it was Margaret who had gone to him, and their open meeting at Quincannon's suggested that the affair had not leaped decorous bounds. Still, Haggard coldly mused, it was time that he used a firmer hand in dealing with Margaret . . .

Tiger Jack Tetlow lounged to his feet and over to the window. He leaned both hands on the sill, staring out at the street, a slim and deadly poise in his stance. He said without looking around, "What kind of deal you got cooking for them farmers' land? Big, huh?"

"Maybe."

Tetlow snorted. "It's big. Otherwise why all the fuss?" He swung negligently around, facing the desk. "What's it worth to you to have 'em off?"

Watching him carefully, Haggard leaned back in his chair and steepled his fingers. "I might pay five hundred for a sound idea."

"You might pay a thousand."

Haggard nodded. "If it gets them off, yes."

Tetlow murmured, "Well, well," as he moved indolently toward the door.

"Where are you going?" Haggard said sharply.

Tiger Jack's chuckle was a dry whisper. "Over to the dance. Got to keep an eye on things." He nodded gently, his pale eyes speculative. "Might get that thousand-dollar idea. You never can tell."

BORG, SUPREMELY WARM and uncomfortable in the stiff black suit he had not worn in over a year, stood by the bar with Abel Jevers, he enjoying a potent *glogg* and Jevers a glass of ordinary fruit punch. It was a strategical location from which Borg could oversee all that went on. By now, though, he was feeling that he could safely relax and enjoy the party.

Quincannon's cowboys had arrived in a solid bunch, washed and curried and carrying themselves with a shy, wary belligerence. Borg, noting that neither Quincannon nor his *segundo* O'Hea was present to keep them in check, had worried that there might be immediate friction. He questioned one of the older cowboys, who told him that Quincannon and O'Hea were burning late oil over the ranch books. "Boss knows we're Texas men and mannerly," the old puncher added dryly.

Borg's concern was pretty well allayed. His own people were well gone in convivial ease, having flocked at once to the hall following the wedding conducted by Judge Haskell in his law office that afternoon. All were set for a lusty good time, and the cowhands, liking their fun high, wide, and handsome, and being primed as Borg suspected by a few drinks, fell quickly into the swing. They danced the settlers' wives and daughters off their feet with the boisterous

173

glee of overgrown boys, while Magnus on the fiddle and white-haired Gust Slogvig, Eric's father, on the accordion made the music lively.

Nathan Dart and his bride stood by the doorway in quiet reserve, murmuring replies to repeated shouts of congratulation, and Borg thought they looked fine together. Dart, sober and staid-looking in his wedding suit, was brought almost to Gurina's height by his new bench-made boots. She, in her colorful bridal dress, was flushed and happy and caught a man's admiring approval as a woman should on her wedding day. Sigrid, busily making up for Gurina's lack of forwardness, had stood by her through the wedding and now hostessed the party with her usual brisk efficiency.

"A gala time," Abel observed.

"We all have earned it. You too, Abel. You're a bold preacher, but shy with girls. Get out and dance."

Abel grinned abashedly and shook his head. "I'm all feet, and the music's too fast. I don't even know what this dance is called."

"A schottische."

Sigrid, satisfied that all was going well, now came up and took her husband's arm. "How long since we have danced?"

"Too long," Borg protested, but she drew him onto the floor, and there were shouts of approval and applause as they led off the dancing couples. Borg, perspiring freely, muttered, "This damn suit is too tight."

"You're getting heavy." She slapped him playfully on the stomach, and Borg, who had not put on ten pounds in twenty years, gave a dry grunt and looked over toward the newlyweds. "They look pretty good."

"*Ja*, they're happy. It's very bad to be alone."

Borg grinned, looking down at her scrubbed and radiant face, her blue sparkling eyes and her hair braided in a shining corona around her head. She looked like a bride herself, and dancing together tonight, the years melted away to another bridal night they had known.

WHEN THE DANCE ENDED, she hurried off to see about preparations for supper, and Borg drifted back to the bar. Magnus and Gust struck up a polka, and the cowboys hit the floor again, each with a sturdy laughing farm girl. The more backward young people sat on the sidelines where chairs and benches were pulled to the wall. Among them Helga Krans and Greta Holmgaard talked quietly together, and Borg was pleased that Helga was coming out of her shell and mixing with other youngsters. Most Scandinavians, having a stolid realism in such matters, accepted the business of unwed mothers as an offhand fact of life. Yet, though she had suffered few social barbs, it was plain that Helga's experience had marked her deeply. She was too young to grieve so long over one hurt, and once more Borg wondered who the man was and what their real relation had been.

His idle attention was pulled back to Helga when a young cowboy crossed the floor and spoke to her. She shrank back a little, shaking her head, and the cowboy, Bert Romaine, being a little the worse for drink, reacted with offended anger. He tried to pull her to her feet, and Greta said sharply, "Go away. She doesn't want to dance."

It drew the attention of the people nearby, and under their stares young Romaine flushed and then turned and walked stiffly, furiously, out of the door.

A glance around told Borg that the music and revelry had served to cover the incident, but Helga looked pale and shaken. A stern realism told Borg it was not good for her to withdraw this way, and he thought, *She should dance, but with someone she knows.*

He looked about at the young men without partners, and his gaze briefly touched on Syvert Hultgren who stood morosely by himself at the end of the bar. Borg shook his head; Syvert had already drunk too much and was plainly lapsing into one of his surly moods. Then he noted Abel Jevers being recruited by two elderly ladies to help bring in the food, and he walked over and took Abel's arm, saying, "Sorry, ladies," and marched him over towards the girls, firmly overriding his objection. "It is time you danced."

Magnus and Gust started a slow waltz, and Abel and Helga fell into awkward time. Borg judged that Abel's embarrassment was due to his banty size, but Helga was about as small for a girl, and quite a pretty one since her health had improved. Not good for a woman to get so peaked and pale. Watching the dawning pleasure of both, Borg nodded his approval—it was fine for the boy to sit up winter nights teaching the girl English, but her English was good now, and there was better use for the spring evenings.

The booming voice of Olof Holmgaard pulled his attention to the entrance, where Olof had bulked stolidly since the party started, checking in the guns of the few who had brought them. Marshal Tiger Jack Tetlow had just entered, and Olof ponderously blocked his path. Borg threaded through the dancers to get over by them.

Tetlow was eyeing Olof with thin amusement. "Do you know who I am, fellow?"

"I know, mister, and what I say is, you check the gun before you come in."

"That's all right, Olof," Borg said, and evenly to Tetlow: "If you're on duty, Marshal."

Tetlow nodded amusedly. "You might say that." He moved away with hands clasped behind his back, shuttling his icy stare over the dance floor.

Olof growled, "By God, that is the last one I would let in with a gun."

"Still he's the law in town."

"I don't like it. Maybe he come to make trouble. You know he pushes us around when we're in town."

"Only when he gets us one at a time," Borg amended grimly. "He will do no pushing tonight."

Supper was set up on a long table, and the music ended as everyone filled a plate buffet-style and afterward sat on the benches and chairs by the wall to eat and chatter.

It was a while before the dancing and the drinking picked up again, but as the evening wore on, the gaiety grew like a happy fever. These were people who labored hard and whose ordinary pleasures were frugal and few; a party was a time to let out all stops. Nearly all the men drank too much and showed it. Some of the cowboys drifted unobtrusively out back of the hall where a jug was produced. The settler men, not to be outdone, brought one of their own out of hiding and joined them.

After a while Borg went out back to check. Some of the men were getting loud and disputatious, but it was all jocular enough, no ruffled feelings. Assured that all was going smoothly, he went back inside.

The music had stopped. Across the floor Magnus had laid aside his fiddle and stood up, raising his arms for attention as Greta joined him. They looked at each other and smiled, and he took her hand, raising his voice now.

"Listen, everyone. I guess you've all wondered whether Greta and I will ever get married. Well, we think this is as good a time as any to say . . . very soon!"

Borg, recovering, pushed his way through a crowd of handshaking well-wishers to reach the couple. Olof was already there, for once speechless, and he grabbed Borg's hand and wrung it. His big Ingrid, with tears running down her cheeks, embraced Sigrid who looked almost stunned.

When the congratulations were done, Borg drew his wife aside, his arm around her shoulders. "Now *litagod,* chin up and be glad."

"I am glad." She started to weep. "Oh, Borg."

"Look now, Gust is playing a waltz—wipe your eyes and we'll dance. Think of what we have, each other and Kjersti for a long while yet. Maybe grandchildren too."

It was a happy thought, and Sigrid was content as they danced. When the waltz was over, Magnus joined Gust in striking up a varsoviana, and Olof Holmgaard whirled Sigrid off. Borg watched it a moment, feeling and liking the warm gay life of it all.

He started toward the bar when the shot came from out back, cutting against the revelry with a flat savage edge. Borg spun about and was threading his way roughly through the dancers as the music and noise ebbed off into a confused lift of murmurs. Before he reached the back door, Oscar Molnar came stumbling in from the yard. His face was pale with alarm as he grabbed at Borg's arm.

"Borg—that damnfool Syvert just killed a man!"

CHAPTER FIFTEEN

IT HAD BEEN A MISTAKE TO RUN, SYVERT HULTGREN numbly realized as he continued to run, stumbling and panting. Two painful falls in the darkness had partially jolted him out of his first drunken panic, but it was too late not to run. He heard an angry shout of "There he goes!" somewhere behind him, and knew that the Singlebit men were gaining on him.

He saw the murky glint of the river ahead, and he slid down a short cutbank and swerved to his right, ducking into a bent-over run. He slogged desperately against the sucking mud, cursing as it balled his boots.

Still half-drunk, he slipped and fell again. From behind him he heard the shouts dwindle off as his pursuers reached the river. Then someone shouted "This way," and he heard them coming fast again.

Abruptly, panting, Syvert came on a narrow finger of sand bar and saw a dark clot of tangled willow brush beyond. He reached it and lunged deep into its cover, sinking down in a tight crouch. His eyes were filmed with tears and his lungs were seared by each gasping breath; months of idleness and steady drinking had left him in sorry shape. He pressed his fists over his chest, fighting to still his breathing and collect his disjointed thoughts.

He had not wanted to shoot the boy—a loud-mouthed Singlebit hand not old enough to vote. It had started from nothing, really. All of them, cowboys and farmers and a sprinkling of townsmen, had been passing the jugs out back of the hall in roistering good fun, except for the one kid who had got mean-drunk on about four slugs of raw whiskey. He had snatched for a jug as it was passed to Syvert, who being in a raw mood himself, had taken offense.

Syvert had concealed his gun under his coat when he had entered the hall earlier, and so had this kid as it turned out. After the short hot exchange of drunken words, the boy had torn open his coat and grabbed for the gun shoved in his belt. With a kind of detached, defensive surprise Syvert had yanked out his own pistol and fired, knowing with the instinctive certainty of a man who has hunted game that he'd shot fatally even as the boy fell. He remembered only seeing the accusing shock in the dozen or so faces turning on him in the dim light from the rear hall doorway before he headed off in the night at a blind and panicked run.

It had taken only a few seconds for the stunned cowboys to rally a pursuit. Their heavy breathing and angry voices were very near now, and then he saw their dark shapes fanning out as they broke onto the pale ribbon of sand bar.

"Over heah—must of ducked into them willows!"

Syvert lurched to his feet in a resurgence of panic, crashing noisily away through the clawing brush. As he broke free of it, they were on him, all five of them, and he lashed out wildly at the nearest one. He felt his fist connect solidly and then another hooked a savage blow to his face and he went down in the cold mud. Two of them grabbed him by the arms and dragged him up thrashing and kicking. He broke one's hold, but someone else swore and hit him. As his senses pinwheeled off and he sagged down, he was seized again by both arms and hauled upright. A fist in his belly jackknifed him, and bent double, retching for breath, he heard their voices.

". . . Good big cottonwood back of the hotel."

"Get a rope, Bert. Meet you there . . ."

The voices broke off suddenly, and Syvert lifted his head. He saw a man coming on a half-run across the beach, a giant of a man with his shoulders hunched and his fists swinging at his sides. Borg was close before the faint light of the quarter moon caught on his long face, but it was a different Borg Vikstrom than Syvert knew. He could see the pale fury that lighted his eyes, the knotted muscle ridging his jaw, even the great vein pulsing in his temple. There was no time to think more because Borg had reached the first cowboy, who blurted, "Heah, you goddam—"

Borg's fist made a solid thunk like a slaughter ax hitting the neck of a calf, and the cowboy went down. Without pausing in his stride he seized the next man by the seat of his pants and his collar and heaved him up and outward like a sack of grain; he lit face-down in the mucky river shallows. The one called Bert swung at Borg as he came wheeling around, and Borg simply swept up a malletlike hand as he turned and clouted him backhand, knocking him flat in the trampled mud.

The two holding Syvert released him and backed warily off, and now Borg halted, his hands settling to his sides. Syvert shared their half-fearful awe as he watched Vikstrom, breathing heavily, master his berserk fury. Borg's glance swung now to the first man out cold in the mud, the second on his hands and knees in the water dazedly shaking his head, and Bert sitting with his head hung, spitting blood. Then he looked squarely at the two on their feet.

"So," he said very softly. "You still want that rope?"

Neither man said anything. Borg, nodding slowly, said with soft finality. "So. Now, Syvert, you damn fool, we go back there, eh?"

Leaving the cowboys to revive their cold-cocked companion, they tramped back through the darkness toward the hall. Most of the people, settlers and cowboys alike, had crowded into the bare lot at its rear, and now came Olof Holmgaard's peremptory bellow: "Here, don't let them kids out here—take them inside, you women!"

Every head turned as Borg and Syvert came up, and the crowd broke apart to let them through. Tom Larned lay on the scuffed earth where he had fallen, and Oscar Molnar was holding high a lamp which sallowed the dead man's face. Syvert looked at it once and shuddered and lowered his eyes.

Tiger Jack Tetlow, squatting by the body, finished his inspection and straightened up. He shuttled a slow glance around the murmuring crowd. "I call it murder. Plain damned murder."

"That's a lie!" The words burst from Syvert with a startled anger. "He went for a gun—"

Tetlow showed his skull-like grin, saying softly, "Did he," as he gestured at the dead man. The skirts of Larned's coat were thrown back, and seeing that the gun shoved in his belt was gone, Syvert felt a clammy sweat break out on his body. He looked wildly about at the stony gravity of their faces. His voice came furiously taut and shrill:

"I tell you he had a gun! Somebody—"

Borg cut in quietly, "Soft, Syvert, soft now. Tell it all from the start and tell it straight."

Swallowing against his cold panic, Syvert told it with halting care. Afterward came a long pause while Borg's glance circled the bystanders. "Who here seen it?"

Four farmers and a couple of townsmen stepped forward. They were in rough agreement with the story,

183

except that no one had seen Larned's gun. Eric Slogvig said hesitantly, "A course it was pretty dark out here an' Syvert was the only one standin' a-front of him. They wasn't six feet apart, and the boy looks like he is going for a gun." He scratched his head vaguely. "A course I couldn't tell so much, and Syvert was pretty drunk." He grinned in mild apology, meeting Syvert's glare.

Marshal Tetlow's dry, cutting voice rose: "I looked around. Only gun out here was Hultgren's. He dropped it when he cut out." He lifted Syvert's .44 Colt from the sagging pocket of his coat. "Fresh fired, one shot. Evidence hardly needed, with a dozen witnesses."

"Nor a trial neither!"

The five belligerent cowboys had straggled up from the river, and Bert Romaine pushed ahead of the others. He stood hipshot, a handsome boy with black curly hair askew under his crushed horsethief hat, holding a bandanna to his mashed lips. He was of an age with the dead cowboy, and probably they'd been closer than most bunkies.

Borg said softly, "You don't want more of what you got, sonny, shut that big mouth."

Romaine's dark, angry stare didn't falter, but he held his tongue as Borg's gaze locked Tetlow's with open challenge. "You are the law here. Is it to ask too much that you keep Syvert safe in your jail till trial?"

Tetlow said almost cheerfully. "Oh, he'll be safe."

Borg gave a gentle nod, saying, "He better be, mister," and took Syvert's arm. "Come on, boy, I'll see you get there."

Magnus and Eric Slogvig and the hulking Holm-gaard twins fell in behind them. Tetlow led the way as the group skirted the building and headed for the jail a block away. Syvert moved numbly to the pressure of Borg's hand on his shoulder, his mind desperately rejecting the savage unreality of the whole business. An insignificant quarrel had flowered into a few fleeting seconds of violence, and suddenly he was a murderer. *But he was not!* The raw shock of it burst fully over him, and he blurted, "There was a gun, I tell you!"

"Easy, boy." Borg's hand turned him toward the small frame building that housed the marshal's office and the jail. Tetlow went ahead to unlock the door and they entered the office then, empty except for a crude plank desk. Tetlow opened a door at the rear and unlocked one of the two large cells that opened off either side of a short corridor. Fighting the deep sickness that dragged his steps, Syvert shuffled in. The door clanged shut.

Tetlow stood watchfully by as Borg stepped close to the bars. "Syvert, listen now. Was it straight about the gun?"

"I swear to God—"

"Tell it straight now. Running off like you done, it don't look good."

"I was drunk," Syvert said miserably.

"So. You was pretty drunk all right. Maybe drunk enough you was wrong about the gun."

"Goddam it, I seen it!"

"All right." Borg's tone gentled. "On this I had to be

sure, Syvert. Maybe, it means someone took Larned's gun in the confusion after you run off, eh? It was pretty dark, so maybe. Only who'd want to make it so bad for you?"

Syvert dropped onto the edge of the board bunk, shaking his head and rubbing his hands over his face. "God . . . I don't know, Borg."

"Look now, I'll ask around and maybe find what's going on we don't know. We got plenty of time, that's something. You sit tight, eh?"

Syvert laughed mirthlessly. "Not much else I can do, is there?"

Borg said steadily, "You got friends working for you, boy. Don't sell that short."

As Borg went out and Tetlow, smothering a bored yawn, followed him, the four young men all came close to the bars. Meeting their sober gazes, Syvert felt an unbidden twinge. He had no close friends, but all of these boys had joined him in a rowdy escapade at one time or another, and with the stubborn loyalty of some-time-comrades would stand by him in his trouble. Simple and stolid Eric Slogvig said low-voiced, "Syvert, you want to bust out anytime now, you give the word."

"You're a big help," Magnus told him.

A brief silence followed. One of the Holmgaard twins broke it awkwardly, shuffling his feet. "Anythin' we can do for you, Syvert?"

"I guess not."

Syvert felt something knot in his chest and ducked his head now, fighting a blur of stinging tears. He thought of his mother and father and how he had failed the trust they had left him, with his petulant rages, drunken brawling, and surly indifference. Arne, infected by his example, was dead. Even afterward, rather than play the man, he had let himself, in a useless welter of guilt and self-pity, sink to worse. He deserved nothing, least of all such loyalty as this.

With the bleak remorse came a wave of crushing hopelessness, and again he dropped his face in his hands. There was too much to make up for, and whatever thin hope Borg's last words might hold out meant nothing. Life was paying him back in the coin he had earned, and with this dismal conviction came the thought of one wrong from which his conscience had shrunk too long. A wrong which, like all the others, could not be undone. But a gesture of atonement was better than nothing.

He lifted his head as Sven-Eric Holmgaard, scraping his boots again, said, "Well," and flipped up a hand in farewell. His brother Charlie said, "S'long, Syvert," and they went out. Eric scratched his head and mumbled, "Guess I'll be seein' you, Syvert."

Syvert's mouth twisted. "Oh, I'll be around."

Eric bobbed his head sadly and trailed after the twins. Magnus, his sensitive face troubled, nodded and started to turn away. Syvert came swiftly to his feet, gripping the bars.

"Magnus—hold up a minute, will you?"

Magnus moved back to the cell door, and Syvert, dropping his voice to a whisper, talked hurriedly for a full minute. . . .

CHAPTER SIXTEEN

TRUDGING ALONG THE EDGE OF HIS FIELDS, BORG thought that the wheat could use a little rain, but somehow the thought was obscure. This morning another gnawing worry occupied the front of his mind. Syvert Hultgren would probably hang for murder, and the settlers were openly outraged. It wasn't that most of them didn't believe him guilty, for they knew his wild hard-drinking ways too well. Syvert was still one of their own, and they bitterly resented his having to stand trial for killing a stranger, a cowboy. The cowboy was the enemy, and the town that would convict Syvert had become the enemy too.

Borg had prevailed on them to have patience and await the result of the trial, but his own hopes had ribboned out. He'd spent hours last night exhaustively querying shopkeepers, bartenders, and other townsmen, anyone who might offer a hint of an unknown reason why someone might want to worsen Syvert's predicament. He had encountered an ill-concealed wall of hostility, for the cattle trade was still the backbone of the town. Could framing Syvert be somehow connected with the destruction of wheat and cattle they had stopped? Borg wanted to dig deeper, but had no idea where to begin.

His earnest effort to knit up the bad feeling between his people and the cowboys had not only fallen flat, but led to worse. Saddled by a gray sense of failure, he felt baffled frustration edging him toward a slow, swelling fury. It was the deep-buried part of him that he feared most, and it had almost got out of hand last night when he had taken Syvert from the cowboys. Above all times he needed a cool head now, and he silently fought down the feeling.

In this mood he swung about and tramped back toward the soddy. He was still a good distance from it when he saw Magnus trot Hans down a hill from the east and rein up in the yard. He swung down and vanished into the soddy. Borg felt a raw irritation that quickened his stride. Earlier Magnus had taken Hans and ridden off without a by-your-leave. He had no damned business traipsing off in the morning when there was work to do. Probably visiting his bride-to-be, but that was no excuse; it was enough that he spent all his evenings at the Holmgaards'.

As Borg came into the yard, Sigrid rushed out of the house in tears. "Look! Look now, mister—ask your son to say about this! Just ask him!"

She was holding some wadded bills in one extended hand, and Borg scowled at them wonderingly, then at her. "What is it?"

"I catch him slipping this money under Helga's pillow in her bunk! He will not say why!"

Borg took the money and thumbed through it. Six soiled greenbacks of fifty dollars each. He crumpled them in his fist and let it fall to his side, feeling a little sick with the significance of this. He looked gently at his distressed wife, then his gaze hardened as it swung to Magnus who had just stepped from the soddy. He

189

halted and glared at them both, then muttered, "Ah, the hell with it," shoved his hands in his pockets and started away toward the riverbank.

Borg, held speechless for a moment, roared then, "Just hold up, sonny!"

Magnus stopped and slowly wheeled to face his father. His hipshot stance was insolence itself, and the stubborn defiance in his face only deepened Borg's first anger. He came up to Magnus and shook the fisted money in his face.

"About this, you better talk, sonny. Now."

Magnus gave him a wintry stare and said nothing. Feeling a wrathful pulse mount to his temples, Borg said softly, "Once more. Where do you got this money? And why put it in Helga's bed?"

"I promised to," Magnus said sullenly.

Borg waited, and when he did not go on, shouted, "What kind of an answer is that, eh?"

Flushing, Magnus shouted back, "That's all I can tell! Damn it, what—"

Borg's hand shot out and caught his shirtfront, yanking him up on his toes. "You give me a civil tongue, boy! And your mother—what kind of bad words did you give her?"

Magnus, choking with anger and Borg's twisting hold on him, sputtered, "You go to—"

Borg let go of him, at the same time fetching him a backhand clout that sent him sprawling on his back. Magnus slowly lifted his head, looking up warily as he wiped his mouth with his hand. Borg moved to stand over him, his fists closing and unclosing.

"Answer me one thing. Are you the father of Help Krans' baby?" He almost added, *Is this why you would marry Greta—to cover the other thing?*

Magnus tightened his cut lips and only stared up, his eyes blank and unblinking. Another time Borg might have felt a perverse flicker of pride at his son's defiant lack of fear, but now it merely goaded the pent fury that had surged in him earlier. He reached down and hauled Magnus to his feet, seeing nothing but his son's face through a red haze, pulling back his fist. Then Sigrid was at his side, tugging desperately at his arm.

"Oh God, no! Have you gone crazy?"

Slowly Borg dropped his fist, enough to let the impulse ebb before he let go of his son. Magnus took a step backward, his face working strangely. Borg said harshly, "Does that matter, woman? Are you afraid of the truth?"

Sigrid said pleadingly, her hands tight on his arm, "It is not worth this. Please—oh, don't look like that!"

Borg breathed in deeply, then declared with a heavy flatness, "It ain't what he done at first. People in this country make a lot of damnfool fuss over the simplest thing in nature. But what else he done, he kept his mouth shut and let someone else carry a burden alone." Borg let out his breath slowly. "A man shares a burden when he's part to blame. He stands up tall and speaks out, he don't shy off like some skulking dog, then sneak the girl a little money and think that makes it all right."

Magnus' face was a mask of bleak defiance now, but behind his eyes glided a dark numb hurt, and suddenly

Borg's anger melted. He wanted to reach out to his son and voice the aching plea, *Don't turn away; at last can't we talk together and not turn from each other?* But his face was a stony dyke against feeling and the moment passed. Magnus' eyes dropped, and he bent and picked up his hat. He slapped it against his pants and clamped it on, then turned without a word, walking away toward the river.

"Where is Helga?" Borg said slowly. "We better talk this out with her."

Sigrid's lips were tight as she shook her head. "She went for a walk an hour ago."

He massaged his forehead with a palm, nodded wearily. "That's right. I seen her."

Sigrid sniffled. "Why? Why this, when we raised him to be a good boy? Our people are great-minded about such things, but you were right. How could he let Helga carry such a thing all alone?" Her eyes entreated him. "And what about this money?"

Borg walked to where he had dropped the green-backs, picked them up and shuffled them together. He shrugged slightly. Magnus could have found the money or somehow saved it up unbeknown to them. There was another possibility too, reflected in his wife's anguished face.

Her hurt and confusion went far deeper than their son's ethical weakness, Borg knew—she was trying in his man's way to reason out the thing, and it escaped her. It had roots in the past, when Magnus had been the firstborn who had nursed at her breast, later a tearful little boy who had brought her his childhood hurts to

192

be comforted. The Magnus she knew belonged to the safe, simple world of her memories; the grown Magnus had grown away from her understanding. *And mine,* he thought wearily.

Sigrid was watching him quietly now, and he surprised a strangeness in her look. He had just seen its counterpart in Magnus, and had put it down to fear. But not from Sigrid.

"What is it, old woman?"

"I don't know," she murmured. "Maybe you. I thought you would hurt him bad."

"I was not thinking," he said roughly. "You know my damned temper. You see it before."

"Not in many years." She hesitated. "Was it only that?"

"What else?"

"I don't know," she said again, still strangely. "Always you are so sure. I think you are right, but now I wonder what it does to you."

Again he thought of the incident last night by the river, but shook his head impatiently. "It's the temper, that's all. I got to watch it. You worry too much."

"*Ja,* I think so." Her face twisted softly, and he felt the wrench of her misery in himself. "Ah, Borg, Borg, what is happening to our family?"

THE DAY WAS ALREADY warm and humid, but it was not only the prospect of a cool dip in the river that had drawn Helga off on her lonely walk. She wanted to think about much that had happened. Walking in the bright clear morning along the low pebbly riverbank, she took off her bonnet and switched it back and forth in her hand, humming an old Swedish air as a warm breeze played with tendrils of her hair.

Thinking of the dance last night, in spite of the trouble it had brought, she smiled with a faint warm excitement. She had thought she was no longer a foolish girt, and perhaps this was a foolishness. Abel Jevers was a preacher and, in some people's eyes, she was a wayward girl. Yet the feeling of flushed warmth held in her, and she let her thoughts stray happily with it.

She reached the cottonwood grove and moved into its dapple-shaded cover, down to the grassy slope above the bank. By the water's edge she found a dense willow thicket. Within its leafy privacy, still humming softly, she slipped out of her clothes, folded them in a neat bundle and laid them on the bank. She went to the water and toed it gently, then stepped in quickly, catching her breath at its first icy shock. Here the river curved deep into the tree-laced shore, and beneath the shading willow the water was unseasonably cold. But the crowding foliage secluded the little pool on three sides, and the river swirled here into a slow backwater that was fairly free of silt.

At first Helga shivered with its invigorating chill, then sank into its trailing coolness with a languorous pleasure. Working up a suds with a piece of yellow soap, she was pleased with the white smoothness of her skin and the new fullness of her slim, yet sturdy, body. She had thought that having a baby at seventeen might spoil her body, and had hardly cared at the time.

Instead, she knew without false modesty, the too-thin waif she had been had become a pretty young woman.

Washing out the light brown hair that fell almost to her waist, she wondered pensively whether it was right to be so happy, with the new trouble come to poor Syvert Hultgren. She thought with humble gratitude of the Vikstroms and all their kindnesses, especially of Inga who had been a true friend and of how at first she had leaned on Inga's strength and envied it. She felt almost ashamed of her newfound happiness while Inga remained snared in lonely bitterness with her great need to give and receive affection. And of course there was Mr. Jevers—Abel. How much she owed all of them for filling her loneliness in a strange new land and making it seem like home. . . .

Startled, Helga froze alert as she heard a crackle of brush high on the bank. Her heart pounded as she listened, holding her breath. The dark water, shafted by mottled sunlight, lapped softly at the bank and a faint breeze stirred the willow leaves, drowsing in the forenoon heat . . . there was no other sound.

Perhaps it had been a bird or a rabbit. Yet suddenly the water felt chilly again, and stirred by a mounting unease, she stepped out shivering and hurriedly toweled herself with a strip of rough cloth.

As she slipped into her camisole, she heard a man's low cough.

Standing motionless against a sudden pulse of panic, she slowly turned her head. There was a loud rustling of the bushes, and then the man parted them and stepped out.

She did not know his name, but she knew enough. She had seen the lanky buffalo hunter in town, and once out walking she had caught him prowling nearby. At the time, being close to the Vikstrom soddy, she had not been very alarmed, though she had realized from the way he had looked at her that he was worse than feeble-witted.

Now, standing a few feet from him and seeing his slack-lipped face and the burning intensity in his dull eyes, she felt her first panic deepen to a sick dread. The seclusion of the little grove had become a trap, and she was too far from the house for a scream to help. Her knees felt weak and boneless: it was only when he took another step toward her that terror sparked her numb limbs.

She turned and darted into a thicket, fighting through the clawing branches. The man overhauled her almost at once, his big fist seizing a handful of her long hair. As he swung her against him, she kicked and struggled vainly, then raked her nails down his face. His pained snarl was like that of an animal. His arms tightened savagely around her. For all his stringy gauntness he was a powerful man, and she felt the breath crushed from her lungs. Dizzily she felt her strength ebb and her body go limp, and she was sick and suffocated by his rough hands on her flesh and the foul stink of his hide coat.

A thought born of cold desperation stabbed into her numbed mind. Blindly her hand fumbled along his belt, closed over the butt of the pistol shoved there. With a sudden twist of her strong young body she wrenched the gun from his belt. She jammed it against his side, thumbing back the hammer.

In the same instant came his half-snarl of rage as he grabbed at the gun, turning it in her hand. Too late, she jerked the trigger. She gasped with the numb blow, but there was no pain, only the mercy of her senses dimming away and then a swift closing darkness.

CHAPTER SEVENTEEN

AFTER THE CLASH WITH HIS SON, BORG HAD NO HEART for work. He puttered aimlessly around till Sigrid called him to the midday meal, then tramped to the bench by the soddy wall and began to wash up. When he heard a team and rig come rattling down over the rutted trail from town, he looked up with only mild curiosity. After noting that it was a buckboard coming, he bent back to his ablutions.

He was toweling his face and arms as the wagon wheeled up in the yard, and was surprised to see Margaret Haggard on the seat. She smiled tentatively as if unsure of her welcome.

"Good morning, Mr. Vikstrom—or is it afternoon?"

Borg said, "Ma'am," with a polite and neutral nod. He was wondering what had brought her here. Of late her husband's attitude toward him when they chanced to meet had been cool—never offensive and not quite cordial. Borg, a direct man, liked open-faced people, and Haggard's manner ruffled him; behind it he sensed undercurrents he did not understand.

Sigrid, hearing their voices, stepped out now. Since what had happened this morning with Magnus, a puzzled sadness had settled into her face, and now it colored with a gentle warmth. "Why, Mrs. Haggard! I have not seen you—"

Margaret Haggard smiled wanly. "I know. Since we met last fall." She hesitated. "I should have come out to visit before, I suppose—"

"Please get down and come in," Sigrid said almost with an eager relief. Mrs. Haggard's visit was a temporary diversion from the household trouble.

"Thank you. I didn't want to intrude."

"We're very happy to have you. You must stay to eat."

Almost belatedly Borg stepped to the buckboard to assist Mrs. Haggard down, and as the two women went inside, Sigrid chatting animatedly, he set to unhitching and watering the team. Finished, he went inside as Mrs. Haggard said teasingly, "Don't you remember me, Kjersti?"

Kjersti held shyly back, biting her thumb with a half-smile. "I guess so."

"Look what I brought you." Mrs. Haggard produced a small flagon from her handbag, and Kjersti's eyes lighted. "Per-fume," she murmured, and accepted it with a proper little curtsy and "Thank you."

Lisj-Per, in the bunkroom, woke from his nap and made his presence known. Inga brought him out. "Oh, may I hold him?" Mrs. Haggard rose impulsively from her chair, not caring that the fine shiny material of her skirt brushed against the sooty stove.

Inga relinquished the baby rather reluctantly, and while Sigrid set the food on the table, the others watched Margaret play with him. Inga's aloof expression softened, and Lars even smiled a little. Her hungry tenderness with the baby was touching and almost pathetic. Borg felt the same wondering pity that was plain in his wife's face.

"Where is Helga?" Inga said worriedly. "She should be back from her walk."

Sigrid, at the stove, said over her shoulder, "It's a nice day, and maybe she wants to be by herself a while, *ja?*"

"She shouldn't walk so far," Inga said sharply. "It's not safe out on that prairie."

Borg grinned. "Only Indian out there is Pawnee Harry." He poured himself a cup of water, drank and added, "I told her to always stay by the river when she walks so she won't get lost. Don't fret, she's a smart girl."

"Not a dumbhead Norskie like you," Inga agreed, and frowned at her plate. "Still . . . I better go look for her."

"Wait till we eat," Sigrid suggested. She set the last dish on the table and seated herself. Borg, reaching for the stew, caught her meaning little frown which meant, *Say grace when we have a guest.* Sunday noon grace was usually said by Abel Jevers, but Abel had not yet returned from conducting his services at the school which this Sabbath morning even Sigrid had been too disheartened to attend. Borg, born the elder son of a strict fundamentalist family, easily ran off the rote grace he had led at meals most of his life and reached for the stew on the "amen."

Mrs. Haggard ate little herself. She fed the baby broth and laughed at his squirming and gulping. She and Sigrid chatted a little, but the talk ran like water over Borg's head. His thoughts were heavy and he ate with little appetite. Magnus had not returned, and he only hoped the boy would not do something foolish. He had gone off somewhere by himself, but being on foot would likely not go far. Somehow, Borg thought, he must undertake to settle the business of his son's relation with Helga Krans, whatever the circumstances behind it. As an issue which involved two people in his own household, it could not be sidestepped. And Magnus would have to explain about that money.

Inga left the table first and went out to look for Helga. Borg, to cover his weighty thoughts, took a second helping of stew and ate it up slowly. Afterward he leisurely lighted his pipe, then stood and started for the door. Passing behind Mrs. Haggard, he noticed for the first time the edge of a dark bruise above the high tight collar of her basque.

He continued out to the yard and paused, drawing thoughtfully on his pipe. Back of the neck was an unlikely place to take a bruise—if a calculating man like Haggard ever beat his wife, he would probably take care to avoid bruising her face. The thought would not have occurred except that Borg had already seen how it was between them. He sighed and shook his head; a wife-beater was not an uncommon breed of man, but a sorry one no less.

He looked about for Inga and saw her standing on a rise some distance from the house. The hill commanded a long view of the river and she was scanning the upstream bank, shading her eyes with her hand. Borg, his eye corners crinkled with thought, tramped along the upper bank till he reached the rise and started up it. Inga, standing alone, made a striking picture, tall and statuesque with that hint of Valkyrian wildness. The brisk wind whipped loosed strands of black hair about her face and molded her dress against her strong full figure.

"Inga," he called, and she lowered her hand and glanced downward. He came up beside her, frowning over his badly drawing pipe. "Go on back. I'll look for Helga. She has likely gone a good ways."

Inga lifted her shoulders in a shrug and started down past him. Her foot turned in the grass, and nearly falling, she caught at him. As he took her arms to steady her, she came fully against him and then brought her mouth up to his in a hard kiss. He pushed her away almost at once, but briefly as it lasted, he felt the wild angry impact of her hunger. She faced him breathing deeply, throwing back her wind-blown hair with a toss of her head, and the bitter half-smile touched her lips.

"Go on down there," he told her harshly and gave a sharp nod toward the house as he spoke. Then had the shock of seeing his brother just outside the doorway, leaning on his crutches with one hand braced against the wall. From here Borg could not tell Lars' expression, but the violence with which he suddenly turned and swung back into the house told enough.

Inga sauntered indolently off down the slope. Whether she had also seen Lars watching, he did not know and did not care. The damage was done. That Lars and his wife had lost whatever they had once felt would not matter to Lars' embittered mind. Over the years his resentment toward Borg for a small part in the incident that had left him crippled had deepened, seeing his brother move through life whole and strong. Yet in these last months Lars had found a new pleasure in work of his own, and Borg had sensed a slow healing of the long-time breach between them. Now, he knew with a dismal certainty, the old resentment would be renewed, perhaps to a real hatred, by Lars' conviction that Borg had taken the woman he'd lost.

First Magnus and now this, Borg thought despairingly, and there came to him his father's words from when the Old Man had been drunk and maudlin once: *My boy, a man laughs sometimes only so that he cannot hear himself cry.* It had been a rare weakness in his father, but remembering it, Borg's jaw hardened. A strong man did not need excuses. He settled the rightness of his way to his own mind and acted on it, and stolidly accepted what came of it, good or bad.

He hunched his shoulders in his dogged way and came down off the rise, descending to the riverbank. He had seen Helga walk this way earlier, headed upstream, and he turned now in that direction. He tramped a rough two miles before a real concern began to furrow his forehead. He had told Helga never to go far from the house, to always stay by the river. He wondered if she had been foolish enough to stray off on the prairie?

In this vast and empty country of few landmarks, losing one's self was easy. The few Indians roving about were peaceable, but there were always rough and lawless white men abroad in the prairie. He'd heard that a woman might move in safety among the worst of frontier desperadoes, but even these were men. Under pressure, as in prison camps during the war, some men could be reduced to lower than animals, and Borg counted generalizations as a lean assurance.

Borg halted now and cupped his hands to his mouth, releasing his breath in a great shout: *"Helga!"* He stood listening for a moment. Fifty yards distant lay the cottonwood grove where he and Dart had once saved Pawnee Harry from being dragged to death by the buffalo hunter. A rustle of bushes drew his glance toward it now, and he saw a wizened form come hobbling out of the grove—old Harry himself. With a crawling sense of urgency that he could not identify, Borg went swiftly to meet him.

"Find girl Vikstrom place," the old man greeted him. "Plenty bad. You come see."

"What is it?" Borg said thickly.

"You come see."

He led off into the grove, then broke trail through the dense willow brush that clogged the riverbank. Helga lay on a grassy knoll down by the water. Her small body in the torn camisole looked huddled and lifeless, one leg twisted awkwardly beneath her. She was lying on her side, and Borg turned her carefully on her back. The left side of her cotton garment was dyed with blood. He felt for a heartbeat and found it faintly. She was unconscious and deathly pale, and Borg did not like the look of it.

He found that the bullet had not inflicted too serious a wound, having taken her on the far left side beneath the ribs, but she had lost a good deal of blood. The powder-burn told him that the shot had been fired at close range and the trampled grass and the bruises on her pale flesh indicated that she had struggled with her attacker, a strong man.

Pawnee Harry told Borg that he had gone farther upstream to check some rabbit snares. Later, returning to his little camp in the cottonwood grove, he had heard a weak cry down in the willows by the water and had found the girl here.

"Harry, you find track good, eh?"

"Huh."

"Look around in the trees."

While Pawnee Harry went over the ground for sign, Borg rigged an improvised bandage with a strip torn from Helga's dress. Afterward he wrapped the dress around her limp body, gathered her up carefully in his arms, and carried her up to higher ground where Pawnee Harry waited stoically. Borg swung toward home at a fast walk, with Harry hobbling at a nimble pace alongside.

"The man, Harry," Borg muttered tautly. "There was a man."

"Findem plenty white man track. Him got horse, tie

'em trees. Girl swim down here. Mebbeso hear girl, sneak up. Shootem girl, him scare, get fast gone."

"That close, if he wanted to kill her, he could not miss," Borg reasoned aloud. "No, she fought him and she got his gun maybe. Then . . ."

"Huh."

Borg persisted. "But you have been around, Harry. You didn't see a man, any man?"

"Think maybe him, not savvy sure. Harry out plenty soon morning. See 'em fella fish by an' by."

"A man fishing? When was this?"

"Huh. Sometime, by an' by." Pawnee Harry knit his wrinkled brow, then swept a hand eastward. "Plenty soon morning, sun there."

That would make it about dawn, first sun. "The man, Harry, eh? You know him?"

"Him one Texas fella, workem mick boss."

Borg said sharply. "A man who works for Quin-cannon, eh?"

"Huh. Him fella Bert Romaine."

To that, Pawnee Harry could add little. He had seen Bert Romaine only once, early that morning, and did not know how long he had remained by the river. But he had been near the grove, and Harry was emphatic that the sign left by Helga's attacker indicated a man of Romaine's size and build.

Bert Romaine had troubled Helga last night at the dance and had walked away angry; later he had spoken for the cowboys who would have lynched Syvert Hult-gren. It told a world about the man, Borg thought, and as always decision settled into his mind with an immovable certainty. As always too, against the stir of iron wrath, a voice of cool instinct warned him to go careful. But for once, there was a strained lack of conviction to it.

Stalking into the house, Borg ignored the flurry of questions as he carried Helga to her bunk. He turned to face the shocked women as they crowded into the sleeping room, saying flatly, "One of you must go for the doctor. I have other business."

Mrs. Haggard said with a cool composure, "Dr. Ledlow is the only doctor in Liberty; he's senile and neglectful and he drinks." As she spoke she removed her small silly hat and began rolling up her sleeves, saying brusquely, "Get some water boiling, Mrs. Vikstrom."

Borg said impatiently, "What do you know, a soft woman like you, eh?"

"It was not only a man's war, Mr. Vikstrom," she said evenly. "In the South, we had few good surgeons and fewer decent hospital facilities. Amputations at line hospitals were more of butchery. The men sent back home needed help. I organized a hospital of women volunteers. And we learned, Mr. Vikstrom." Briskly she stepped past him to Helga's side.

"Oh, what has happened?" Sigrid cried.

"A bad thing. I don't know all of it, but it looks like a man of Quincannon's is to blame."

She wrung her hands, following him from the bunkroom. "Now it comes, all the trouble!"

Borg said, his tone hard and level, "That depends on Quincannon. I will see him. Meantime Lars and Harry

206

will go to every home and fetch all the men. Bring them to Holmgaard's place and wait for me there."

"Then you do think this is trouble!"

"I don't know. I think this: there were cowboys last night who wanted to lynch Syvert. Some of our men were mad about that, maybe mad enough they'll go half-cocked when they hear about Helga. This way, they get it from me, and I can talk them out of foolishness. But first I see Quincannon." His glance sharpened on his brother, slumped in a hand-carved chair by the stove. "You hear what I say, Lars?"

Lars raised his head, saying surlily, "I hear you."

"Then get going. You can sit a horse."

Borg pivoted on his heel and walked to the wall, lifting his rifle off its pegs. He took a box of cartridges from a shelf and rammed it in his pocket, then stalked out. A moment later Lars heaved up on his crutches and swung after him.

There were only two horses, so Borg dispatched Pawnee Harry off on foot to alert the nearest families, cautioning him not to tell them the reason for the meeting, but to make sure that they understood the urgency of it. Afterward Borg got the mare out of the small corral and saddled her. He hoisted Lars into the saddle and Lars rode off then without a parting word or glance. Hans was in a refractory mood, and Borg spent several sweating, cursing minutes roping him and throwing on the rig.

He set a hard-driven pace for Singlebit, and Hans was wet and blowing when he finally reined into the ranchyard. As he swung down and tied the reins, Quincannon opened the door and stood on the threshold, his bulk filling the doorway. A glance told Borg that his mood was an ugly one. No doubt his crew's version of Larned's shooting had placed an incontrovertible blame on Syvert. Borg, expecting as much, knew he must keep a close leash on his own contained fury.

Quincannon leaned his shoulder against the doorframe, saying with a brittle softness, "You want to talk about last night, I'll advise you not to waste breath. Your man's guilty as sin, and he'll hang for it."

Borg kept his voice cool. "You have decided the sentence, then?"

"Like you decided Robles' last year."

"That was not the same, maybe."

"Maybe," Quincannon echoed derisively. "But like I say, don't waste your breath."

"I am not here for that." Borg moved forward and lifted one foot to the lowest step, leaning a big hand on his knee. "A girl in my household has been shot. Maybe she will not live. And maybe one of your men done it."

Quincannon's iron face altered slightly to the brutal gravity of this, and then he straightened slowly up. "You had better back that." He bit the words off hard.

Borg talked, watching the cold rejection of the charge form in Quincannon's face. "You wouldn't be suggesting," Quincannon murmured ominously, "that I turn him over to you, would you now?"

"No. But that he be taken to town and held for trial. I don't say he's guilty, but that the evidence—"

"What evidence, for God's sake!" Quincannon's

hand made an impatient chopping gesture. "An old whiskey-shot Injun saw Bert Romaine fishing earlier near where the girl was shot? You call that evidence? I know Bert; if he asked the girl to dance and she was standoffish, little doubt he got warm under the collar. That's Bert's way, and no denying it. But it's a far shout from this—"

Borg cut in, feeling a slow heat swell into his neck. "Quincannon!" He controlled his voice with an effort. "A girl has been shot, and she may die. If she comes to her right mind, she can tell the truth. But I think she may not live, nor can I wait to let her killer get away. Now. If your man is not afraid of the truth, let him come forward and say it. Let him go to town and wait for trial."

Quincannon eyed him a long moment, his hard stare not relenting. "If you know anything at all about Texans, Vikstrom, it's a damn fool you are to even suggest it. You've done worse than accuse a man, you've offered him a deadly insult. No man'd gainsay the bad of this thing, but there's the point. I know Bert Romaine well, and for all his bad temper, I don't guess, I know, that this was not his doing."

"I'm asking you to tell this in court, at his trial."

"You're asking too damned much!"

"No less than you demand for Syvert Hultgren!"

"There's a difference—eleven witnesses saw him kill Tom!"

"Syvert says Larned had a gun," Borg said doggedly.

Quincannon gave a short harsh laugh. "From all I hear, your Hultgren is a mean hard-drinking lad, and he was drunk last night. A drunken liar, to boot."

"All that might be said of your Romaine," Borg said softly, feeling the slow flood of his anger coming to full tide. "For the last time, I ask you—will you bring him to trial?"

"I'm telling you, no. I'll offer no such insult to any man of mine, even if every man on my crew wouldn't quit me for tryin' it!" His voice became very soft. "And now, Vikstrom, I'll thank you to get off my property. You're trespassing here."

Borg swung away and walked to Hans and untied him. He stepped into the saddle, then quartered around to face the Irishman. "Quincannon," he said low-voiced, "I thought you and me could live side by side with justice between us. But today I come for justice, and what I get is the gospel according to Quincannon. This is not a little thing over cattle or wheat. You think one of our women gets attacked by a man, we just shrug it off, eh?"

Quincanmon said stonily. "If that's a threat, I'll give you back as good—don't try to take him. We'll be ready for you."

"Take him?" Borg shook his head gently. "You don't know how I fight. You will not like it, mister. You will not like it at all."

CHAPTER EIGHTEEN

"I NEED SIX," BORG TOLD THE TWENTY-FIVE MEN assembled in Olof Holmgaard's yard. "Only six. The rest of you go home and wait. Stay inside with your families and wait."

They stirred restlessly, exchanging glances and low mutters. There had been an outraged response to Borg's news, and all were in agreement of retaliation after he had laid out the issues at stake. Barring reference to a higher court of judgment, a man could only settle the morality of his way according to his own lights, and to Borg the issues were clear-cut. A young girl had been criminally assaulted, and the little evidence pointed directly at Bert Romaine. Bare justice demanded that Romaine's guilt or innocence be established in open court, and Quincannon had arrogantly sneered at the notion.

But the whole issue went far deeper, he had told them: for some it might seem simpler to back off from immediate trouble by letting the matter pass without a murmur. However, should they do so, what kind of a life would there be afterward here for any of them? Thus far he had successfully called Quincannon twice, first on Arne Hultgren's killing, then on the depredations against their wheat, each time toeing a hard but reasonable line that had forced Quincannon's yielding to a middle ground. This time Quincannon had not yielded, and if the business was let to slip by, the other times would amount to an empty bluff. Quincannon respected nothing but a hardheaded toughness that matched his own; let such a man trample your rights once and get away with it and soon he would push you into a corner.

But many here, being slow and cautious men, would not respond outright to the drastic idea Borg had proposed to meet the situation. Knowing this, he wanted only volunteers. He had made clear to them that there would be some danger, and now he was watching their shifting expressions as they slowly and methodically turned it over in their minds.

"I'll go," boomed Olof Holmgaard, and his two sons followed suit. Eric Slogvig made a fourth. Borg's glance moved to Nathan Dart, a good man to be sided with in any venture. Dart was standing off from the others, his seamed face still and thoughtful.

"How about you, Nate?"

Dart shook his head, saying in his dry meager way, "Count me out, hoss. Seen too many prairie fires in my time. You don't know what that means out here. Worse'n the end of the world."

"The end of Quincannon's world—maybe. It's hard to count you out, Nate."

Again Dart shook his head. "Hate to run agin you. But I growed up runnin' cattle on Texas grass. I'd a sight rather shoot at a man than burn off his graze."

He was eying Borg steadily, and something in his regard touched Borg with a baffled irritation—had he seen that look in Sigrid's face only this morning? In Magnus it had been fear, in his wife loving worry, and in Dart a cool, narrow-eyed assessment. In each case it was as though they were reshaping a part of him to their own minds, not liking what they saw. Angrily he shook away these thoughts.

A renewed strain of mutters ran through the men, and his hard blue glance swept them. "Well?"

"I'll go," Oscar Molnar growled.

Borg, sensing his residue of cautious reluctance, said, "Not unless you're sure, Oscar."

"*Helvete,* I'm sure."

"All right," Borg nodded. "Who—"

"I'll go."

Startled faces swiveled toward Lars Vikstrom, sitting his horse behind the crowd. Only Borg interpreted the glowering emotion that flushed his gaunt face for what it was.

He said quietly, "You'll have to stay on your horse. You think—"

"I think I can do any goddam thing you can."

Lars' response came low and flat and faintly slurred, making Borg think coldly, *Ah, so now he hates me that much.* So much that Lars' newly fired resentment had carried him from the opposite of his old apathy, to a sullen and raging determination to match whatever his brother might do.

Borg gave a curt nod and swung away to mount Hans. As the men started to break up, Abel Jevers pounded up on his whey-bellied nag. He flung himself breathlessly out of the saddle and walked over to Borg's stirrup, his thin face full of trouble.

"Pawnee Harry found me over by the school and told

213

me and I went to see about Helga—"

"How is she?" Borg interrupted.

"Still unconscious. I couldn't tell much else. She looked so pale—" Abel swallowed, then straightened up. "Listen, what do you have in mind?"

Borg told him. Abel Jevers stepped backward, looking shaken. He turned to include them all in his passionate plea: "For the love of God, don't do this thing! You're decent people, Christian and civilized, not bloodthirsty savages. Think, men; think what this can lead to. There has to be a better way than this, else every ethic you profess is a lie."

"Go stay with the women," someone hooted, but Borg's dark frown killed the outburst of jeers. "Abel," he said quietly, "would you forget what happened to Helga?"

Abel's eyes burned in his white face, and he said softly now, "If you have to ask that, then every sermon I've preached went for nothing."

There was a motionless silence as he walked to his horse, mounted, and started away.

"Abel."

Borg spoke quietly, then ranged Hans up alongside Abel's horse and lowered his voice for Abel's ears alone. "Abel, I have listened to you as I would to any man, for whatever good I can find in his words. But no man tells me my way. I follow mine, you follow yours. Let it be that way. Go stay with Helga now and say your prayers for her."

Abel lifted his face, and Borg saw the open misery working in it. Behind him someone snorted derisively and without turning, Borg raised his voice: "If any man thinks this is funny, it will please me to smash his jaw."

Abel reined away, and Borg felt a fleeting compassion for how shabby life must seem at times to someone so young and earnest and with self-set goals so high. Automatically his thoughts veered to Magnus, but then hardened with bitter anger. Magnus too would follow his own way, and be damned to him. Borg swung brusquely back toward the others, watching them mount their horses.

His six volunteers, Olof and the twins, Eric, Oscar, and Lars, fell in behind Borg as he led the way, heading east. In the latening sunlight of midafternoon, the virgin sweep of dipping and swelling prairie was much as they had seen it on that afternoon of their arrival in Eben Haggard's country, months ago. The buffalo grass, already turning buff-brown in the heat of early summer, was mellowed to the hue of old gold. The wind rising off the river flats to the west, soughing through the deep grass and pressing it down like a gentle hand, riffled Borg's hair against his sweating forehead. Its touch did not cool the hot decision rooted in him.

Deep in Singlebit range, he called a halt, there dispersed the men with curt orders. They were to keep to open flats against the likelihood of being discovered by nearby Quincannon riders; the fires would be spotted soon enough, but being set at seven widely separated points, they could not all be stopped. They were to roughly correlate the action for twenty minutes from now, and afterward to get out as fast as they could.

The men nodded understanding and broke apart in divergent directions. Borg himself, after checking his watch, rode on due east. When he next fumbled the watch from his vest pocket, it was almost time. He halted and turned about in his saddle. His companions were all lost to sight, and there was no sound but the sigh of wind in the grass, nothing to be seen on the rolling emptiness of prairie but the distant dots of grazing cattle.

Borg dismounted, wet a finger and made a final check of the wind. It was holding strong from the west. He dug out a match as he studied the parched terrain with cold satisfaction. There had not been rain for a long time; the prairie would take fire easily. Burn off Quincannon's graze upon which his precious cows depended—then see how long he would hang on. If he wanted to carry the fight from there, he would get all he wanted. For Borg's decision, once made, was mercilessly single-minded: Quincannon's attitude had made it clear that they could not live side by side; one of them would have to go.

Borg squatted down and snapped the match alight with his thumbnail, cupped the spoon of flame between his hands and touched it to the tough dry grass. The flame spread swiftly outward in a thin scorching wave, shimmering but invisible in the blazing sunlight, and Borg stood and stepped back and watched. One by one the grass stalks blackened and collapsed and then the bright orange flames took shape, licking and curling avidly for new fodder.

So quickly did it take then, exploding before the wind, that Borg fought down an alarmed impulse to stamp it out. Already it was too late; the fire was leaping to right and left in a livid sheet as it blew eastward with a terrifying speed. The first gray curling tendrils of smoke belched into sullen billows and were windborne ahead of the flames.

A thin backfire ate into the grass by his feet, and it was time to be moving. Borg stepped into saddle and watched a moment more, now with a thickening worry for his companions. The responsibility was his, and he had better check on them.

As he struck south now he saw other pillars of smoke that belched distantly along the prairie and were quickly tattered before the wind, and the incredibly rapid spread of the smoke blanket bore home to him the appalling enormity of the deed. He held his mind to its grim necessity, and was only glad that their own fields were enclosed in plowed firebreaks, for the fire would work backward during every break in the prevailing wind.

He saw Slogvig trot over a rise, pulling up his horse when he sighted Borg, but Borg waved him on home with a swinging motion of his arm, and Eric kicked his animal on without hesitation. A little farther he met Oscar Molnar, who rode up suddenly out of a draw and drew rein beside him. Oscar sleeved a rivulet of sweat from his gray face, staring at the holocaust. The westward sky was darkening with the rise of scattered smoke, and vast tongues of flame rose and fell with a crackling roar amid the churning dark clouds of it. A winddrift of fluffy ash spiraled down out of the sky on all sides; it sooted their sweating faces and their horses' coats.

"*Helvete,* man—it's something we started!"

"Yah, but ride on now, Oscar. Get back home and stay inside."

"Man, you better come too. I seen some Quincannon men riding up from the east. I don't think they can stop it, but they will be happy to stop Vikstrom, eh?"

Borg shook his head. "I got to see about Lars."

Oscar lifted his hand in a wry brief salute and rode away. Borg pushed on, hoping that Olof and his boys had made it out safely. These three had worked out south from his own central position, but they were not his first concern. For Lars had ridden off the northern-most way; should Lars lose his horse, he would be stranded and helpless. But even that concern was trivial to the basic fact.

No matter what else, Lars was his brother.

He scanned the prairie to northeast, straining for a sight of Lars, and soon made out a lean spout of black smoke, far off from the others. Borg swore aloud as he realized that his brother, goaded to prove himself, had ranged dangerously afar to set his fire. Unless Lars pulled back quickly, he might be sighted by Quin-cannon riders. Or be caught in the path of one of the other fast-merging fires, racing with a wind-fanned fever into Singlebit's five thousand acres of virgin grass.

The wind had slackened off, and that would somewhat slow the headlong rush of flames. Borg swung deep north around the seething heat and smoke of Molnar's fire, hoping that he would soon meet Lars returning. Ahead suddenly he heard the panicked lowing of cattle, and he felt impatient pity. Like the prairie wildlife, the bulk of Quincannon's scattered stock would stampede away before the flames, but a few bunches would probably mill stupidly till they were ringed in.

He put Hans into a lunging climb of a steep rise. Beyond it he could hear the bawling cattle. He heard something else too, that made him pull up. He flung himself out of the saddle and went on foot to the top of the hill. A group of riders were hoorawing off a bunch of steers, their shouts carrying hoarsely from smoke-raw throats. Three men were on foot; they had killed two steers and split their gutted bodies in half. As Borg watched, two riders secured ropes around the neck and foot of a half carcass, then rode at a gallop along the edge of the flames, dragging the carcass between their horses with the raw side down.

He understood their purpose: to smother the fire over a wide swath while the wind held low and save Singlebit's north range. No doubt others were doing the same along the south range, location of the ranch headquarters. Perhaps, if they were lucky, only the central graze might be gutted. Already, where the fire had passed, a lake of virgin grass had become a blackened, smoking wasteland. Watching the furious activity as others followed the first two, dragging the split bloody carcasses across the fringe fires, Borg wished these blistered, besooted men no ill.

One rider, spotting Borg now, reined up with a shout. Sunlight glinted on his rifle as he swiftly unsheathed it. It was a pretty far range, Borg thought, but all the same he turned to drop back down the rise. He felt the blow and burn of the slug, the rifle's savage crack echoing the stunning impact.

He staggered and fell. He lay on his belly and shook his head, not quite sure what had happened. Then, feeling a hot trickle along his scalp and temple, he touched it with a hand which came down smeared with red. Borg heaved to his feet with an angry grunt, and a wave of dizziness darkened his eyes; he fell again and plunged down the slope, rolling.

This time he lay for a while, blinking, till vision swam back. He fought against a grip of rising panic; if he could not sit his saddle, or could not ride fast enough, the broadening belt of fire would catch up with him shortly. He planted both palms firmly against the ground now and pushed upward, getting a knee under him. He came slowly to his feet, battling the surging nausea that qualmed through him. Hunching his head doggedly between his shoulders, he moved at a stumbling walk toward Hans, who was fiddlefooting uneasily.

Borg cajoled him with soft and careful words as he approached, and Hans steadied. After picking up the reins, Borg sank down on one knee, resting to let the dizzy sickness recede enough for him to muster strength. He raised his head with a sluggish effort, hearing a horse canter up from a valley fifty yards away, then halt. Borg's bleary gaze focused on the rider, not quite making him out. But he knew the bright sorrel mare. He opened his mouth to call but his voice was a hoarse croak.

Lars did not move. Borg saw his tense posture and, without effort, knew his thought. The hated brother who had wronged him was in trouble, and why not let the encroaching fire settle the grudge? Yesterday, or even tomorrow, Lars might have moved to help, but the strong immediacy of seeing Borg with his wife still lay raw and bitter in his mind.

Go on, ride off, damn you: a man can make it on his own. Borg lowered his head and closed his eyes, breathing strongly for the attempt. He straightened his knees and caught the saddle horn and got a toe in stirrup. With a massive heave that seemed to burst his head, he threw his weight across the saddle, straddling it.

For a moment he rested, his chin sunk on his chest, fighting for shuddering breaths. Then, feeling a hand on his bridle, opened his eyes and raised his head.

"Can you hang on if I lead out?" Lars said.

Borg jerked a nod of assent, and his brother wheeled the mare out ahead, pulling Hans along. Borg gripped the horn tightly in both hands, his head bowed. The nausea washed gradually away, and now a pounding ache began to jar his head at every hooffall. The wind returned and shifted; black smoke blew about them and hazed the landscape. Fitfully coughing against its acrid suffocation, they moved on. The smoke thinned and ahead of them, Borg saw with relief, lay open prairie.

When they came to the first firebreak that edged Slogvig's fields, Lars drew rein and said, "We rest now." Borg laboriously swung himself to the ground and braced himself, panting, against the stirrup, then sank to his haunches. Lars dismounted just as carefully, saying, "Should we lay up at Slogvig's a while, or can you go on?"

"We'll go on home. We—"

Borg broke off. Lars was walking, awkwardly and gingerly, the few steps to his side. He sat down with a vast sigh and dug a bandanna out of his pocket, eying Borg's scalp. "That's a lot of blood. Better tie it off, eh?"

"You walk?"

Having said it, Borg felt a little foolish. Lars nodded, gripping an end of the bandanna in his teeth and tearing it across. His pale brown eyes were musing in his sweaty, soot-blackened face. "Funny thing . . . made myself walk back there, gettin' down to lay the fire. Maybe I was only so mad, I had to get down. All I knew was, I could do it. Funny though"—he paused, knotting the bandanna strips together—"it was easier just now, and I wasn't mad."

Borg was silent as Lars tied the bandanna around his scalp, then: "Lars, thanks for that."

"You would of made it out by yourself maybe."

Borg almost said, *Maybe,* and did not; for once it was he who had needed Lars, and maybe that meant something.

Lars said slowly, "It's like something that was all tied up in me let go. Just let go, like that."

222

"When you decide to help me, eh?"

Lars met his gaze soberly, all the bitter rancor gone from his face. "Maybe. Can you make it up?"

"Yah, sure."

Both men clambered into their saddles awkwardly, as if using the untried muscles of infants, and again they looked at each other. Lars' gaze was wondering, and Borg could only shake his head.

Probably there was no miracle about it, except in the way that all life was a miracle. Borg remembered Chris Mikkelsen back in Koshkonong. Chris had come home after the war with two useless legs, and one day two years after Appomattox, he had simply stood up and walked away from his wheelchair. For such things there must be reasons that were not apparent. But Lars had not been in the war. Or maybe he had been involved in a war of his own, fighting his way to a finding of himself as a man.

A trace of the old bitter tension marked Lars' voice when he spoke again. "What I see with you and Inga— how much does this go on?"

"Never before. It wasn't my doing, Lars. Only listen, it's been hard for her."

"I know." A flurry of gray ash drifted out of the sky, and Lars watched it settle. "It's funny, like maybe a man can dig a grave for himself and not know it, till he looks up and sees the sky. And now he wants only to climb out and live again."

"It's like that, being a man."

Lars looked at him and nodded yes, and they rode on.

CHAPTER NINETEEN

WHEN THEY REACHED THE SOD HOUSE, EVERYONE WAS gathered outside, facing eastward. Gripped by a sober hush, they watched the dark pall of rising smoke haze in a murky smear across the sky. Nathan Dart and Gurina were there, and so was Pawnee Harry, his wrinkled face a stoical mask against the old story of the white man's destruction of his beloved prairie. The women had drawn close together, as women did to ally themselves in their mutual trouble. Kjersti, frightened without knowing why, pressed close to her mother's skirt. Lisj-Per napped contentedly in Inga's arms and ignored everything.

Sigrid's hands were twisted in her apron and her face showed open distress, as it did when alien passions disturbed her comfortable world. She came quickly over to Borg as he stepped down. "Oh, what's happened to your head?"

"Nothing much. It's a good thick one."

Inga was thoughtfully eying her husband as though sensing something about him that had never been, and now with almost elaborate casualness, Lars dismounted and took a few careful steps.

Sigrid gasped, "Why, Lars, look at you!" She turned to Borg in confusion. "Why, look at him!"

Borg nodded dourly. "He walks pretty good."

Inga tried to cover her amazement with an offhand shrug. "I always said he could if he wanted."

Lars gave her a long hard look, then said grimly, "It's time you and me talked." He hobbled over and took her arm and moved her firmly off from the others.

Borg said soberly, "How is Helga?"

"Not awake yet, but she's resting good." Sigrid gave a little smiling nod. "Mrs. Haggard thinks she will be all right."

"Ah, good. Good."

Borg became aware that Mrs. Haggard was watching him intently, her face holding a mute and pale accusation. Suddenly she came over to face him, her voice low and impassioned: "Did you have to do this to him? Did you?"

"Who?" Borg asked blankly.

"Linus! Linus Quincannon! He has so much to bear—now this."

"This," Borg echoed dryly, "you had better explain, maybe."

Her face colored and slowly her eyes fell. "I—yes. I'm sorry. You couldn't know." She made a small weary gesture. "We were engaged to be married. That was in Texas, a long time ago, before I met Eben."

Borg and Sigrid exchanged startled glances, and Sigrid said quietly, "My husband had no choice, Mrs. Haggard."

"But he's not really like this, not hard and bitter," Margaret went on with a soft insistence. "You don't know him as I did—before—"

Borg said gruffly, "His arm? The war maybe?"

Mutely she shook her head, then brushed a hand across her eyes. "Oh, why are men such fools!" She turned blindly away into the house, and Sigrid looked after her with distressed compassion, then at Borg. He gave a baffled shrug, thinking tiredly now, *All this, and the day is not ended.*

Sigrid laid a hand on his arm, saying gently, chidingly, "I think a good bandage on the *dumskalle* head, now."

"Small difference," he growled. "There's not much to leak out any more."

They went inside and he sat at the table, patiently bowing his head while she undid the crusted bandanna and began with firm fingers to explore his scalp for the damage. Nathan Dart came in from the yard, his wife with him, and Dart observed, "Caught some Texas mad, eh, hoss?"

"Too much mad for straight shooting," Borg grunted, and lifted his head to say more, but Sigrid pushed it firmly down. "*Gud,* but you're a shaggy one. Ah, here it is, just a little nick." She went to the stove for hot water, and Borg looked up with a reproving frown.

"Nate, you should not have brought Gurina here. You know this is where Quincannon will come first."

"Reckon that's why. The woman an' me talked it over. I was some put out, you firin' up that grass. Only what's friends for, if not to stand by?"

Gurina linked her arm with her husband's, saying with an emphatic nod, "Sure, that is what I tell him."

Dart grinned. "Let her come because he won't move agin the families, not womenfolk an' kids. Reckoned you figured as much."

"I would have got the women and kids away first, otherwise," Borg said sharply. "Still, it's in your head I was wrong, Nate, eh?"

Dart's gaze was cool and unruffled. "Takes a long while sometime to judge how wrong a man was. Point that troubles me, you didn't wait to see how right you was."

Borg's big hand knotted to a stubborn fist on the table. "I was right."

"Maybe so," Dart said quietly, dryly. "For all I seen, you're pushing pretty damn' hard. Granted Quincannon's a hard devil to deal with, I'd say he's got plenty excuse to run his herd over your wheat on today's account should he take a mind. I seen men get all sorts of mean burrs under their saddles, and yours is still stuck tight."

Borg said thickly, "You better make that plainer."

Dart glanced at Sigrid as she came to the table and set down a basin of hot water, a deep trouble in her face. "Ain't my place to say. Said too much already. Anyways, I taken my side."

"Please," Sigrid said softly. "You will say it, Nathan."

"Put it this way. Man who takes a leader's way has got more than others to watch. Feel of power is a funny thing, may get out of hand before a body knows it. Might not even show except by his conduct." Dart paused. "I'm a blunt-spoke man. I don't put things kindly, even to a friend."

The words flagged down Borg's first anger, and he only said, "All right, you have said your mind. We'll say no more on it." He looked at Sigrid, trying to read her face. She did not see things as he did, that was all, went his iron-set thought. A man must do what he thought right.

He said brusquely to Dart, "You know Quincannon a little. How will it come?"

"It's a man's fight, and I reckon his real accountin's with you."

"Good. I will keep the others out of it."

"Won't be hard. Touch his pride, make it personal between you and him." Dart eyed him soberly. "Better think about that some. He's a big mean man and I allow he'll be a sight meaner after this. Anyways you tackle it, you're in no shape for mixin' with him."

"On account of a scratch?" Borg snorted, and winced as Sigrid began to clean the scalp wound. When she had finished and affixed a clean bandage, Borg rose and discovered that he was pretty light-headed yet. He went into the women's bunkroom to check on Helga.

Helga, her face now holding a little feverish color, was sleeping quietly, her breast gently rising and falling to her steady breathing. Abel Jevers was hunched on a stool pulled up by her bunk, his elbows on his knees and his hands clasped loosely together, watching her. He glanced up gloomily as Borg entered; he did not speak. Borg felt Helga's forehead and thought there was not too much fever.

His own head was swimming, and he went to his bunk to stretch out and rest awhile. Only for a minute or so, he thought drowsily. . . .

He roused out of his blank doze with a fitful start. Nathan Dart was shaking his shoulder, saying tersely, "Man's comin' now, hoss."

Borg swung his feet to the floor, rubbing his rough horny hands over his face as a goad to bring full wakefulness. His head still ached, but he felt alert and steady. He went out to the common room and found Lars standing by the open doorway with Borg's rifle in his hands. Nathan Dart stood beside him with his Springfield, squinting off toward the eastward hills. Pawnee Harry had disappeared. Inga and Sigrid behind Lars, peering past him, and Margaret sat listlessly at the table while Kjersti stood by her chair, studying her gravely.

Borg moved to the doorway, took his rifle from Lars and stepped outside. He saw them coming and they were already close, a tight-riding bunch pushing their horses down the first slope toward the southeast. Borg planted his feet apart, his rifle slack in the crook of his arm, and waited. The sun threw the long shadows of a waning day across the yard as they swung into it, Quincannon in the lead.

The Irishman raised a hand and halted his men perhaps a half dozen yards away. They pulled their horses around in a half circle, facing the house. Borg felt his nerve ends tingling with alert tension, and every sight and sound bored into his brain with a crystal clarity. The lean-faced riders motionless in their saddles and their silence stressed by a solitary chink of spur and the creak of leather, the slobbering snort of a horse and the shuffle of hoofs. The small stilling noises of a dying day, the restless stir of grotesque and lengthy shadows thrown by riders and mounts, the moiled dust making a golden haze in the sunlight and settling softly. They came to a man at rare times, Borg thought obscurely, those scenes that would hold strong forever in his memory.

Quincannon stepped from the saddle and tossed his reins to Dennis O'Hea without looking at him, pivoting in the same vicious movement to stalk across the yard. He wore a gun, but his hand swung empty at his side. The granite set of his face was broken at last by scarlet fury, and the gray frost of his eyes was like hot gunsteel.

Borg was aware that both Lars and Nathan had stepped quietly out behind him, and Dart said mildly and soberly, "Never seen a man looks as mean as El Capitan when he's het up. You mind yourself now, Borg."

Margaret Haggard's slender form slipped suddenly past Borg, moving quickly to meet Quincannon. She caught his shoulders, and her words came tense with a desperate pleading. "Linus, don't!"

Quincannon came to a dead stop, his stare blank with fury and fixed above her head. "Woman, get out of the way. Damn it, have you no shame left?"

"No more." Slender and delicate against his great bulk, she tilted up her face, her hands against his chest. "Linus, if ever I meant anything to you—please!"

Slowly he looked down at her then and his eyes never softened; he said softly, bleakly, "Get away now, Maggie. I mean it."

After a long moment she dropped her hands and stepped aside. Quincannon came on, stopping within six feet of Borg. His bullish shoulders were hunched and his head thrust truculently forward on his short neck. "What kind of low dog are you, to burn off a man's graze and starve his cattle?"

"I told you, you wouldn't like the way I fight," Borg said quietly. "Now you know."

"Ah, so you did. Now tell me another thing. Have you the guts to go off from these women and meet me man to man?"

"I hoped you would want that."

A bleak and wicked smile touched Quincannon's thin lips. "Did ye now," he said softly. "You'll get that wish."

Nathan Dart had moved up beside Borg with his rifle barrel canted idly to cover the riders, and Borg handed him his own rifle. "We will not need these, Nate."

"Good," Dennis O'Hea called softly, sitting blocky and solid on his horse reined out ahead of the others.

"Vikstrom," Quincannon said with a savage calm now, "it's plain we can't both share this range. You can burn off my grass, but I can stampede a herd across your wheat as easy. Little sense that makes, so let's give this fight a reason. Loser pulls his stake. Me and mine, or you and all of yours. Agreed?"

Borg said without hesitation, "Yes," and to Dart then: "Nate, get a piece of rope. Tie my right arm behind me."

Quincannon's one arm half-lifted, the hand forming a fist. His voice came as flat and hard as a slap:

"There'll be no need for that!"

"It will be this way."

"Be a fool then, and divil take you!"

With swift, furious motions Quincannon stripped off his shirt, and Borg did the same. Dart then cinched his hand down to his belt at his back. Sigrid had come out to stand quietly by her man, and now Margaret Haggard said frantically, "Oh, Mrs. Vikstrom, can't you stop it?"

Still-faced and grave, she shook her head. "No."

"Look at them—look at their faces! They'll kill each other!"

No matter what Sigrid's misgivings, only a deep quiet pride marked her voice. "My husband will do as he thinks best."

They headed off together onto the narrow strip of prairie downstream between the river and the fields. The sinking orb of the sun laid its molten dye across the wind-stirred grass as their feet swished through it, their shadows moving alongside like dark elongated specters. Neither man looked back at the silent assembled people watching from the yard. A hundred yards off from the soddy, Quincannon halted.

"This will do."

Borg nodded once, saying nothing while he flexed his free hand for the feel of a one-handed fight. He felt awkward and exposed, and knew that Quincannon, accustomed to his condition, had an advantage now. Yet he waited for the Irishman to carry the rush, and almost at once Quincannon bulled full against him with a savage slash at Borg's face.

Borg did not even try to step away from the blow; he turned his head enough so that it only rocked his jaw, and that sledging impact was enough to goad his own long-pent rage. Burning off the graze he had regarded as his simple right; it had let little out of his system. Now he could fight for himself, and he let thought of all that had happened in these few days fuel his ferocity. Here was an equal foeman at last, one against whom he need not pull his punches. On the heel of Quincannon's try, he chopped his fist into the rancher's belly and drew a savage grunt.

They stood almost toe to toe then and simply hammered at each other. It was a contest of bone and sinew and muscle, elemental and brutal, with neither man attempting to cover up, neither giving quarter nor asking it. The differences that had fostered their quarrel faded away, and they became two primal giants alone on a vast and lonely plain in the dim dawn of creation, each with one common snarling goal: to outlast a powerful opponent and batter him into submission. The drive of their feet churned the sod to dust; sweat and blood grew in grimy patches on their woolen underwear. Their breathing was a guttural, gusty sound punctuated by the sodden strike of fists.

It could not last forever. Borg gave back a step, and then leaned into a long slogging smash and Quincannon went down on his knees. He wrapped his arm around Borg's legs and tried to heave him over. Borg's raging exertion had torn loose his bound hand, and now he grabbed a handful of Quincannon's hair and wrenched his head back and hit him again.

"Arraaggh!" It roared out of Quincannon's lungs as, goaded to a final effort, he got a foot under him and bulled his head into Borg's middle and carried them both over backward. They rolled apart slowly, their movements clogged by the drag of exhaustion, and came staggering to their feet. Borg squinted at Quincannon's giant form limned against the fiery eye of the sun where it arced a last bloodshot glance above the rim of prairie, and then he hunched his shoulders and moved in for the kill.

"That's enough," Nathan Dart said quietly.

His noiseless trot had brought him up unseen, and now he halted almost between them, dwarfed by their hulking bodies, his voice seeming to float from a great distance away. Both antagonists, weaving on their feet and fighting for great gasps of lung-searing air, eyed him without comprehension in the dregs of their berserk blood-madness.

Dart said dryly now, "Reckon you boys called a wrong turn."

Quincannon rasped between labored breaths, "What?" His underwear shirt, fouled with blood and dirt, was torn half off and great bruises welted the pale skin exposed. His eyes glared wildly from the puffy flesh of his cut and swollen face, and his teeth were bared in an unconscious snarl. Borg, bearing his dim gaze to focus on his opponent, wondered if he looked like that and knew that he did.

He frowned, fumbling for Dart's meaning, and the words left him as a husky croak: "What is it, Nate?"

"Gal just come to and says it wa'n't Bert Romaine

shot her. Say it were the tall skinny gent in a fur coat. That d be Panjab Willin'."

A shudder ran through Quincannon's bull-shoul- dered frame as the tension drained from it. He sank down on his haunches, fighting for breath, and then his glare lifted to Borg. "You were wrong, Vikstrom. You were wrong."

Borg stared at the ground, his breathing a labored sweep, tasting a cold and brutal realization now. Dart put in dryly, "Scour your pots 'fore you name any ket- tles, mister."

Quincannon's glare seemed to turn inward as it low- ered to the torn sod. "Aye. I'd forgot something I once knew better than most men. Three years ago I went down to Mexico only because that something was burning in my guts. It was more than my arm I lost down there." He sighed deeply. "No man's an island; his best interest is the interest of all. Romaine's not guilty, but it remains that in the eyes of some he might have been. While that large doubt remained, the way to absolve him was by a lawful trial."

Borg sank down on his haunches facing Quin- cannon, letting the dizzy ache of his head subside. He picked up a handful of dust and crushed grass and scowled at it. "There's a thing I forgot lately too. Today, burning off your grass, I give myself a lot of reasons first. A man always does. But it was in the back of my head to get back at you, worst way I could. I would not even wait to see if Helga could clear Romaine. For this, one of us might have killed the other, eh? Today it was close, too close."

"Not a lot burned, and for the rest, there's new grass every spring," Quincannon said. Their eyes met for a long and measured moment. Quincannon extended his hand, and with hands griped together, they came to their feet.

Borg's sober glance found Nathan Dart. "Too close, all right, Nathan. And you were right."

Dart gave a polker-faced nod. "Kind of make you wrong, wouldn't that?"

Borg forced a slow and painful grin. "I got pretty bigheaded, all right. Like you said once, Scandies is like mules. A mule needs a kick in the belly to knock the wind out of him."

Dart chuckled. "And quite a few more places, from the look."

Borg nodded wryly. But the bruises and scars of the fight would fade. What would remain with him all his days was the rough lesson that no man could bull ahead with regard to his own will alone, not when the welfare of so many depended on him. He had known the travail of leadership without realizing its danger. No, he would not forget.

"There is still Panjab Willing. Where will we find him, Nate?"

"Hard sayin' that. Prowls the prairie a heap. Of an evenin' a man's likely to find him drownded in whiskey somewheres in a back alley."

"Tonight?"

"Depends. If he knows the gal ain't dead an' can talk, he'd make tracks for the tall brush. T'other hand, if he thinks he killed her he'd likely be shook enough to find hisself a bottle in Liberty. This's supposin', Borg."

"I think maybe a good guess," Borg nodded. "We will try town. If he's not there, tomorrow we start looking on the prairie. One way or the other . . ." His raw-knuckled hand formed a slow fist.

Quincannon said quietly, "We'll look as long as you, my boys and me."

"No need."

"It's as I said, Vikstrom. You don't know Texans. A woman's honor's been affronted. I'd have offered as much before, savin' you were rough about Bert. We'll look too, with you or without you."

"With us," Borg said. "And if we find him, what?"

"Jail for him."

They eyed each other in sober agreement, and then the three of them tramped back across the stretch of prairie lying dark and windless now in the pearl-tinted twilight. Nearing the soddy, Borg saw that the silent and waiting group comprising his household and the Singlebit men had been joined by the settler men from every farm. Some of them must have seen Quincannon and his men pass by enroute to the Vikstrom place, and these had alerted the rest. Remembering the reluctance of many of these men at the war conference this afternoon, Borg felt a strong pride in them now; they were not ones to back off when the chips were finally down.

Sigrid stood waiting almost meekly, as an obedient wife should, but seeing him close then, her composure broke and she ran to him. "Oh! Your poor face," she began to weep, but quickly salvaged her usual briskness. "You come inside now and we will clean this mess off you and see what is left. Never in my life—!"

"Later, old woman." Borg walked to the washbench, filled the basin from a pail of water, and splashed it on his face. The lukewarm water brought every cut and bruise painfully alive, and then the air against it was like a cooling balm. He poured the basin out and refilled it for Quincannon, then turned about to face the expectant lot of them.

"Quincannon and me," he said quietly, "we're going to town to look for the man who shot Helga Krans. How many will come?" A murmur of response swept among the men, and Borg, not missing the ugly under-tone of it, raised his hand. "Good. It's good we all go, to show the vote of decent men. But one thing. We take him for trial."

"That's right," Quincannon said shortly, eying his own men as, wincing, he patted his face dry on the towel. "Ye'll bear it in mind, all of you."

Margaret Haggard had moved up beside him, her touch timid on his arm, and a soft quaver in her voice: "Linus?"

Quincannon's bruised face withdrew behind its stony mask; his glance at her was brief and his words so low that Borg, at his side, barely caught them. "I'll thank you to bear another thing in mind, Mrs. Haggard." He balled the towel and flung it on the bench, then pivoted on his heel and walked away to his horse.

Borg, starting toward the corral to get Hans, paused to catch the eye of Bert Romaine. The young cowboy

238

was standing ahead of the others, watching him with an angry truculence. Borg tramped over to him, facing him squarely in the fading light.

"For what I thought, I apologize now."

Romaine said thickly, "You damned well better."

Borg had started to turn away, and now he swung back. "A word of advice, sonny," he said steadily. "Don't wait till you're my age to learn what bad judgment can do. You maybe will not live that long."

CHAPTER TWENTY

ABEL JEVERS, LEANING IN THE DOORWAY WITH HIS HEAD bowed, listened to the rattle of hurrying horses and tag-ends of angry voices die off in the prairie dusk as the settlers and cowboys rode away in a solid body toward Liberty. Helga's revelation had pulled these raging and embattled men together, but only to vent their smoldering wrath in a different direction. They would tear the town apart to find Panjab Willing—and then God alone knew what. He had been sitting inside with Helga and had not heard their plans for Willing, but their behavior so far indicated another savage reprisal, and Abel felt heartsick.

For him, the bleak knowledge that this raw and lawless land had shaped of necessity a harsh code of retribution against itself was no comfort. To him the gentle tenets of his faith were absolute, not merely applicable in the convenience of civilized times and places. Yet how could he condemn these men when he had himself so much to think about still, so much to understand?

He sighed and dropped his hand from the doorframe, turning back into the room. At the table the women were murmuring quietly together, Inga rocking the baby in her arms. Sigrid, her tone hushed as she tried to explain all this to her troubled little daughter, now raised her voice a little, looking at him.

"Abel, will you hitch up Mrs. Haggard's team, please? She is going back to town."

When he had done so, Mrs. Haggard, with a bare word of thanks in her obvious agitation, sent the team off at a fast clip. Abel watched her go, then wandered disconsolately back into the common room. Sigrid, regarding him compassionately, suggested, "Go sit with Helga some more, now she is awake."

Abel went into the sleeping room and pulled the drape shut. A lamp burned on the stool where he had sat his vigil, and Helga lay with the yellow light soft on her wan face, her eyes open and grave on him. Uncomfortable under her searching gaze, Abel set the lamp on the floor and eased himself onto the stool, leaning his elbows on his knees and staring glumly at the floor.

She said softly, "They are all gone after him, all the men?"

Abel could not bring himself to meet her eyes. Suddenly the words of confused and bitter self-reproach burst from him: "I know how it is with them—I felt it when Pawnee Harry told me what had happened to you. I wanted to find the man myself—" He swallowed hard, and his eyes, filled with a numb misery, lifted almost pleadingly. "It can't be that way, not with me. Do you understand, Helga? Can you understand?"

"I think so. *Ja,* I do." She looked very young, with the soft light hair framing her small face, but there was a woman's compassion in her look. "I know you pretty well, I think. Now life looks very bad to you, *ja?*"

"I guess so."

"It will be better, you will see. I know. It all seemed so bad once—" Her eyes darkened with memory, and she murmured then, "It was very bad. I have not talked of it to anyone. Now I tell you, Abel. I went walking with—a boy. I thought he was nice. He dragged me into the bushes. He hit me till I had no strength." A thin shudder ran through her. "Now it was done, and I could not change what happened and, oh, I wanted to die. So much shame, I could not tell anyone. And soon, I found there would be the baby and everyone would know. For a long time I wanted nothing, only to die."

"Hush," he begged. "Please don't."

"Is it so bad? Will you hate me now?"

"No—oh Lord, no. I love you." The words long-dammed by shyness broke from him. She smiled and lifted her hand from the blanket, laying it gently on his shoulder. "Poor Abel. I don't hurt any more, but how much you hurt for everyone. So much the preacher always, *ja?*"

"No, you're wrong. Not that, Helga."

She met his earnest look a long moment, then raised her head. "Inga," she called softly. "Bring the baby."

241

Inga parted the drape and entered with Lisj-Per, her face expressionless. "Give him to me," Helga whispered, and Inga carefully laid the sleeping baby in the circle of his mother's arm. She straightened, looking briefly from Helga to Abel and then, without comment, left the room.

Helga's gaze was misty and warm on her baby, and it did not change, lifting to Abel Jevers' homely, pugnosed face. "Look now, Abel, look very hard. You the good preacher, what do you see?"

"What God sees, I hope," he said truthfully. "If you know me, Helga, did you need to ask?"

Smiling she sighed and brought up her free hand to his head, drawing it nearer. "No, but sometimes you're a very slow man."

IT WAS ALWAYS THE SAME DREAM, repeating itself with an unvarying clarity of detail that haunted his waking hours. About him on every side rose the shabby tenements of his slum boyhood, and from them came a thousand mingled sounds of misery which grew louder and louder till he clapped his hands over his ears to shut them out. Then the walls began to move in on him like a massive vise of squalor and poverty and ugliness, and he scurried about to find an escape and there was none; then they were pressing in on him and smothering him, crushing him . . .

At this point as always, sweat-drenched and trembling, Haggard woke. He sat up then, staring wildly around the dusk-filled parlor . . . he had lain down on the divan after supper and had dozed off. He came slowly to his feet and ran a hand through his hair. From the kitchen came the ordinary clatter of dishes and Juanita singing pensively as she washed them. He adjusted the damp collar of his shirt and straightened his tie, then walked out to the kitchen.

Juanita turned with a startled quivering of her vast bulk. "Ah, meester. It is only you."

"Only I," Haggard agreed dourly. "Has the señora come home?" At her negative shake of head, he snapped, "Where the devil did she go?"

Juanita shrugged expansively and turned her back on him, clattering the dishes in the pan. "*Quien sabe?* She goes off this morning, saying nothing. Out on the prairie where is more nothing, maybe."

Haggard's irritation deepened. "I wish you'd try to dissuade her when she takes a notion to go off alone, and I'm not here. The prairie isn't the safest choice for a Sunday promenade, particularly with that prairie fire that was sighted off southeast this afternoon."

Juanita glanced over her shoulder, an open irony in her round brown face. "Maybe here's not so safe for her no more."

"Remember your place, woman, and mind your tongue," Haggard said coldly.

Juanita gave a careless shrug, rattling the dishes loudly. "I don' care one way or another, *patrón*. I know how men are. My papa use to beat my mama alla time. And Solice Mendoza, my little hosbond who is dead, he was a mean one. He would drink much and think he was a big man. He never dare to beat Juanita, not him. I am too big of a woman. One night he got full of tequila and hit me and I bend the kettle over his head. Oh, how he squealed . . ."

The stream of her chatter flowed on as Haggard impatiently left the kitchen, heading for the front door. He set his hat on his head and stepped out into a cooling evening blurred by the first gray seep of dusk. He walked down toward Main Street, his head bent in frowning thought. Apparently Margaret had not learned her lesson . . . was she still seeing Quincannon?

He had spent the day worrying over various ways to precipitate a final break in the tense relations between Singlebit and the farmers. Syvert Hultgren's killing of the young cowboy had almost led to an open clash last night. Once more it was Vikstrom—damn his guts—who had prevented it, this time by quelling the attempted lynching of Hultgren by the five Singlebit hands. And today Haggard had received a letter posted from Wyoming. It was from John Trevelyan, stating that he would return to Liberty in two weeks and hoped that Haggard might have good news concerning his prospective land buy.

Time was running out, and unless those farmers were pushed off and their land repossessed by him, the ripe plum of Trevelyan's offer would decay on the limb and his future plans would be crippled. The tensions revived by the killing of Tom Larned gave him a ready-made fuse; he needed a spark to ignite it. Mulling over the possibilities, Haggard had come back repeatedly to Tetlow's suggestion: put Vikstrom out of the way for good. It was a fact as old as human history that the assassination of a beloved leader could fuse his followers into die-hard resistance, and Haggard had rejected the idea for this reason.

He had been thinking too deviously, he thought now; the raw, stark simplicity of the proposition had led him to overlook the equally simple corollary that would make it workable—he had only to make it appear that Quincannon was responsible for Vikstrom's death and afterward let human nature take its course. It would have to be set up more carefully than any machination of his yet: a man who pledged himself to raw murder was staking his own life. A cold-blooded thoroughness was needed, and obviously there was only one man for the job . . .

Heading up Main Street for the marshal's office, he sniffed the night air and felt a warm relief that the tinge of smoke present earlier was gone. Apparently that prairie fire of this afternoon had died away. It had seemed to be near or on Singlebit range, which was no concern of his so long as his town was not endangered.

Passing Lavery's Saloon, he sent a casual glance over the horses tied in front, picked out in a soft out-wash of lamplight from the half-frosted front window, and noted that one of them was Panjab Willing's gaunt nag. It reminded him that he had asked Willing to keep an eye on his wife's comings and goings; he might have spotted her on the prairie today, and it would do no harm to check.

Haggard angled onto the boardwalk and pushed through the batwings, seeing Willing seated at a front corner table. An empty bottle stood by his elbow, and an abandoned shotglass. He was hunched over the table with a bottle, three-fourths empty, clenched loosely in one rawboned hand, and now he lifted it and took a deep pull, his stringy neck muscles working, and set it down with a convulsive shudder. He was gasping shallowly and a thin line of spittle crawled down his chin. Haggard wondered narrowly what had gotten into this purposeless halfwit; he was far gone in his drunken torpor, his eyes glazed and unseeing, yet there remained a harried intensity to his drinking.

Haggard shrugged; no point in trying to get anything coherent out of the derelict hide hunter now. Tomorrow would be soon enough. He left Lavery's and headed on to Tetlow's office. The door was open against the heat, and Haggard went in.

Tiger Jack was seated in his back-tilted chair, his feet propped on the desk and his polished jackboots catching a dull sheen under the light of the desk lamp. He was carefully paring his nails with a Barlow knife, his head cocked critically to one side. Haggard shut the door behind him, at which Tiger Jack lifted a bleak and irritated glance. Haggard ignored it, giving a curt nod toward the closed door leading to the jail behind the office, from which he could hear a murmur of voices.

"Who's in there?"

Tetlow's lip curled faintly. "Some snorky kid callin' on Hultgren. Magnus Vikstrom, says his name is."

"Vikstrom's son?"

"Reckon. Didn't ask. Don't favor his pa noways."

Haggard eased a hip onto the desktop and leaned forward, lowering his voice to a murmur. "You want a job?"

Tetlow blew speculatively on his nails, studying them. "Got a job."

"Only this one was your idea."

Tetlow's chill opaque stare lifted without expression, and Haggard said softly, deliberately, "I want Vikstrom dead."

Tetlow swung his feet off the desk, thumping the front legs of his chair to the floor. He placed both hands palm down on his desk and studied the backs of them, again lifted his colorless stare. "Brace him?"

"Deadfall him. Hit him from ambush and rig it so it's found to be Quincannon's dirty work."

Tetlow smiled his understanding. "How you figure I do that?"

A corner of Haggard's mouth twitched wryly upward. "Bushwacked during the war, didn't you, for that Jayhawker scum? I won't presume to tell you your trade. Particularly when you may as well work for your fee, which will be exorbitant."

Tetlow leaned back and tucked a thumb in a button-hole of his vest, one finger idly toying with his watchchain. "What about last night?"

"What about it?"

"Framed up Hultgren for you, didn't I? Offered me a thousand, didn't you?"

"For an idea that'd move the farmers off," Haggard contradicted him coldly. "They haven't moved."

"You figure killing Vikstrom'll move 'em?"

"It'll move them against Quincannon, and in an open

fight Quincannon'll run 'em off for me. Damn it, man, do I have to draw a map?"

Tetlow grinned wolfishly. "Let me draw one. You offer a thousand for a sound idea. You say killing Vikstrom is a sound idea and you admit it was mine." He lifted his hands, gently touching one index finger with the other. "Framing Hultgren helped set up some bad will to start with, so say you owe me a bad will offering." He ticked off a second finger. "Now. Say I wrap it all up by deadfalling Vikstrom and riggin' blame on Singlebit, call it a bargain package for three thousand dollars."

Haggard said thickly, "Go to hell."

"Why, I'm much a down-Easter as you, born and bred." Tetlow's wicked grin came and went. "Horse-trade me. Go ahead."

Haggard could hear the heavy pound of his own heart in the warm silence of the room. What had he come to, bargaining with an ice-blooded killer for a man's life as you might bargain for a butchered beef? And then he almost laughed aloud. From legal and extra-legal chicanery to hired murder was a natural step, and when had he ever troubled to fortify his own conscience with the illusion of respectability he wore for the world?

He was about to reply when the low-pitched voices from the cell block rose in angry debate. Tetlow lounged to his feet, saying lazily, "I'll break that up while you're thinking about it."

He picked up his keys from the desk, then paused and cocked his head alertly, listening. "What's that?"

Without waiting for an answer, he stepped swiftly past Haggard and opened the door. Haggard moved up behind him, peering out.

"I'm damned," Tiger Jack murmured. "Look at them. The whole she bang, cowherds and clodhoppers."

Seeing the strung-out crowd of men riding up the street, Haggard felt the breath of sudden guilty panic fill his lungs with a cottony suffocation. What could have brought Vikstrom and Quincannon riding into town together?

Then he saw the group swing to a halt in front of Lavery's Saloon a block down. The outstreaming light picked out the huge and solid form of Vikstrom as he reined over to the tie rail.

Haggard caught the marshal's arm. "Get over there," he ordered flatly. "Find out what's happening."

THE RAWBONED PAINT tied at Lavery's rail had taken Borg's attention at once, and he dismounted now and handed his reins to Dart. There was a stir of movement among the mounted men, but he said, "No. One man can take him without a fuss."

Borg unbooted his rifle, skirted the tie rail, and looked above the batwing doors. He ran a brief eye over the jostle of evening activity in the long vaulted room, then saw Willing at his table. He parted the batwings and went in, his rifle angled toward the floor. He would not need it, he thought, with Willing collapsed drunkenly across his table, snoring.

He walked over and nudged the sodden hide hunter with his gun barrel. Willing stirred torpidly and Borg said coldly, "Get up," and jabbed again.

Willing raised his head, sniffling, his muddy eyes finding a bleary and bloodshot focus on the man looming beside him. A bright terror lay quick in his face, and his reaction was instant. His chair crashed forward to his sudden rise, and he lunged around the table to bolt for the door.

Borg intercepted him in a leap and caught him by the neck, then leaned for balance as he wheeled Willing in a savage half-circle and flung him away. Willing's arms flailed wildly as he kited into a table and carried it to the floor with him. He lay belly down, groaning, and then Borg bent and dragged him bodily upright with a hand fisted in his collar. The men at the bar stared, their talk dribbling off.

Borg hiked Willing helplessly onto his toes and marched him toward the doorway. There he set his foot against Willing's rear and propelled him through the batwings in a floundering run, as if shot from a cannon. He lost footing, and momentum carried him clear under the tie rail in a skidding, face-down sprawl.

Borg stalked out, crossed the sidewalk, bent and grabbed him by the collar and the seat of his pants. He hoisted the feebly struggling man in an easy heave, carried him effortlessly to the watertrough nearby, dumped him in and held him under with one hand. Willing thrashed feebly, then with a convulsive panic, and Borg let up. Willing's head popped clear with a strangled yelp, and Borg gave him a few seconds' sputtering respite and ducked him again.

The cowboys and farmers, dismounted now, gathered silently around as he hoisted Willing out and set him on his feet. Held up by Borg's fist around his collar, the half-drowned hide hunter reached for deep retching breaths, his long lank hair streaming water. His vapid eyes shuttled wildly about, and he gave a faint whinney of fright.

"Talk," Borg rapped harshly, shaking him. "The girl has talked, now you talk."

"God's sake," neighed Willing. "I 'uz jis'—you gonna string me up, that what you gonna do?"

"A man cannot always do what he wants," Borg said tightly, but he felt a sudden pity for this palsied, drink-addled halfwit. "No, you will not hang. This I promise. But talk now."

Willing seemed not to hear him. He sagged bonelessly against Borg's hold, his teeth chattering. "Oh yes, I done it. She 'uz sich a purty little thing, all white an' pink like. I 'uz jis' watching. Uh—she come outen the water, an' she 'uz so purty—" He sniffled violently, and waggled his limp head and wept. "I didn' wanna hurt 'er. All them cows me an' Lutey shot, that 'uz mean doin', but this here—"

"The cows," Borg broke in softly. "What of the cows, and the wheat?"

Willing gulped deeply, his head waggling on his chest. "I dunno," he whimpered. "Mr. Haggard tol' us t' do it. He give us gold. I dunno . . ."

"Haggard," Quincannon said, "Haggard then," with a flat edge of finality. His words were echoed by a rising, ugly swell of mutters from the flanking men.

"Easy," Borg told them, "none of that," and shook Panjab Willing again. "Why? You will say why."

"Let up, hoss," Nathan Dart said meagerly. "Eb Haggard's the man with the answers. I make it so is Tetlow."

Borg quelled the hard core of wrath he felt, thinking afresh of Haggard's changed attitude, and of Marshal Tetlow's recent brutality toward the settlers. "But it makes no sense."

"Does to Eb. He'd have a good reason for crowding you boys to a fare-thee-well, you can bet."

Bert Romaine chuckled, "Well," and grinned about him. "That bastard marshal is bumped heads aplenty hereabouts. I d fancy bumping his."

There was a chorus of happy assent, but Quincannon's steely glance cut it short. "Vigilante law's all we got now. And Kangaroo court too, that shyster judge being Haggard's man. But they'll get their proper due of that much, ye hear me?"

The muttering became subdued, and Nathan Dart said then, "Seen Tetlow standing by when you was questioning Willing. Next I looked, he was gone."

Borg thought it over quickly. Tetlow, seeing the drift of Willing's panicked confession, must have gone at once to warn the man who paid him. It would give the two a few minutes in which to try a break from town. They could escape easily on foot under cover of darkness—but with the nearest settlement a hundred miles away, they could be tracked down and quickly overtaken. On horseback they would stand a good chance, putting many miles between themselves and town while darkness held—but that would mean the delay of getting horses from the livery and the risk of being shot at before they got clear of Liberty.

Borg said as much in a few words, then told the men to spread out up and down the street; two of them were to watch by the livery stable. He turned to Dart. "Nate, take Willing to the jail and lock him up."

Quincannon and Dennis O'Hea were talking low-voiced, and he caught the rancher's soft, "If Maggie knew—"

"You're daft," O'Hea snorted. "You know her better—"

"All right," Quincannon snapped, and looked at Borg. "We'll try Haggard's house, you and me."

"Good."

Nathan Dart steadied Willing as he maneuvered the stumbling hunter away, commenting dryly, "No wonder the poor soul busted all up. First bath he ever had."

CHAPTER TWENTY-ONE

HAGGARD HAD PULLED BACK INTO THE DEEP SHADOW of the alley between the jail and the feed company, watching tensely as Tetlow sidled around the edge of the grouped men, listening. Abruptly he turned and came back at a fast walk. He halted in the alley mouth, and his grin held a hint of feverish, shocking pleasure.

"I'm on the run. So are you. Let's move."

Haggard grabbed blindly at his shoulder. "Damn you, what is it?"

"Someone shot one of them snorky girls—she named Willing. Damn' fool's went crazy scared, babbling on as how he's the one done it—then he run on about shootin' Singlebit cows. They'll have the whole story in a minute, so I didn't wait around. He gets done talkin', they'll be set to run me out on a rail and string you up. Maybe me too. We best stick behind the buildings till we reach the stable . . ."

Haggard was no longer listening. His thoughts ribboned off against a blank wall and his mind turned the first words over unbelievingly, trying to pick a shred of meaning out of them, and then he knew the answer. He was finished here; it was as simple as that.

As the spur of panicked urgency drove home to him, he pushed past Tetlow toward the rear of the alley. He cut through the darkness at a blind angle across the empty back lots, running, tripping, and falling, scrambling up, the breath clawing in his lungs. He paused a panting moment to get his bearings, saw the lighted windows of his own house, and made directly for the back door.

He lunged into the kitchen past the startled Juanita and through the now-lighted rooms to the staircase. He went up the steps three at a time and burst into his room. He forced his hands to steadiness as he lighted the lamp on the commode, then dropped to his knees by the small safe in one corner and began to twirl the dial.

It was not up with him yet. Money . . . there was

always a chance if a man had money. Make a clean escape, lie low for a while, start over elsewhere under an assumed name. It would take only a minute to clean out the safe, leave by the back door, and slip around to the rear of the livery stable. He could get a horse, wait till the fools went to search his house, then ride casually out—

A shadow loomed in the doorway and Haggard jerked half-erect . . . it was Tetlow. The interruption and the uncertain light had caused him to miss a turn, and he swore and bent back to it with a sweating concentration.

Tetlow lounged a shoulder against the doorjamb, saying with an amused and feverish relish, "Think you can get far enough?"

"I will," Haggard muttered between his teeth, not looking up. "Wasting time, aren't you?"

"I don't reckon. Mentioned once you keep all your money up here . . ."

"A two-way split, eh?" Haggard muttered, squinting at the dial. There . . . a final turn. He swung open the safe door, then took a deep breath and glanced up. "Well, you can go—"

He broke off, seeing the dragoon pistol in Tetlow's fist.

"Salted up a hundred thousand dollar so far, didn't you say once?" Tetlow said gently. "One-way split on that's worth a bullet and a runnin' start, way I look at it."

It clotted thickly in Haggard's throat, all the unrequited bitterness of his life never to be requited, and it made a dark, wrenching sickness in him. He leaned a hand on the safe and started to his feet.

"No," he said thinly.

Tetlow fired.

BORG AND QUINCANNON were a block from Haggard's, just swinging off Main onto Bison Street, when they heard the shot. It brought both men to a halt, listening to the whipcrack echoes die off in the evening stillness. Quincannon said, "What the hell," wincing with the effort of speech to his cut lips.

"From Haggard's maybe," Borg said, and broke into a loping run. He had the grim thought that they might never know Haggard's reason for wanting to drive them out—that could have been a suicide shot.

As they neared the house, a woman's scream knifed across the night. With Quincannon on his heels, Borg quickened his run, lunging up the path and into the lighted parlor. He ran full into the fat Mexican cook on her way out, and she promptly went into shrieking hysterics. Borg shook her angrily. "What is it? What is it?"

"Oh, *Dios, Dios!*" Juanita's chins trembled and tears streaked her brown cheeks. "I hear the shot and come see and there is the señor dead on the floor and the *mariscal,* Tetlow, robbing the safe—oh, *Dios—!*"

Borg pushed her aside and bounded up the stairs. Seeing a door ajar in the hallway, he veered into the room, his rifle lifted. He saw Haggard's crumpled body and the open and ransacked safe, then the open window with its curtains bellying gently inward on a breeze. He went to the window and peered out, straining his eyes against the growing night. Tetlow was gone. He would be a murderer and a fugitive now, but probably a damned rich one. Except that first a fugitive had to escape.

Quincannon bent briefly over Haggard, then straightened up. "The man's done." He looked at the open window. "Got away, hunh, Tetlow?"

"Not if he is stopped," Borg said flatly, and made for the doorway.

Tetlow was daring enough to try for a horse. From here the livery stable was two blocks away, and likely Tetlow would cross the back lots and come up on it from the rear to avoid the street.

Both men, already hurt and exhausted by their brutal brawl, were laboring for breath as they jogged into Main Street and swung toward the stable. Abruptly Borg hauled up in the street, raising his hand. Quincannon panted, "What—" and broke off.

There was enough light to identify the man pacing a horse slowly out of the livery archway . . . Tetlow. Ahead of his horse, tense with the threat of Tiger Jack's leveled gun at his back, walked another man. Borg did not move and scarcely breathed. Tetlow's hostage was his son, Magnus.

"Vikstrom!" Tiger Jack's thin shout carried down the street, and the farmers, cowboys, and citizens gathered in muttering knots along the walks fell into silence and every glance was pulled toward the stable.

Tetlow reined to a stop outside the archway with a sharp, "Hold up, boy." He lifted his voice again. "Your boy, ain't he, Vikstrom? You want him alive, I ride out free, turn him loose later." His long pause filled the dead stillness. "All right, Vikstrom?"

"Yes," Borg called hoarsely.

"Quincannon?"

"Stay set, men, all of you," Quincannon shouted.

After a moment Tetlow said with flat clarity, "All right, boy. You keep on ahead of me. Turn left and walk slow."

Magnus, moving with a stiff jointed care, started down the center of the street toward its north end. All of Borg's senses ached with a terrible tension as he watched them come slowly abreast of where he and Quincannon stood. Once Magnus' face, white with strain, turned toward him and their eyes met. Again the boy looked dead ahead as they went on past. Tiger Jack held his horse at a measured pace behind, and he briefly shuttled a glance of cold jeering at Borg and Quincannon.

The situation washed through Borg with a full, tiding sickness. This Tiger Jack Tetlow had never been more than a mockery of a lawman, living only to inflict hurt and death. He had seen a few such men in the army, a breed set apart from the others. Such men, always, had a coldblooded indifference to risk, yet would court danger with a restless savagery if things got too tame. In some warped way Tetlow was enjoying this, and it came strongly to Borg that once he was safely away, the man would kill Magnus with a casual pleasure. Now he was a murderer in the open, with nothing to lose.

It was a clammy fist knotted around Borg's guts, the knowledge that he must stand helplessly by and watch his son walk to death, when any action by him would only trigger that death at once.

Someone else had another idea.

A man standing on the sidewalk in a square of out-thrown lamplight made a furtive movement; a bright streak raced softly along the rifle barrel as he arced it up to sight along Tetlow's back. Borg, in a frozen instant, saw that it was reckless Bert Romaine. Quincannon, spotting him at the same time, bellowed, "Bert! No!"

Tetlow twisted in his saddle with a snakelike swiftness, half-wheeling his horse about, as Romaine fired. The shot bucketed sharp echoes against the buildings as Tetlow's horse, seared by the bullet, plunged and reared. Tetlow fought him on a tight rein, but his control of the animal was gone, and then he could only trigger off two wild shots at Borg as he lunged forward.

Dennis O'Hea was nearer, standing directly to Tetlow's left with some other punchers, and he reached the plunging horse in two long strides. Tetlow twisted again and his gun roared, and the bullet's impact smashed O'Hea over backward.

Magnus had wheeled, tensed on the balls of his feet, as Tetlow's horse started to plunge, and he moved in the same instant O'Hea did. Even as the Singlebit *segundo* went down, Magnus leaped from Tetlow's other side and grabbed his belt and yanked, spilling him out of his saddle into the dust.

Tetlow's horse bolted, and three of the punchers pounced on the fallen marshal; two of them dragged him to his feet. The third picked up Tiger Jack's gun and cocked it, lifting it against his face. "This's for Denny, you goddam——"

Magnus batted his arm down, and the puncher wheeled on him furiously. Then Borg loomed between them; he wrenched the gun away, and pivoted to face the rest of the angry punchers as they surged forward. "No more!" he roared. "We had enough of that!"

Every man stopped dead in his tracks. Borg slowly raised his arm and pointed at Romaine who stood ahead of the others. "You," he said softly, "you could of got my boy killed. You maybe saved him though, so I call it even. But you cross me now, mister, it's the last time for you."

"Get out of here," Quincannon told them quietly. He had come up now, staring at the silent form of O'Hea. "Get out of here, the lot of you."

One by one they pulled back, moving away. Borg collared Tetlow and rammed his own gun in his back, forcing his stumbling steps toward the marshal's office. Entering, Borg kicked the door shut and pulled Tetlow around facing him, fisting a hand in his pleated shirtfront.

"I have thought a lot about last night, man. It was you sneaked off Larned's gun. You had the chance and you had the reason."

Tetlow grinned faintly, his icy poise unruffled. "Maybe I threw the gun in the river."

"You are a damned mean man, enough you will not

talk though you have no more to lose by telling, eh?"

"What do you think?" Tetlow grinned.

Borg shook him gently. "I think mister, I can break the bones of your arms and legs, one at a time, if you don't talk. And I will not get a bit mad doing it."

Tetlow sighed profoundly. "It was a chance to hit you squareheads hard, break you down by framin' one of you for murder. Reckon only Hultgren and me seen Larned grab inside his coat—the others was all standing back of him. While the ruckus was still on I slipped out Larned's gun and stuck it under my coat."

"And threw it in the river later."

"How'd you guess?"

Borg pushed him over to his desk and shoved him into the chair. "You will write all that out. Make it clear Hultgren shot in defense of his life. And you will sign it."

For the next few minutes, except for the sounds of belated excitement drifting in from the street, only the scratching of Tetlow's pen filled the silence. Afterward Borg glanced over the confession, pocketed it, and prodded Tetlow to his feet. He searched his pockets and found, along with a knife and hide-out derringer, a canvas sack bulging with Haggard's money. He dropped the knife and gun on the desk, stuffed the money bag in his pocket, and motioned Tetlow ahead of him into the cell block.

Syvert Hultgren was standing with his face pressed to the bars of his cell door. In mute surprise he watched Borg lift the bunch of keys from Tiger Jack's belt, unlock the door, and shove Tetlow in past him.

Syvert only stood, his face working in disbelief as he stared at Borg who still held the door open.

"Well, come on, Syvert. You want out or no?"

Syvert found his tongue, stammering thanks which Borg brushed aside, as the two of them left the office. When they stepped onto the sidewalk, Magnus was waiting. He tried to speak, but his lips only quivered and formed "Pa" soundlessly, as they had long ago when a hurt little boy had run to his father's knee.

Borg felt something in him give way like a log-jam breaking up, and his arms went tightly around his son. "Two grown men don't cry, boy, they talk. It's time for that. A little later, eh?"

With Syvert, they walked slowly back down the street, somewhat awkward in this unfamiliar closeness. People milled about or stood in small groups, and there was much talk, but none of it very loud. Nathan Dart moved quietly into step beside them, and only now did Borg recall how Dart had been at his side, a gray small shadow of a man with ready rifle, when Borg had confronted the cowboys. Lars, too, had been close by, armed with their father's old pistol.

Borg said now, "Nate, it has got to where I talk too much, thanking you all the time."

Dart gave his dry nod. "Can't say I didn't side you this time."

Borg sighed and shook his head. "Burning off that grass was a fool thing."

" 'Pears he's lost a sight more." Dart motioned toward Quincannon, and they all stopped and looked. The big rancher was standing by O'Hea, looking down at his dead friend, and his rock-graven face was still and without expression in the lamplight from the big front window of the hotel.

"Never let it out of him, that man," Dart said slowly. "All the same, he's recallin' a lot they went through together. 'Member how it was when we all sojered with Shelby in Mexico. Closer'n any two brothers."

A buckboard had pulled to a stop downstreet, and now a woman was coming from it and Borg saw that it was Mrs. Haggard. She must have just arrived and did not yet know about her husband. She would hear it soon enough, and little blame to her if she felt less grief for Eben Haggard than for Dennis O'Hea. She stood by Quincannon and looked down too, her face sad and composed though her cheeks were bright with tears. It struck Borg that she would know everything about Quincannon from the past, perhaps better than he knew himself.

Her words came low and barely audible. "Linus—Linus, how much can a man lose before he knows his need?"

Quincannon looked at her for the first time. "A man can always know, Maggie, and be too proud to say it." His hard face broke as something that it had masked broke inside him, the protective pride that had been a part of him, and with it came the terrible and wracking sobs of a grown man who had carried too much hidden hurt too long.

Borg turned away, stung by disgust as he eyed several avid onlookers, weak men relishing a strong man's weakness. The rest had the decency to look away now. Borg said gruffly to his son, "Sometimes there are things not to look on. Now we'll go home. We've both made enough worry for your mother for one day."

CHAPTER TWENTY-TWO

BORG LOOKED AROUND FOR LARS AND SAW HIM standing with Molnar and Olof Holmgaard by the livery. As Borg started over toward them, a group of muttering cowboys broke up and came forward to confront him. Bert Romaine, always the feisty spokesman, pointed belligerently at Syvert Hultgren. "What's he doin' out?"

Borg explained very briefly, showed them Tetlow's confession, then took the sack of money from his pocket. "You, being always the do-gooder, Romaine, might like to give this to Mrs. Haggard later, eh?"

Some of the farmers had already left, and the others fell into a loose group behind Borg and his son as they rode out from town, Magnus on his livery-rented nag. A few men ranged up beside Borg, wanting to talk, and he put them off with curtly terse replies. He was tired, bruised and aching in every muscle, and there was still a matter to be settled with his son. After a while, when he and Magnus had fallen back behind the others, he said low-voiced, "Now it's time we talk. About Helga and her baby."

Magnus said nothing, and Borg glanced at his dim shape in the windless darkness, feeling the old rise of baffled anger. Was it to be the same thing all over? Then Syvert Hultgren, riding just ahead of them, reined back beside Borg. He cleared his throat hesitatingly. "Overheard you, Borg. You're dead wrong. Magnus won't tell you because he give his word."

"To who?"

"Me. Uncle Syvert." Syvert gave a wry, painful smile. "Just thought of that. Hell of a thing." He went on quickly, telling how he had confided to Magnus that Arne, his dead brother, had fathered Helga Krans' baby. Syvert had known the truth long before they had departed Koshkonong; in fact he had browbeaten the story out of Arne on that very evening Arne had gone walking with Helga and had come home afterward, scared and unnerved by what he had done. Syvert had covered up for Arne when it became apparent that Helga would not betray him; he had continued to do so after hearing that she was pregnant.

It was not until last night, finding himself faced by a murder charge and a hangman's noose, that all the sick and bitter regret for his past mistakes had overwhelmed Syvert. Had he made Arne accept his due blame, it might have made a man of him and he might now be alive. It was then that he had confided the truth to Magnus, also telling him of the three hundred dollars of his savings not yet drunk up which was buried in a tin box under the floor of his soddy. He had asked Magnus to get the money and give it secretly to Helga. It was a poor amends, but it might help her and the baby. He had sworn Magnus to secrecy in the matter, feeling that no good could now be served by making hearsay of the truth that would tarnish his dead brother's name.

Syvert said awkwardly now, "I'll leave you here, cut over to my place. Try to get the girl to take the money, if she will. God knows it's little enough. Borg, Magnus—about all this, it's small return to say a man's sorry."

"Maybe," Borg said quietly, "it worked for the best, Syvert. Good night."

Syvert left them, and they jogged on for a time in silence. Slowly then, and haltingly, Magnus began to talk. This morning after getting the money for Helga, being caught by his mother and misjudged by both parents, he had gone off seething. He had wanted only to be alone, and he had tramped for hours, heading in a generally northerly direction that took him far past Liberty town. Much later, after seeing the distant smoke of Quincannon's burning graze and thinking he might be caught in the way of a widespread prairie fire, he had turned back toward town. By this time a furious and juvenile determination had rooted in him: he would ask Syvert to release him from his promise, then go throw the truth in the faces of his father and mother, laugh at them, and walk out for good.

Reaching town, he had gone directly to the jail. There he had argued bitterly and briefly with Syvert who had flatly told him that he was lucky to have two parents so fine and that he was a damned fool. Angrily he had stalked out, ignoring all the commotion in the street, and had gone to the stable to rent a horse for the ride home, for his legs were aching and rubbery from his long fast hike. Tetlow had come in through the rear archway leading to the horse corral, commandeered his horse and made him a hostage.

As he finished, Borg said abruptly, "How about now. You still want to leave us?"

Magnus said hesitantly, "I don't want to be a farmer, Pa. I guess you know that."

"So? Like I tell Abel, each to his way. What you want to do—draw pictures, eh?"

"Maybe." Magnus' voice in the dark held a smile. "But I'm not going off half-cocked. Whatever I do will probably mean study. Back East, or even Europe. I'm going to ask Greta to wait till I'm sure—she'll understand. Then we'll plan and do together."

"That's good. Man should make a plan to reach what he wants and stick with it all the way. He don't, he winds up like Syvert, a man with no purpose, maybe drinking himself to death."

"Syvert's changed, Pa. What happened—"

"Well, Syvert learned a mighty hard way. Anyway, son, what I got is yours. It ain't much, but you want help, it's what a man owes his son, like you'll owe your boy one day, too. When you know what you want, come to me, eh?"

As the three Vikstroms and Nathan Dart rode into the Vikstrom yard, the cheery warmth of lamplight from the open door flooded it and made, with the warmth of homecoming, a completeness in Borg's tired mind. Sigrid and Inga and Gurina were waiting in the yard, and even Inga could not hide her relieved anxiety. Borg and Sigrid and their son stood together for a time, and listening to her husband's low words, Sigrid blinked away tears of mingled relief and pleasure.

She said briskly, "So. Good. Now you, Magnus, march to bed, and I will fix your father's face." She turned to the Nathan Darts. "Nathan, you must come early tomorrow to help build one of your fine dirt soddies. There is a nice hill over there."

She pointed, and Nathan Dart nodded dryly. "Yes'm. Who for?"

"Lars and Inga," she said, adding stoutly, "it is not right a man and wife don't have a place of their own."

"Oh, hush up, Sigrid," Inga said, a trifle flustered. . . .

When all the questions had been asked and answered and the good change in things was a settled fact for everyone, the whole household retired except for the family head and his wife. Borg sat patiently at the table while she, mildly scolding, tended his cuts and bruises. Afterward, since the night was warm and they were not at all sleepy, they strolled outside.

Arm in arm they walked in the thin moonlight to the edge of the fields and watched the silvered wheatstalks pressed by a soft wind which blew coolly against their faces, so that the rich ripeness filled the night.

"This stuff is ready for harvest soon," Borg observed. "Early next month I think we cut."

"H'm," Sigrid murmured, busy with womanly thoughts. "What about that Quincannon? You think maybe we can get along with a man that mean if he marries Mrs. Haggard now? I mean, how will—"

"Gossip, gossip, when does a woman stop? *Gud*

bevara, give them time, eh?" Borg laughed and pulled her against him and she put her arms up around his neck, smiling.

She teased, "And Syvert? What about Lars and Inga and Abel and Hel—"

"What about us? We're getting pretty old."

She turned her face against his shoulder, laughing softly. "You feel old, mister?"

He moved his hand down the deep curve of her back and smiled, knowing the full-breasted strong-hipped body of her as well as he knew his own, knowing too the great good luck that was his. The bad times had been and would come again along the current of life, but the whole of it had been good because he had known what loneliness was only through seeing it in others. Some of them, it was true, had lost and then found again, like Lars and Inga, like Quincannon and his Maggie. But what a waste of years had gone between. Yes, Borg Vikstrom had been very lucky.

She stirred in his arms and turned, looking out again over the fields and the dark prairie lost beyond them, and her murmured words were sober. "How quick life goes on. So much to happen, so much. And where is it all now?"

He thought about that. "Part of us, I guess, *litagod,* if we remember. Nothing good comes an easy way. This is a young land we have helped break a little, and we have left some blood and a lot of sweat in it and I've seen us grow better for it. We should see our kids remember too, and their kids, so they will know what the good life costs. Long after this is settled country they will have their own troubles to meet. All we can do is help them be ready."

Her eyes, holding that hint of kind and troubled warmth that he loved so well, lifted to his. "And that? It will be enough?"

"Why," he said gently, "it has always been."

Center Point Publishing
600 Brooks Road • PO Box 1
Thorndike ME 04986-0001 USA

(207) 568-3717

US & Canada:
1 800 929-9108